Rafael strolled to the back of the car and reached in to emerge again with a bottle of vintage champagne and two glasses.

'We're celebrating?' Once again Harriet was thoroughly disconcerted. She was starting to appreciate the strong streak of unpredictability that made Rafael Flynn such a powerful competitor in the business world. In old-fashioned parlance, he was a law unto himself—for he had not once reacted as she'd expected him to. It was, she reflected headily, an incredibly unsettling attribute.

Breaking open the champagne, Rafael sent the golden liquid foaming down into the delicate goblets. 'Let's drink to mixing business with pleasure.'

'But *I don't…*' Tiny bubbles burst and tickled Harriet's upper lip as she sipped.

'Neither do I—usually.' Setting down his glass, Rafael moved lazily closer. 'But I get a kick out of breaking rules.'

A tiny twist low in her tummy filled Harriet with restless heat…

Emerald Mistress

Lynne Graham

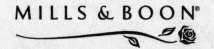
MILLS & BOON®

*First published in Great Britain 2005
Harlequin Mills & Boon Limited,
Eton House, 18-24 Paradise Road, Richmond, Surrey, TW9 1SR*

© Lynne Graham 2005

ISBN 0 263 84578 8

135-1005

*Printed and bound in Spain
by Litografia Rosés S.A., Barcelona*

CHAPTER ONE

IN AN INSTANT of searing honesty that came between sleeping and waking exhausted in her Manchester hotel room, Harriet Carmichael recognised that her life was not at all what she had once dreamt it would be. But she still hadn't the slightest suspicion that she was about to face a day when her every worst nightmare would come true.

In any case, on her seventh birthday her stepfather had taught her to count her blessings when her exquisite mother had failed once again to put in a promised appearance. Those constant disappointments had hurt so much that Harriet had soon learned the art of looking on the bright side. That was how she protected herself. Negative thoughts were banished with a rousing mental mantra of all the things that she felt she should be grateful for. Right now there was her fantastic fiancé, Luke, who had fallen for her in spite of her imperfections. Then there was her wonderful and glamorous extended family. She also had a great job, which earned her a terrific salary and which had finally persuaded Luke to put marriage on the agenda.

A starry smile tilted her generous mouth now. Awash with feel-good buoyancy, Harriet reached for the television remote and flicked on the business news.

'Following a recent drop in share prices, Rafael Cavaliere's arrival in London is fuelling rumours of a crash in the electronics sector.'

Harriet sat up in bed with a jerk to study the camera shot of the notorious Italian tycoon at Heathrow Airport. As usual his staff and his bodyguards surrounded his tall, commanding figure while a posse of frantic paparazzi bayed for attention. In the midst of this mêlée, however, Cavaliere strode along without haste in an apparent oasis of personal peace. The iceman cometh, Harriet thought grimly. Although he was only in his mid thirties he emanated the brutal assurance of a powerful male at home with the raw politics of the business world. His enormous wealth and brilliant financial acumen were laced with formidable ruthlessness. Behind the shades he always wore his lean, dark and compelling profile was as unreadable as a granite wall. A disturbing little shiver ran down her spine.

With an impatient hand Harriet thrust back the tumble of rich dark red hair falling across her pale brow, the soft contours of her rounded face taut with disapproval. Ten years earlier Rafael Cavaliere had acquired the pharmaceutical company where her stepfather had worked. Stripped of its every asset, the ailing firm had ceased to exist. Subsequently unemployment had devastated the rural town where she had grown up, and wrecked more than one previously happy family. She despised everything Rafael Cavaliere stood for: he did not create, he simply destroyed, and all in the very convenient names of progress, efficiency and profit.

In those days Harriet had been a country girl, never happier than when she was helping out at the local riding school, and her sole ambition had been to work with horses. Which was exactly why she had been so very unsettled only two months ago, when she'd become the fortunate recipient of a most unexpected inheritance: a relative she'd never met had left her a small livery business on the west coast of Ireland. Initially astonished and ecstatic at the news, Harriet had been downright irritated to be told that a handsome offer had already been made to purchase the property. In fact she had been mad keen to book the first available flight to Kerry. Unfortunately for her, however, absolutely nobody else in her life had shared her enthusiasm for exploring either her Irish legacy or her Irish heritage, she recalled heavily.

Her mother, Eva, had fled Ireland and her family for London as a pregnant teenager. Eva's memories were bitter and unforgiving, and she had always refused to tell her daughter who her father was. Harriet would have dearly loved some encouragement to visit the village of Ballyflynn, where Eva had grown up, and would have welcomed the chance to see if she could discover for herself the identity of her birth father. But fate had decreed otherwise, for tomorrow contracts were to be exchanged for the sale of the livery stable. Urged to be sensible rather than sentimental, Harriet had given way to pressure and had agreed to sell her inheritance sight unseen. After all, to do otherwise would have entailed turning her life upside down.

Her mobile phone rang. Though discomfited by her somewhat downbeat reflections, Harriet answered it with concentrated brightness.

'Harriet…do you know if my Armani suit is still at the dry cleaners?' Luke enquired tautly.

'Let me think.' Harriet thought back to the weekend, which had raced past in her usual feverish fight with the clock as she struggled to meet all her obligations. Luke had asked her to pick up his suit if she could manage it, and she had said she would. But had she actually done so? Since working overtime had begun encroaching heavily on her weekends, she had found it increasingly hard to factor in the time to take care of the ordinary things of life.

'Harriet…' Luke pressed. 'I'm running late—'

'I definitely picked your suit up—'

'But it's *not* in the wardrobe!' Luke was as clipped and cutting in his impatience as only a lawyer could be. He had been equally blunt when it came to pointing out that the Emerald Isle was famously green because it rained a lot there, and therefore it was not at all his idea of the perfect setting for a holiday home.

'So where is it?'

Harriet pictured him with his streaky blond hair swept back from his brow, his tanned, lively features lit by light green eyes. Love made her feel hollow with longing. With effort she retrieved a recollection of staggering into his apartment laden with shopping bags, the Armani suit draped over her arm. 'Give me a minute. I'm thinking.'

'Why are you always so disorganised?' Luke condemned with sudden unexpected anger.

Taken aback by that unfair criticism, Harriet squeezed her eyes tight shut and with a meteoric effort remembered. 'Your suit is hanging on the back of the kitchen door.'

'It's...*where?* Oh, never mind,' Luke said un-gratefully.

'That is the last time I do a favour for you on a Saturday, just so that you can meet your friends at the gym,' Harriet declared. 'I'm not disorganised, just run off my feet!'

A sudden silence hummed on the line.

'I'm sorry. I was out of order,' Luke told her quietly. 'Will I see you later?'

'No. I'll be lucky to make it home before midnight.' Even when she got back to London she would still have to call into the agency, brief her boss, Saskia, and write up a detailed report. The monthly meeting with the executives at the Zenco headquarters in Manchester was the most important date in her diary.

'That's a shame, because I miss you,' Luke asserted with easy charm. 'However, I do have a lot on today too. So don't worry if I switch off my phone. Just leave a message. Look, I have to rush...I'll call you tomorrow, babes.'

Babes? Replacing the handset, Harriet was surprised by that particular term of endearment, for it had a frivolous edge that was not in his usual style. Her half-sister Alice used that expression too. But then Alice was an It-girl with a trust fund and an aptitude for always being at the cutting edge of the latest trends. Harriet smiled fondly. She was very proud of the younger woman and thought, not for the first time, that it was a great shame that two of her favourite people, her sister and her fiancé, could hardly stand to be in the same room together.

Her mobile shrilled once more, just as she was about to head out for her meeting.

'Are you watching the news?' Her boss hissed in a frantic tone of urgency.

'No…why?' As Saskia was a natural-born drama queen, Harriet turned on the television news again in no great hurry.

'Zenco has gone down…' Saskia framed harshly.

Harriet's stomach flipped. She stared transfixed at the screen. Crowds of employees were milling around the pavement in front of the Zenco building. Some people were banging on the entrance doors, but nobody appeared to be getting inside. Expressions reflected anger, bewilderment and blank disbelief. The camera lingered lovingly on the face of a young woman sobbing.

'You deal with Zenco's people all the time. Why didn't you realise that there was trouble brewing?' Saskia condemned, slashing like a knife through Harriet's horror at the drama that was unfolding on screen. 'If you'd warned us we could have pulled back!'

Unprepared for this attack, Harriet was bemused. 'But, Saskia, how could I—?'

'Right at this minute I'm not interested in listening to your excuses,' her boss spat, with an almost hysterical edge to her voice. 'Get over there and pull every bloody string you have to and find out what's happening. Then come back here as soon as possible! Without the Zenco account you can't afford to be running up expenses like some lottery winner.'

In the aftermath of that unreasonable accusation, Harriet pressed cooling hands to her hot cheeks. The brunette was well known for her acid tongue, but it was the first time that Harriet had personally felt its effects. Until this morning she had been a favoured employee, riding the crest of the wave on Zenco's ever-increasing marketing budget, she acknowledged grimly. If Zenco was in trouble, so was she.

Two years had passed since Harriet had joined the staff at Dar Design. Back then the Zenco account had been small, but they had liked Dar's creative department's campaign and Harriet's enthusiastic presentation skills—and the rest was history: the agency had expanded fast to meet the advertising needs of the giant multinational company. What if the gravy train had shrieked to a sudden halt?

Six hours later, Harriet crossed Dar Design's elegant reception area. An eerie silence hung over the office. Hovering colleagues peered out of doorways and looked away again hurriedly. Nobody knew what to do or what to say. Before Harriet had even boarded her flight back to London Saskia had phoned her four more times. Everybody must have heard Saskia screaming at the top of her voice that Zenco owed the agency so much money Dar Design would go to the wall with them. Harriet's attempts to talk to Luke had been foiled when, on calling his secretary, she had discovered that he would be at a legal conference until six; and his mobile phone was switched off, just as he'd said it would be.

An emaciated brunette in her forties, clad in a pink tweed suit, thrust wide the door of her office. '*So?*' Saskia demanded caustically.

Harriet breathed in deeply, walked in and closed the door behind her. 'It's not good. The rumour is that there's a black hole in Zenco's accounts and investigations are pending against three of the directors.'

Saskia uttered a very rude word and studied Harriet with raging resentment. 'Why the hell am I only hearing about this now?'

'Corruption in high places isn't a topic of conversation amongst the Zenco personnel I've dealt with,' Harriet pointed out as quietly as she knew how. 'They don't have the connections and neither do I.'

* * *

Despite the long estrangement that had existed between Valente Cavaliere and his son, Rafael chose to attend his father's funeral.

Rafael believed family hostilities were not for public parade or debate, and he saw no reason to offend tribal traditions. Certainly it was inconvenient for him to leave the UK at the moment that Zenco went into its death throes, but he was still well on track to make another few million pounds in profit from other people's stupidity and greed.

A silence filled with awe and respect greeted his arrival at the chapel in Rome. He marked the older man's passing without visible emotion or sentiment. His impassive demeanour was a fitting footnote which his late parent would have very much admired. In seventy odd years of fully indulging his own essentially vicious nature, Valente had never once managed to match his son's cold, proud detachment.

In a thwarted rage at his inability to intimidate Rafael, Valente had fought continually with him. He had competed in corrupt and underhand ways for his son's every prize and had on many occasions attempted to bring the younger man's business empire down. In defeat, Valente had learnt to his own astonishment that he was very proud of his own flesh and blood. Rafael was fiercely intelligent, icily self-controlled and lethally unemotional. By the time of his death Valente had come to believe that he had bred a king among men by the Irish wife who had so grievously failed to meet his expectations

Rafael's reflections at the graveside were not of a religious or peaceful nature. By then memories sharp and sour as bile were afflicting him.

'Your mother is a slut and a junkie. Don't believe a word the lying bitch says!' Valente had warned Rafael when he was seven years old, and he had gone on to carefully explain exactly what those words meant. 'When you visit her never forget that you're a Cavaliere and she's Irish trash.'

Valente, however, had truly surpassed himself when Rafael had fallen in love for the first and last time at the age of fifteen. He had paid a remarkably fresh-faced hooker to charm and seduce his impressionable son over the space of a week.

'I had to make a man of you and she was impressed. Tasty, wasn't she? I should know. I tried her out before I picked her for you,' Valente had chuckled. 'But you can't love her. She's a whore and you'll never see her again. All women are sluts under the skin when it comes to men with money and power. '

That devastating news had been delivered with tasteless hilarity in front of an appreciative audience of his father's closest associates.

'There can be no sentiment in business,' Valente had

explained when the father of Rafael's best friend had shot himself over a deal that went wrong the week after Valente reneged on it. 'I look after me and, as long as you are loyal, I look after you. That's *it*. Family and friends don't count unless I get something out of it.'

Not long afterwards Rafael had received a lecture on the respective values of abortion, denial and intimidation in respect of unplanned pregnancies. That ironic recollection almost made Rafael smile for the first time in days. Valente had fathered a child in Ireland, during a brief encounter with the widow who had once acted as the caretaker at his wife's ancestral home, Flynn Court. Now Rafael had a half-sister, a lively fifteen-year-old girl with a brash, mouthy manner and big scared Cavaliere eyes. He'd been paying for her education at select boarding schools for almost the last four years. It wasn't a sentimental attachment, though. There was always purpose in Rafael's actions. His generosity had embarrassed and enraged his father and done his own image no harm whatsoever in the eyes of the once suspicious locals in Ballyflynn.

He tossed a copy of a faded photo of his mother and the neglected Flynn Court into the grave with Valente. May she haunt you through purgatory and hell, he urged grimly…

* * *

At Saskia's command, Harriet finished work earlier than she'd expected and went home. By then she was fully aware that, with Zenco about to go down, her career would divebomb with it. In the short term a period of unemployment would not create a serious problem for her as she was financially secure, she reasoned, striving to be upbeat. But Luke, who was always cautious, would undoubtedly decide that setting a date for their wedding was out of the question.

Harriet tried not to think about the prospect of another couple of years spent concealing her secret addiction to bridal magazines and smiling with valiant unconcern when people asked when the big day would be. She would have cut off her arm sooner than let Luke guess just how keen she was to buy into marriage and eventually motherhood, because she did not want him to feel under pressure. But they had been together five years and engaged for two; at twenty-eight she was ready for the next step.

Once home, she listened to a message on her answering machine.

Alice's beautifully modulated speaking tones, honed to an aristocratic edge by her expensive education, filled the room. 'I thought we could do lunch…but obviously you're off doing your big business bit somewhere. Shame! Catch you another time. I'm off to Nice tonight.'

Harriet suppressed a disappointed sigh just as the doorbell sounded. Lunching with her glitzy kid sister and hearing all about her wonderfully exciting life was always entertaining.

It was Juliet, the pneumatic blonde glamour model who lived across the hall. 'I'm moving out this evening.'

'My goodness, that's sudden—'

'I'm off to Europe with my bloke and I have a favour to ask…' Juliet, who never came to Harriet's door for any other reason, displayed perfect teeth in an expectant smile. 'You have such a soft heart, and you're fantastic with animals. Would you give Samson a home?'

Harriet blinked in dismay. Samson was Juliet's chihuahua, purchased as a girlie fashion accessory when the film *Legally Blonde* had been in vogue. Harriet realised she'd not seen the little dog since another resident had reminded Juliet of the no-pets clause in her rental agreement. 'I didn't know you still had him.'

'He's been living a life of luxury in a posh pet hotel and costing me a bloody fortune,' Juliet lamented. 'But I don't have time to sell him.'

'I'm sorry—I can't help.' Harriet hardened her heart against the thought of poor neglected Samson and felt very much like shaking his feckless owner until her pearly teeth rattled in her selfish head. 'Couldn't the kennels find another home for him?'

'No, they'd rather hang on to him to make more dosh out of me!' Juliet wailed accusingly. 'You've got to help me with this. Danny's picking me up in less than an hour!'

'I'm afraid I don't have anywhere to keep a dog either.' Harriet steeled herself not to surrender to the blonde's steamrolling personality; Luke was not a dog lover, and had vehemently objected when she had once taken care of Samson over a weekend.

An hour and a half later, having changed into a blue dress that was a particular favourite of Luke's, Harriet was on the way over to his flat with the intention of surprising him—his conference would have ended by now. She clutched the ingredients of an oriental stir-fry; he loved her cooking. Would it be manipulative to feed him before she mentioned the giant black cloud hovering on her career horizon? Her scrupulous conscience twanged. She was also being haunted by an image of Samson, small enough to sit in pint jug, being bullied by other larger dogs in some gloomy canine holiday home. But the chihuahua was not her responsibility, she reminded herself hurriedly. Luke got really irritated when she plunged headfirst into helping other people solve their problems.

She let herself into his ultra modern apartment and went straight down the hall and into the kitchen. A burst of giggling from the open plan living-cum-bedroom area made her still in surprise. She moved to the door.

'We called her Porky Pie when we were kids,' a familiar female voice was saying. 'Ma was so ashamed of Harriet that she once pretended that she was the housekeeper's child. She was plump, and she talked with a horrible country bumpkin accent. She might have slimmed down since then, but she's still got a fat face and a bum the width of a combine harvester.'

Harriet was welded to the spot by astonishment. What was Alice doing in Luke's apartment, and why was her sister saying such horrible things about her? Was she trying to amuse Luke? Once or twice she had heard Alice being cruelly sarcastic and funny at the expense of others, but had put it down to imma-turity since the girl was six years her junior.

'Alice,' Luke chided, in an inexcusably indulgent tone.

'"My name is Porky Pie and I am so boring. I talk about recipes and am so desperate to be liked that I am a total pathetic doormat to everyone around me,"' Alice proclaimed, mimicking Harriet's burr well enough for her shaken victim to wince and turn even paler as she moved forward hurriedly to reveal her presence before anything more could be said. 'Would you prefer a slice of my chocolate cake or another shag, babes?'

'Do you need to ask? Open those beautiful legs…'

Harriet's own lower limbs set like lead beneath her. Her stomach churned like a whirlpool while she stared across the spacious stretch of polished wood flooring in utter disbelief. Luke was lying back on the bed stark naked and he was pulling her equally naked half-sister down on top of him! Giggling with carefree abandon, her pale blonde silky hair rippling across her slim tanned shoulders, Alice moved straight into a much more intimate pose with the ease of habit and confidence.

'I love your dainty little boobs…' Luke groaned with pleasure, stretching up greedy hands to the pert mounds jutting over him as Alice arched her spine with taunting sexiness.

Harriet was frozen to the spot in sheer shock at the graphic scene before her. 'Not like mine…' she heard herself say flatly, and out loud, her own voice sounding curiously detached and lifeless to her ears.

The lovers froze with an immediacy that might have been comic in other circumstances. Luke reared up off the pillows. *'Harriet?'*

'How long have you been seeing each other?' Harriet enquired with revulsion, her hands knotting into fists as she physically forced herself not to avert her gaze from their intimacy.

Alice detached from Luke with unhurried grace and angled a bright look of defiance at Harriet, her brown eyes sparkling, her beautiful face expressing unashamed challenge. 'Months. He can't get enough of me, in bed or out of it. I'm sorry you had to find out this way. But that's life, and it's tough on all of us. I haven't enjoyed sneaking around like I'm doing something to be ashamed of.'

Striving to pull on his trousers with something less than his normal assurance, Luke harshly told Alice to keep quiet. Harriet recoiled from that pitying intervention from her fiancé. Only he wasn't her fiancé any more, she told herself starkly. When he had slept with her sister he had made a joke of their engagement. Rigid with the effort of self-control required to keep her emotions from betraying her, she turned round in a stilted movement and walked straight back out of the apartment.

She couldn't catch her breath at first. She felt like someone had locked her in a little black box and deprived her of oxygen. She was fighting off the urge to panic and scream. Her mind kept on feverishly replaying what she had seen, what she had heard and been told. The words and the images were like serrated knives, twisting ever deeper inside her. The pain was unbelievable, for she had adored Luke for what felt like half of her adult life. She could not imagine living without him. She could not bear the knowledge that he had made love to her sister, had laughed and listened to Alice's degrading comments. What had happened to loyalty and decency?

What had happened to the dislike that Luke and Alice had been so keen to parade previously, their snide comments about each other? Luke had called Alice a spoilt little princess and had scorned her life of carefree self-indulgence. Alice had often referred to Luke as a pompous prat. Had that supposed animosity only been put on for Harriet's benefit?

When Harriet had first met Luke at university she had been his mate when she'd wanted to be so much more, a rank outsider forced to smile on the sidelines while he dated and bedded prettier and slimmer and more sophisticated girls. But through friendship she had won his trust and affection. Love had blossomed when he'd begun to look for her when she wasn't there, and had shared his hopes, failures and successes with her.

She had starved herself down two full dress sizes to meet Luke's standards. Indeed, this was the worst of moments to appreciate that she had honed herself into a different person simply to make herself more attractive to the man she had set her heart on holding. But maybe that had been trying to cheat fate. Maybe she and Luke had never been meant to be. Certainly she could not compete with Alice, who was six inches taller and a naturally slender blonde with a fantastic figure. Alice was truly beautiful, and she did not have to work at self-presentation.

Wanting Luke, Alice had just reached out and taken him without apology. She had probably picked up that simple philosophy of life from their mother, Eva. The older woman had left her humble beginnings behind in Ireland and had missed no opportunity to better her prospects. Now based in Paris, and on her third marriage, to a Norwegian shipping magnate, Eva had attained all her goals in life. Harriet was her eldest child and had been raised by Eva's first husband. Eva had had Alice, and Harriet's younger half-brother Boyce, with his successor.

'You only get one life,' Eva had remarked without regret when she walked out on her devastated second husband for his younger, richer and more powerful replacement. 'Sometimes you have to be totally selfish to make the most of it. Be true to yourself first.'

That had been a foreign creed to Harriet, who had been forced to put other people's feelings and needs ahead of her own. But now that her own world had come crashing down around her she could see how self-interest could pay off, and how it might give her another desperately needed focus. It was to meet Luke's expectations that she was living in the city and working in a high-powered job for money that gave her very little satisfaction. Suddenly she was seeing how her broken heart might be turned into something much more positive.

With Luke out of her life, and a career that was fast fading, she was free to do exactly as she liked, she told herself fiercely, determined to find a source of optimism in the savage, suffocating pain she was struggling to hold at bay. If losing Luke to her half-sister meant the chance to downshift to a simpler lifestyle in the Irish countryside, should she not snatch at that opportunity? After all, there would never be a better time to take such a risk. She was young, single, solvent and healthy.

She was taken aback to find Samson the chihuahua parked outside her front door in his pet carrier. A box of doggy accessories, which included his fake diamond collar collection and designer coats and matching boots, was placed beside him. She rummaged through its contents: there was no feeding bowl, no food, not even a lead. The tiny animal shivered violently at the back of the carrier, enormous round eyes fixed to her in silent pleading.

Harriet suppressed a groan of angry exasperation. How could Juliet abandon her pet when she knew that Harriet didn't want him? Samson had been dumped, just the way she had been, Harriet recognised painfully. Dumped when he fell out of fashion and a more promising prospect came along. She had always wanted a dog—but a big, normal dog, not one the size of a tiny stuffed toy. But didn't that make her guilty of body fascism? How had she enjoyed being judged against some impossible marker of physical female perfection and found wanting by Alice? She squirmed with guilt and frustration. It wasn't Samson's fault that he was very much undersized...

The ivy-covered tumbledown wall of an ancient estate bounded the road for what seemed like miles before a roadsign in English and Irish Gaelic alerted Harriet to her arrival in Ballyflynn.

Her heart started beating very fast. A very old stone church appeared in advance of the first houses. Had her mother worshipped there as a girl? Trying as she was to look in every direction at once, Harriet slowed her car to the speed of a snail. Buildings painted in ice cream pastels lined both sides of a wide street embellished by occasional trees. It was distinctly picturesque if sleepy little village.

Parking outside McNally's, the solicitor dealing with her late cousin's will, she lifted her designer handbag. Luke had bought it for her birthday.

Suddenly she had a flashback to the photo of Alice and Luke that had been printed in a gossip column two weeks earlier. Her tummy gave a sick lurch of remembrance. Luke had always been ambitious and he would be thoroughly enjoying his new public profile. Hungry for the offer of a partnership in the legal firm where he worked, he had told Harriet that appearances were all-important when it came to impressing the senior staff. Alice had to be the definitive image enhancement, with her beauty and her entrée into more exclusive circles. Harriet snatched in a shaken breath. It was only seven weeks since they had broken up and the pain was still horribly fresh. But she was going to get over it without turning into a bitter, jealous monster, she urged herself.

Eugene McNally, the portly middle-aged solicitor, handed over the keys to the late Kathleen Gallagher's property with wry reluctance. His disappointment had been palpable when Harriet had stated her complete uninterest in discussing or even hearing about the increased offer that had just been made for her inheritance. However, although she had already received copious details in the post, Harriet did have to sit through a further recitation by Mr McNally of the liabilities which were still being settled against her late relative's estate.

'Your legacy is unlikely to make you rich,' the

ruddy-faced Mr McNally warned her. 'It may even cost you money. Making a profit out of horses is not easy.'

'I know.' Harriet wondered if he thought she was the type to chase foolish rainbows. Of course her last-minute change of heart about selling must surely have caused considerable annoyance and inconvenience for both him and the prospective buyer, she allowed guiltily. But she'd been hugely apologetic when she'd explained on the phone that an unexpected crisis in her life had made her rethink her future. The buyer she had let down was a business called Flynn Enterprises. Obviously a local one, she reflected ruefully, and treading on local toes was not the way to make friends. Yet, while moving to Ireland was an admittedly bold and risky move on her part, she was convinced that her nearest and dearest were wrong in believing that she was making the biggest mistake of her life....

'Are you doing this to punish me and make me feel bad?' Luke had condemned resentfully when he found out.

'All of a sudden you seem to have gone haywire,' her stepfather had muttered worriedly. 'You're acting like a giddy teenager!'

'A hair shirt and a spell in a convent would be more exciting than burying yourself alive in that hick village at the back end of nowhere,' her mother

Eva had warned in exasperation. 'I couldn't wait to get away. You'll hate it. You'll be back in London within six months!'

But what Harriet had chosen to do felt very right to her. In fact she felt different, and she didn't quite understand why. But she did appreciate that for once she was in complete control of her own destiny, and that gave her a wonderful sense of freedom. She could hardly wait to meet the challenge of running her own business and was quietly confident that, with hard work, she could make a go of it.

She drove very slowly out of Ballyflynn. The same estate wall that had greeted her arrival still stretched before her in an even worse state of repair. There was a tight knot of anticipation in the pit of her tummy. Eugene McNally's helpful receptionist had given her exact directions: travel about half a mile past the hump backed bridge and turn sharp left down the lane behind the chestnut tree.

The lane was rough and winding, the tall hedges on either side so overgrown that any view was obscured. The verges were lush and green, the floating tumbrels of Queen Anne's lace moving softly in the slight breeze. She wasn't expecting too much, Harriet reminded herself. It was so important not to have unrealistic expectations. The lane fanned out into a concrete yard surrounded by a collection of old sheds and stables fashioned of a variety of materials and not at all scenic. Obviously repairs were on the agenda. Well, she had a little money to spend, and two hands to work with.

She drove on round the next corner and lost her heart within thirty seconds flat. In a grove of glorious trees a little whitewashed cottage sat below a thatched roof so endearingly steep it resembled a witch's hat. Worn red paint picked out old-fashioned mullioned windows and a battered wooden door. Utterly astonished by the sheer eccentricity and apparent age of the building, Harriet blinked and stared. Then she slammed on the brakes, thrust aside her seat belt and climbed out to explore.

The key turned in the door's lock with ease. A good sign, she thought, buzzing with anticipation. She stepped into a dim interior and was struck by the evocative smell of beeswax and flowers filling her nostrils. A tiny fire glowed in a massive smoke-blackened fireplace, which still rejoiced in all the black metal fittings that had once functioned as a cooking range. The light of the flames gleamed and danced over the dark wood patina of a centrally positioned table, on which was placed a bunch of misty purple lavender spikes and soft pink roses in a chipped crystal vase.

There were two doors, the first of which led into

a small room dominated by a high brass bed and a massive Victorian wardrobe. The other led into a much more recent extension to the cottage. Here, the kitchen housed an Aga and had an office corner that accommodated a very cluttered desk set against walls papered with tatty rosettes and faded photos of racing events and horses. Another bedroom led off a small rear corridor. Praying that the final door next to it led into a bathroom that enjoyed full washing facilities, Harriet depressed the knob.

'Go away…I'm in the bath, Una!' a startled male voice yelled in protest.

Almost simultaneously Harriet heard a door open off the kitchen and a girl shouting, 'Fergal…there's a strange car out front. Forget having a soak. If that's the Carmichael woman arriving, she'll not want to find a strange fella in her bath!'

A tall whip-thin teenager in dirty jodhpurs focused on Harriet with sparkling brown eyes and thumped a dismayed hand to her full mouth. Her spiky black hair was threaded with purplish streaks in true gothic style, but she was without a doubt an extraordinarily pretty girl.

There was the sound of a body hastily vacating sloshing bathwater. 'How do you know? I have a way with women,' Fergal quipped cheekily. 'She might be glad enough to find me here—'

'I can't give you an honest opinion on that score until I see you,' Harriet murmured truthfully.

A silence that screamed fell, and then the upper half of a young giant with a tousled blond head twisted round the door to peer out at her. He had navy blue eyes and an unshaven chin. Even though Harriet was thoroughly irritated to find her magical cottage invaded by strangers, she was not at all surprised at Fergal's belief that he had a way with her sex. In his early to mid-twenties, and with a smile that could strip paint, he was very handsome.

'Bloody hell…I'm sorry!' Fergal groaned, and slammed the door fast.

'I'm Una Donnelly…your part-time groom,' the teenager announced, tilting her chin pugnaciously.

'I didn't realise that anybody else had keys for this place,' Harriet remarked carefully.

Una reddened. 'Fergal's not anybody,' she proclaimed defensively. 'He's like Kathleen's unofficial partner and he's always made himself at home here.'

'Only not now that there's a new owner!' Fergal called hurriedly from behind the door he had opened a crack.

'I assume I have you to thank for dusting and lighting the fire in the hall.' Harriet walked back into the kitchen to fill the kettle and put it on to boil. She was very tired and extremely hungry, and she needed to get Samson out of the car. After a crack-of-dawn start yesterday, she had driven her packed car from London to board a ferry in Wales. After spending the night on Irish soil in a bed and breakfast, her subsequent journey across the midlands to the Atlantic west coast had been long and draining.

'No. Why would I do that?' Una asked in a startled tone that suggested such homely domestic tasks were alien to her.

'Well, someone did.'

'But I didn't know for sure when you were coming—'

'Good heavens!' Harriet lost interest in that minor mystery when she looked out of the window for the first time. A simply huge mansion sat on the hill above her new home. Silhouetted against the dulling blue sky, the house was as pure and classic an example of Georgian architecture as she had ever seen, and the setting was spectacular. 'What's that?'

'Flynn Court.'

Harriet tensed. 'Any connection with a business called Flynn Enterprises?'

'Big connection,' Una emphasised at her elbow. 'With Rafael Flynn on your case you don't need to worry about us. We don't want you out. We're on your side. We think it's great that you want to make a go of the yard.'

'I'm delighted to hear it.' Smothering a yawn, Harriet trekked outside to release Samson from the captivity of his cosy carrier and bring in the groceries she had bought on the road. Did this Rafael Flynn want her out? She winced. Obviously he had tried to buy her out already. But he couldn't achieve that without her agreement, so why should the teenager's words leave her feeling threatened?

Samson danced round her feet, tossing a half-hearted bark of greeting at Una, but reserved his main enthusiasm for the food and water that Harriet was placing outside for him.

'I've never seen anything that tiny,' Una gasped. 'Is it a dog or a rat? You'd better watch out for it in the yard. Horses spook easily.'

'Samson will learn. He may be small but he has the heart of a lion.' Harriet made a determined attempt to build up the chihuahua's profile.

Unimpressed, Una frowned in wonderment at the lion-hearted miniature dog. 'Don't let him wander. The wolfhounds up at the Court would eat him up in one big bite.'

Fergal reappeared, fully dressed in the shabby gear of a horseman. With his damp blond head hovering within inches of the low ceiling, his blue eyes anxious, he held out a huge hand. 'I'm Fergal Gibson, Miss Carmichael—'

'Harriet,' she said automatically

He put a set of keys down on the table with a definitive snap. 'I wouldn't have been using the facilities if I'd known you were arriving today. There's the spare keys back.'

'But you can't just surrender to her like that!' Una launched at him fierily. 'Like this place is nothing to you and you don't care that you're losing a fortune. Kathleen never meant for this to happen—'

'Stay out of this, Una,' Fergal cut in with frank male embarrassment. 'Harriet's only just got here, and I'm sure she'd prefer to be taking stock of her new home without uninvited visitors. I'll lock up the horses for the night, shall I?'

Uncertain as to what to do and say at that moment, Harriet walked out in to the yard with Una in the young blond man's wake. As her mother's cousin had died nearly four months earlier, it had not occurred to Harriet that there might still be livestock on the property. Certainly none had appeared on the inventory of assets. What exactly was the role of an 'unofficial partner'? Encountering a truculent look of suspicion from the hot-headed teenager, Harriet suppressed a groan, for she was beginning to suspect that nothing about her Irish inheritance was likely to be as straightforward as she had fondly imagined it would be.

At the back of the cottage a new barn and a row of state-of-the-art stables greeted Harriet's astonished scrutiny. Her attention skimmed over the floodlit sand paddock with jumps sited towards the rear and what looked like the entrance to an indoor arena.

'Kathleen and Fergal split the costs of construction. He did the actual building himself. It took three years, and he worked all the hours of the day to afford his share. He bought in young stock and he trained them to sell on as four-year-olds. The horses are his.' Una spelt out that information with the curtness of youthful stress. 'But he owns nothing else because it's all built on your land, and he's got no right to compensation, either.'

Harriet drew in a long deep breath and slowly exhaled again. 'I'll handle this with Fergal direct,' she countered gently. 'Give me time to get settled in.'

Spirited brown eyes sought hers. 'I just want you to do what's right. Kathleen was very fond of him, and he kept the yard going for her when she was ill.'

Discomfited, Harriet nodded and wandered over to the stables to escape any more argument. Fergal gave her an admirably cheerful introduction to the three inmates that dispelled her unease. There were two brown geldings and a huge almost black stallion of about seventeen hands. Sighting Harriet, the big horse gave a nervous whinny and pranced restlessly in his box.

'Watch out for Pluto. He can be a cheeky devil,' Fergal warned her. 'Don't try to handle him on your own.'

'He's superb,' Harriet acknowledged, impressed by Pluto's undeniable presence.

'He's the one I'm hoping will make my fortune,' Fergal confided with a sunny smile that lit up his open tanned face. 'Don't be listening to Una. She means well but she's too young to understand,' he added in a rueful undertone. 'This is your place and Kathleen always meant you to have it.'

'I didn't even know she existed. I wish we'd met.' Harriet grimaced. 'I'm not only saying that because I think I should. Ever since Kathleen Gallagher remembered me in her will and I had to ask my mother who she was I've been eaten with curiosity about Kathleen and a side of the family I never knew.'

'Let me tell you, in some cases never knowing your relations could be a gift,' her companion opined wryly, surprising her with that hint of greater depth than his candid expression and easy smile suggested.

A couple of hours later, with Samson at her heels, Harriet took a rough tour of the fields that were designated as hers on the property plan. A wave of happiness and enthusiasm had temporarily banished her exhaustion. It was on this fertile ground that she would build a viable business that would still allow her the time to savour life. It didn't matter that the fencing needed to be renewed, or that the outbuildings that had not been built by Fergal were badly in need of repair: she had enough money in the bank for now to take care of things. The green rolling countryside ornamented by scattered groups of stately mature trees was truly beautiful, and that was infinitely more important to her.

The smell of the sea was in the air when she followed a winding uneven track that took her right down to the seashore and a stretch of glorious white deserted beach that disappeared into the distance. With the sun setting in crimson splendour it was breathtaking. The sound of the Atlantic surf breaking against the silence of true isolation enclosed Harriet and she smiled. Tomorrow she would deal with any problems, but this evening was just for celebrating—not only the joyful surprise of ownership but also a new beginning and an independence that she had never known before.

Back at the cottage, she unpacked only the necessities and enjoyed a quick supper of soup and a roll. She thought how comfortable it was not to have to stick to a strict diet or feel the nagging need to retire still hungry from the table. Not having a man around had advantages, she told herself with determined good cheer as she went into the bedroom: she didn't care that she had put on weight since breaking up with Luke. She pulled on a floral jersey camisole and matching shorts and sank into the blissfully soft brass bed with a sigh of grateful contentment. Cosy comfort and a full tummy felt good.

It was daylight when she wakened with a jolting start and sat up. From somewhere she could hear a loud clattering and banging noise. Alarm made her tense. Scrambling out of bed, she raced through the kitchen to look out into the stable yard. Her breath tripped in her throat in dismay when she saw the door of Pluto's stall swinging back on its hinges in the stiff breeze. How the heck had he got out?

Yanking open the back door, she hauled on the muddy Wellington boots she had worn while she walked the boundaries of her land the evening before. As she hurried round the corner of the cottage she was just in time to see Pluto sail like a ship on springs over the fencing that marked the division between the livery yard and the grounds of Flynn Court. Saying a rude word under her breath, Harriet threw herself at the fence and clambered over it to set off in keen pursuit...

CHAPTER TWO

JUST AFTER DAWN, Flynn Court was wreathed in a sea-fret that semi-obscured the classic elegance of the great house and concealed the worst of the dilapidation inflicted by decades of neglect. As the sun broke through the mist, Rafael settled his helicopter down on the landing pad situated to the north side of his ancestral home.

Ireland felt cool and airy and fresh after the heat of the Caribbean sun. Emerging from the helicopter, his current lover, Bianca, had a dramatic fit of the shivers and announced that she was freezing. As Rafael had warned her already that accompanying him to the wilds of County Kerry would involve a degree of physical hardship, a total absence of luxury and no exclusive social outlets whatever, he ignored the complaint. On Irish soil he always relaxed, secure in the knowledge that the local community respected his privacy and that the paparazzi who had finally connected his dual Irish-Italian heritage would receive no assistance and even less encouragement to pry further.

Breakfast was brought up to the master bedroom suite by one of the staff he'd had flown in to make the house ready for occupation the previous week. Barefoot, his shirt hanging open, Rafael sprawled along the window seat with his coffee and feasted his attention on the rolling parkland that ran down to the jagged rocks and the sand dunes that bounded the bay where he had played as a child.

In his father's home in Italy he had been watched every hour of the day by nannies and bodyguards. The staff had walked in fear of Valente's violent temper and had restricted Rafael's play in an effort to protect him from even the smallest injury. Only at Flynn Court had Rafael had the chance to get dirty and paddle, fishing in rock pools and building dams. With his mother too out of it to know what he was doing most of the time, Rafael had run wild and free on the windswept beauty of the beach at the foot of the hill.

'This is sublime…' Bianca employed her favourite word, which she used to distinguish everything from a good meal to phenomenal sex and expensive perfume.

Rafael had forgotten her presence. She had little stimulating conversation, so tuning her out was not a challenge. Previously he had decided that the ability to emulate wallpaper was a something in her favour. Now, blonde hair trailing into a flowing mane over one shoulder, she was reclining on the bed. As befitted a supermodel who was internationally renowned for her beauty, she looked as inhumanly perfect as an advertising hoarding. She was posed for maximum effect, her flawless body arrayed in silk lingerie the colour of a café latte, artfully dampened nipples poking through the lace for his admiration. Oozing confidence in her manifold attractions, she stretched out languid legs that were an incredible thirty-six inches long. But Rafael wasn't a photographer, and he liked his sex a little less choreographed. At this moment he felt nothing and knew that, once again, he had become bored.

Anyway, Bianca's green eyes, smoky with smudged kohl, were fixed with mesmeric intensity on the true object of her desire. She smiled a Helen of Troy smile of unsurpassable luminosity that lit up the exquisite symmetry of her face. Rafael watched this display of blatant self-love that no mere man— or woman—could ever hope to equal. Bianca shifted position, skimming a light, caressing hand down over the smooth sculpted line of her slender thigh.

She was enthralled to the point of ecstasy by her own beautiful reflection in the eighteenth-century mirror on the wall opposite.

A sudden noise from outside sent Rafael's attention flying back to the tall sash window. A horse was galloping at breakneck speed across the field below his lawn. His interest was caught; he was a great horse-lover, and the owner of an internationally acclaimed stud farm in Kildare. He stood up for a better view; a flutter of colourful movement behind the lower hedge that bounded the field made him reach for the binoculars on the pier table.

A woman was fighting her way through the hedge. She was wearing a quite bizarre outfit: a camisole and shorts fashioned of fabric decorated with large pink flowers. Pyjamas? Worn with green Wellington boots? An aristocratic black brow climbed. A stray shard of sunshine made her hair shine as bright as polished copper in firelight. It was an amazing colour, red as the richest wine against her pale skin. Could this be the tough and savvy London career woman who had refused to sell the Gallagher property back to the Flynn Court estate? The woman who wanted to downshift to the idyllic illusion of rural simplicity? Rafael grinned. One more dreamer bites the dust....

'If the mountain won't come...' Bianca giggled

and let intimate hands stray below his shirt to trace his muscular back and then sink below his waist.

Rafael's even white teeth gritted and he shifted to dislodge her. He wasn't in the mood. After a week on the yacht in which Bianca had entertained his entire crew by walking around nude at every opportunity she had lost all mystery and allure. He had shagged her on the plane to pass the time. Perhaps out of guilt over his essential indifference now that desire had fled. Why did he get bored so easily? Why was the chase always so much more exciting than the sexual catch? But then, honesty urged him to admit, when had he ever had to mount a pursuit to score with a woman? Or employ the tactics of charm and persuasion?

His intent gaze narrowed on the woman charging across the field full tilt. Her firm round breasts bounced with unfettered abandon. The stallion soared like a great bird over the fence onto the rolling lawn. The redhead flung herself sideways over the same barrier, got into difficulties and virtually fell down the other side. She had a generous bottom, shaped like a heart. In fact, he acknowledged, his interest fairly ensnared, the body below that clinging jersey fabric was as lush and ripe with curves as an old-fashioned hourglass. That voluptuous hint of pure feminine abundance was distinctly sexy.

Without any warning, she achieved the effect that Bianca had failed to rouse. His slumbering libido kicked in with a surge of sexual enthusiasm that startled him.

'There's a fat woman running round your garden!' Bianca exclaimed in disbelief.

Fat? Rafael would have laughed out loud had he not at that moment registered that the stallion was frantically rolling its eyes in fear and panic. In that state of terror the horse was as much a danger to himself as to the foolish woman chasing him. Without hesitation, Rafael raced for the stairs.

'Pluto...shush, there's a nice boy,' Harriet wheezed, struggling to make her voice calm and comforting, but so out of breath that her lungs felt strangled.

Showing the whites of his eyes, Pluto careered round like a crazy mechanical bucking horse, and then he started coming right at her and she froze. Out of the corner of her eye she caught a flash of sudden movement, but that was the only warning she got before she was snatched off her feet and pinned face down to the damp ground, her ribcage momentarily squashed flat beneath a powerful masculine body. The thunder of hooves passing too close to her ears for comfort made her appreciate that she had very nearly been trampled.

'Stay here,' an accented male voice growled, and the weight on her back lifted again as he tugged Pluto's head collar from her loosened grasp.

Harriet flipped over and watched him approach the sweating, snorting stallion. He was very tall and his movements were incredibly quiet, assured and graceful. His black hair was cropped short, his feet bare in the dew-wet grass. His blue shirt fluttered back in the morning breeze from the soft, well-worn denims that hugged his narrow hips and long powerful thighs to reveal a hair-roughened bronze torso that was as sleek and hard with muscle as the proverbial six-pack. She flushed at her straying attention and then noted that he was talking softly to Pluto. He knew his way around horses all right. The huge stallion trembled. The man reached up and, still talking with soothing cool, slowly and deftly slipped on Pluto's head collar. In silence she watched as the stallion calmed down beneath much firmer handling than she would have dared to attempt.

Prior to this point she had only seen her rescuer's bronzed profile, and now she saw him face-on. Her blue eyes widened and her heart began a slow, heavy beat that echoed her growing tension. He was drop-dead gorgeous, and for an instant she thought there was something eerily familiar about that stunning bone structure of his. Frowning, she discarded that unlikely notion, but still she stared at him, drinking in every vibrant aspect of him with a hunger that was startlingly new to her. His high cheekbones framed brilliant, dark golden eyes, divided by a strong masculine nose and completed by an aggressive jawline.

'Thank you,' Harriet said unevenly.

'So you're the lady who is planning to get back to nature and raise organic vegetables on my doorstep,' he husked. 'I'm Rafael Flynn.'

'Harriet Carmichael.' Only when she encountered that mocking scrutiny did she finally recall that she was wearing her comfy floral pyjamas, which could not be said to flatter the fuller figure. Her face coloured up and burned with embarrassment. She was furious with herself for blushing. After all, only a bikini would have shown more flesh. 'Sorry about all the fuss. I don't know how Pluto got out—'

'If your horse had strayed onto the road he would be dead,' Rafael Flynn slotted in smoothly.

Feeling that it was grossly insensitive to point out the obvious, Harriet stiffened defensively and resisted the urge to inform him that Pluto did not belong to her. Technically the stallion had been in her charge, and she was not one to duck responsibility. 'But fortunately he didn't,' she countered tightly, while also trying not to wonder how long Pluto would have had to hang around the very quiet road to get run over by passing traffic.

A weather-beaten older man in a dark suit hurried round the side of the house towards them and came forward to take charge of the stallion. 'Tolly will ensure that Pluto is brought back to you in a horsebox,' Rafael Flynn asserted.

Harriet bit her lip, feeling like a schoolgirl being rebuked for imprudent behaviour. She would dearly have loved to seize hold of Pluto herself and frogmarch him back to his stable. But there were too many barriers to be cleared, and she was too sensible to even consider taking such a risk with a horse too powerful for her to hold. 'I'm sorry you've been inconvenienced.'

'Relax… I would have been gutted had I missed out on those enchanting pyjamas,' Rafael murmured silkily.

His heavily lidded dark eyes roamed with unashamed intent over the jutting swell of her ripe breasts and lingered there with wicked appreciation before he directed his attention back up to the wonderfully voluptuous promise of her full-lipped pink mouth. If it had not been for Bianca he would have invited his neighbour to join him for breakfast in bed. At the same time, he knew that with regard to Harriet Carmichael he had to take care of business first. He never, ever allowed anything to deflect him from his goal. And she was in for a rough and rocky passage if she continued to oppose him.

Wholly unprepared for his comment and appraisal, and interpreting both as derisive amusement, Harriet flung him a look of angry disconcertion. 'Very funny. Don't let me keep you!'

Taken aback by that inept response to a mildly flirtatious comment, Rafael frowned as Bianca chose that inopportune moment to stroll out of the house. 'The countryside is sublime,' she sighed, invading his space.

The statuesque blonde was so beautiful that Harriet simply gaped, only glancing away uncomfortably when she appreciated that the other woman was virtually naked below the silk wrap that she had forgotten to close over. The possessive hand she curved over Rafael Flynn's arm made Harriet feel equally uncomfortable. Had she been guilty of casting admiring eyes over another woman's husband?

'Miss Carmichael…' In a fluster, Harriet focused on the silver haired older man, who had passed custody of Pluto over to a younger man in working clothes. 'I'm Joseph Tolly. Forty years back our families were neighbours. You have a great look of your mother.'

A huge smile of surprise and pleasure momentarily banished Harriet's discomfiture. 'Honestly? My goodness, you must have known her. I would really love to hear what you remember about those days.'

'You'd be very welcome to visit me this evening,' the old man told her warmly.

'I'd be delighted. Where do you live?'

Unaccustomed to being ignored, Rafael watched the exchange of civilities between his usually correct butler and his new neighbour with grim amusement. Bianca was flouncing back and forth like a child threatening a tantrum, because nobody was demonstrating the slightest interest in her either and attention was the oxygen of her existence. With that example before him, Rafael was able to concede that the ability to enjoy a friendly chat whatever the circumstances was inimitably Irish. He could even afford to smile with benevolence at such sentimentality between strangers. Having refused his generous offer to buy her property, his sexy neighbour was about to pay the price for that defiance in what would be a rather less civilised second act. When necessary, Rafael played a long game, and a deep one, and he did not stop playing until success was his.

Encountering Rafael Flynn's glinting dark, reflective gaze, Harriet felt chilled. A split second later, discarding that sensation, she recalled that she was still standing on the front lawn of his fabulous Georgian mansion, and mortification threatened to eat her alive. How could she have forgotten for one moment that she was parading around in her pyjamas? Was it any wonder that Rafael Flynn was looking at her as though she had escaped from a zoo?

'Excuse me…' she muttered, turning hurriedly on her heel to trek rigid-backed down the hill. Every big gaudy rose splayed across her bottom felt like a stabbing source of personal torment. The arrogant louse had laughed at her! But, she reflected uncomfortably, he could hardly have missed the juvenile way she had blushed and stared at him with eyes on stalks. Any guy that handsome had to be aware of his effect on women, so he was certain to have noticed. What on earth had come over her? She cringed with chagrin.

As if that were not bad enough, that crack about organic vegetables had hit her on the raw as well. Why shouldn't she want to have a bit of a go at growing things? It seemed Mr McNally, the solicitor, had repeated everything she'd said—but then why should he not have? She had not asked the poor man to keep her aspirations to get down and dirty in the vegetable patch a big dark secret. Since when had she become so over-sensitive?

After a quick shower, and an even faster breakfast, Harriet began to plan the rebirth of the livery yard in greater detail. A proper name for the business and a sign out on the road would be the first step. Lost in thought, she stroked Samson's silky ears until the little dog sighed with contentment. She would have to do some research to see which services were most likely to be in demand locally and check out the competition. She also needed to get moving on a repair programme, and talk to Fergal to find out exactly what his unofficial partnership with Kathleen had entailed. Someone to supply help and cover in what was basically a twenty-four-seven business would be very useful, Harriet conceded thoughtfully.

Fergal Gibson drove into the yard just as Pluto was being led out of the huge horsebox that had arrived from Flynn Court.

'What happened?' he exclaimed. 'How did Pluto get out?'

'The stable door's damaged,' Harriet told him. 'I think he kicked his way out, but I have no idea why.'

'It could have been Flynn's helicopter coming in.' Fergal ran careful hands over the restive stallion in search of injury and with a relieved sigh put him into another stall. 'I'm really sorry. I'll put up another bolt. Catching him must've been a nightmare.'

'Rafael Flynn caught him,' Harriet admitted ruefully.

Fergal chuckled. 'Women and horses. Now, there is a guy with the magic touch. I hear that he can make them do anything for him.'

Her blue eyes gleamed. She was tempted to quip that that was no doubt why Rafael Flynn appeared to have such a good opinion of himself. 'Is he married?'

'Are you joking? I hear his latest lady is some famous fashion model.'

Thinking of the woman she had seen, Harriet thought that figured, and she told Fergal to come inside for tea when he had finished in the yard.

'One of the local farmers has been looking after Kathleen's animals for you,' he informed her then, washing his hands at the sink with the ease of someone very much at home with his surroundings. 'You'd best decide what you want done with them.'

'Animals?'

'Kathleen has a soft touch for strays. There's an old mare called Snowball that she rescued, and she can still be ridden. There's a pig too...oh, yeah, and chickens, ex-battery farm inmates,' Fergal explained ruefully. 'We're talking pets and charity cases here, not pedigrees. I had them moved before Eugene McNally did his inventory because he would've had them put down. Now you can make the tough decisions.'

Harriet was already smiling at the prospect of a readymade family of livestock which would provide a vital link back to the cousin whom she had to thank for her inheritance. 'If they had a home with Kathleen they'll have a home with me.'

His tanned face broke into a warm, attractive grin.

'Right.' Harriet curved her hands round the mug

of tea in front of her and breathed in deep. 'You're using the stables here…'

'I was hoping we could come to an arrangement,' Fergal admitted.

'I'd like that if it is possible,' Harriet told him honestly. 'But I do need to make a living, and right now I don't know if the figures will add up with your horses using that amount of space—'

'I could start work on fixing up the old stables and move the geldings in there instead. That was phase two of Kathleen's expansion plan. But the new stables were essential to bring in the owners who wanted their mounts to have only the best.'

Talking to Fergal was easy. He was straightforward, and happy to talk about her late cousin's original plans. Having been priced out of the riding school business by the high costs of insurance and the seasonal aspect of the tourist trade, Kathleen had hoped to build a livery yard that would be upmarket to attract new clients and increase her income.

'She must have had savings or something, because she really did spend a mint here,' Fergal advanced. 'She bought that pick-up brand-new, and the horsebox arrived only the week before she had the first heart attack.' His cheerfulness visibly ebbed at that sobering recollection. 'She was sixty-three and seemed as fit as a fiddle. She was waiting for surgery when she died.'

Harriet watched Fergal swallow thickly and knew that he had been genuinely fond of the older woman. He reminded her of a big, blond good-natured bear, slow of speech and thoughtful and kind.

'You should come to the Point-to-Point races with me tomorrow. It's the last meeting of the season,' he told her with enthusiasm. 'I'm running Tailwind. I can introduce you around. People need to know you're open for business.'

'I'd like that.' Belatedly conscious of the speculative masculine look of appreciation she was receiving, Harriet glanced away and tried not to smile. She was flattered that he appeared to find her attractive. But she suspected that Fergal Gibson might be a wild flirt, and if she responded it would probably wreck any prospect of their establishing a good working relationship. Unless she was reading him wrong, it would be easy come, easy go with Fergal, and that had never been her style. But maybe a silly rebound fling was what she needed right now…after all, she had been extremely sensible and cautious all her life and where had it got her? Luke, she reminded herself squarely, was with Alice now.

'What's your interest in Harriet Carmichael?' Rafael asked his elderly butler smoothly, while Bianca chatted to a friend on the phone about how sublime Ireland was—with the exceptions of the weather, the absence of large shopping outlets and nightclubs, Rafael's cold and comfortless ancestral home and the amount of time he spent in the stables.

Tolly gave him a little smile. 'Now, wouldn't that be telling?'

Rafael laughed with true appreciation, for only Tolly would dare to tell him to mind his own business. 'What do you know about her?'

'That she'll not be single for long,' the older man forecast with assurance, his blue eyes twinkling.

Rafael elevated a mocking black brow. 'On what do you base that belief?'

'She's a fine-looking girl with a lovely smile and land and a business. When it comes to a good catch the local lads are neither blind nor stupid. No, that little lady will be snatched up and off the market by the winter.'

'Maybe she craves something rather more exciting?' Rafael murmured softly.

Tolly's weather-beaten features stiffened. 'I don't think so, sir.'

Sir? Rafael wondered why the old man should be so thin-skinned about a young woman he had only met that day. Was it because Tolly had once known her family and already considered her part of the community? Or was he simply showing his disapproval of Rafael's infinitely casual attitude to women and sex? Whatever, Rafael was very much amused by Tolly's sudden formality. Across the room, Bianca was now dancing, her hips shimmying to the driving beat of the music she had put on. She shed her jacket slowly, provocatively tugged her suede belt free of her tiny mini-skirt and treated herself to a seductive appraisal in the vast gilt mirror. Rafael decided that his next lover would be less vain and more intelligent and switched on the business news.

Joseph Tolly lived in a small, incredibly neat gate lodge beside the distinctly ruinous rear entrance to the Flynn Court estate. For all his arrogant confidence, Harriet reflected, with a stab of wicked satisfaction that shook her, Rafael Flynn was clearly too poor to adequately maintain his ancestral home. So why the heck had he attempted to buy Kathleen Gallagher's property from her at such a healthy price?

The old man appeared at the door before Harriet even reached it. 'Come on in,' he urged with a broad smile of welcome.

She was touched to see the careful preparations he had made for her visit. A snowy white lace-edged cloth had been laid on a tray that bore old-fashioned floral bone china and a luscious chocolate cake. The simply furnished room was immaculately tidy and every wooden surface gleamed.

'Will you tell me everything you remember about my mother's family?' Harriet urged her host eagerly, and then, rather more self-consciously, her cheeks colouring, she added, 'You must be wondering why I'm asking a stranger when she's still alive. My mother isn't very nostalgic about the past.'

'Perhaps there wasn't much for her to be sentimental about,' Joseph Tolly said gently. 'In those days this community was struggling to survive. There wasn't much employment. Even now the tourists need encouragement to travel several miles of twisting road from the nearest town to visit Ballyflynn. Have you been to see the old place where your family used to live?'

'I don't know where it is.'

'Your mother's family lived a field away from mine, on a smallholding about two miles out of the village. The house is derelict now, but I'll draw you a little map so that you can go and have a look around.'

'Thank you...I'd love to do that,' Harriet confided.

'Shall I tell you what I remember best about your mother?'

Harriet nodded very seriously and offered to pour the tea.

Watching her take charge of the tea tray, Joseph

Tolly smiled and settled himself more comfortably into his shabby fireside chair. 'Your mother must have been about fourteen when she decided she didn't want to be known as Agnes any more, and she started calling herself Eva instead.'

Harriet blinked in surprise, for she had not known that her parent had chosen that name for herself. Agnes? But then all she had ever known of Eva's history was the absolute basics: that her mother was the daughter of a small farmer who had been widowed while she was still a child. Her older teenaged brother had been killed in a tractor accident.

'What a rumpus she caused!' Tolly chuckled. 'The nuns at the convent school had no tolerance for girls' fancies, but your mother defied the lot of them—even the cantankerous old priest that we had then.' His expressive eyes invited her to enjoy his warm humour. 'Unfortunately I think she paid the price for it, because your grandfather took her out of school early and she was a bright girl.'

'What was my grandfather like?' Harriet prompted eagerly.

'Dermot Gallagher had a mean temper on him,' Joseph told her, with a look of honest apology at having to make that admission. 'He wasn't a lucky man, and his disappointments soured him and made him a harsh parent. He wouldn't let your mother have a life like other girls, so when she ran away nobody was that surprised. If she wasn't working on the farm, he hired her out to work for other people and kept her wages.'

Harriet was sobered by what she was learning, and finally appreciated why her mother might have preferred to leave that distant past buried. 'I wish she'd told me what it was like for her then. I had no idea her childhood was that tough.'

'Your cousin, Kathleen, once told my late wife that when your mother tried to stand up to Dermot he would threaten to have her locked up with the nuns. That may sound unbelievable to you, but right up until twenty years ago certain convents ran commercial laundries staffed by young women who had been put in their charge because they were supposedly a threat to decent society. More than one disobedient daughter ended up in those unhappy places, and some of them never came out again.'

Harriet lost colour when she made the connection. 'You're talking about the Magdalene Laundries?'

'Yes.' Tolly nodded grave confirmation. 'Life was very different here then. No one would have dreamt of interfering between a father and his child. '

'She must have felt so alone…' Harriet thought that it was hardly surprising that when Eva had finally escaped her father's threats and restrictions, partying had held rather more appeal for her than parenting.

'Hasn't Eva the life now, though?' Joseph remarked in a determinedly cheerful change of subject that suggested he was more comfortable skimming the surface of her mother's past. 'I saw a picture of her in an old magazine last year. She looked like a queen in a ballgown at some charity do. She's come a long way from the young woman who used to help out in the village shop.'

'Could you give me the names of any of her schoolfriends?' Harriet suspected that the key to discovering her father's identity would most likely be found amongst her mother's contemporaries.

'I was acquainted with the family situation, but not with much else. We were of different generations.' His eyes veiled, he served her with a mouthwatering wedge of chocolate cake, and for a few minutes there was silence as Harriet did justice to it.

'I imagine that there was quite an uproar after my mother ran away.' Harriet was thoroughly relaxed, and happy to match Tolly's frankness with her own. 'I'm very keen to find out who my father was.'

Clearly unprepared for that admission, Joseph looked startled. 'But surely your mother—?'

'No…she's always refused to say,' Harriet admitted ruefully.

'But you can hardly go around asking awkward questions of people you don't even know,' the old man pointed out. 'You could cause offence, and you might also cause trouble by casting suspicion on an innocent party. I would strongly advise you to speak to your mother again.'

Harriet suppressed a heavy sigh. She was not close to Eva, and worked hard at conserving the relationship she did have with her. The last time she had tackled the older woman on the score of her parentage Eva had taken strong umbrage.

Joseph gave his guest an anxious appraisal. 'I think you also need to ask yourself what you're hoping to get from the information you seek. Your father may be a man who let your mother down when she most needed his support. He might have no interest in knowing you.'

'Yes, I accept that.' Harriet was, however, studying her companion with increased interest. The very urgency with which he spoke made her wonder if he knew rather more about her background than he was willing to admit. 'Were there rumours at the time?' she pressed more boldly. 'I mean, people must've talked.'

'People always gossip, and rarely with kindness or commonsense,' Tolly responded steadily. 'It would be wrong of me to repeat idle chatter. If your mother was seeing anyone it was kept very much a secret.'

Harriet let the subject drop there, guiltily conscious that she had said rather too much for so short an acquaintance, and listened as her host talked gladly about less contentious issues. It had gone nine when she drove home in a deeply pensive mood. What *did* she hope to achieve from establishing the identity of her father? She knew that she had a deep need to know exactly where she had come from. But wasn't it more than that?

Harriet had never really felt that she belonged anywhere. In the same way she had never known what it was to have a parent who was absolutely hers...at least not for long. As a child she had been hurt and confused, because she'd rarely seen the mother she adored. She had then had to adjust to the cruel reality that Eva could somehow manage to be a full time parent for her younger son and daughter. But perhaps it had hurt most of all when Harriet had finally discovered that the man she had grown up believing to be her father was not her biological father after all.

Eva had been six months pregnant when she'd married Will Carmichael, a research scientist a decade older. Seemingly she had snatched at the chance of a wedding ring and a name for her unborn child. A quiet, studious man, Will had been besotted with his youthful Irish bride, but the union had been a disastrous mismatch. Walking down a London street one day, Eva had been stopped by a talent scout and discovered as a fashion model. Hiring a nanny to take care of her baby, Eva had flung herself into the excitement of fame, fortune and foreign travel. The unequal marriage had disintegrated without fanfare.

Even after the divorce Will had been left to shoulder the burden of raising Harriet while Eva concentrated on her career. And when Harriet was five years old her mother had remarried and become a society wife. The wealthy English businessman with whom Eva had had her younger children, Alice and Boyce, had not encouraged Harriet's visits to his country home in Surrey. He had disliked such an obvious reminder that his beautiful wife's past had featured other men, and in the interests of marital harmony Harriet had been virtually airbrushed out of her mother's life.

Harriet had been thirteen years old when she'd overheard a devastating exchange between Eva and Will on the phone.

'I wanted to tell Harriet the truth years ago, but you wouldn't agree,' Will had been saying, with unusual curtness of tone for so mild-mannered a man.

'She thinks of *me* as her father, and finding out that I'm no more her father than the Easter bunny will be a nasty shock! Teenagers are vulnerable, Eva. I don't care if your therapist believes that coming clean on that score will benefit you; I'm more concerned about how it might affect Harriet.'

Harriet had been shattered by the revelation that the father who had brought her up with so much apparent love and sacrifice was not even a blood relation. Even though Will had repeatedly assured her that he loved her just as much as any biological parent, Harriet had still felt like a cuckoo abandoned in his nest. In her heart, where she had used the salve of her father's love to compensate for her more distant bonds with her mother, she had felt utterly crushed. A kind and gentle man, Will Carmichael had taken on a responsibility that was not his and done his best by her principally because he had had no other choice. Her mother's refusal to finish the story by telling Harriet exactly who her birth father was had not helped.

The following morning dawned bright and breezy, and Harriet scrambled out of bed with a little frisson of anticipation: it was an absolutely perfect day for the races. A veteran of such country pursuits in her early teen years, and well aware of how rough and ready such events could be, she dug out warm comfy clothes and thermal socks to go with her Wellington boots.

Samson trotted round her feet and fussed until she set out his breakfast.

'You're a real little tyrant,' she told him fondly.

Out in the yard it was all go, and Harriet resolved to rise from her bed earlier. Fergal was cleaning up a dilapidated horse trailer and Una Donnelly was busy in Tailwind's box, engaged in plaiting his mane into intricate knots. Harriet leant on the stall door to watch. 'I was never very good at plaiting.'

The teenager looked across at her with a surprisingly ready smile, her liquid dark eyes full of pleasure, as if such compliments rarely came her way. 'It takes a lot of practice,' she confirmed. 'But I could teach you if you like.'

'OK…did Fergal bring you over?'

'No, I've got a bike.' She grimaced and lowered her voice to an exasperated whisper. 'He passes our door but he won't give me a lift because he's scared of folk talking about us. He's dead silly about stuff like that.'

Harriet gave her a non-committal smile.

'You should let Fergal use the horsebox,' Una added. 'It'll make the yard look better. You've got to think of your image in horsy circles.'

Harriet went pink and hurried over to Fergal to

urge. 'I never even thought to say…for goodness' sake, use Kathleen's horsebox!'

'If I do, will you do me the honour of walking Tailwind round the paddock for me before the race?' Fergal asked with a grin.

'I'd be delighted.'

'You can't let Harriet do it!' Una wailed incredulously. 'That's my job!'

As Harriet parted her lips, to hastily disclaim any desire to usurp the teenager's place, Fergal caught her eyes with a meaningful expression in his and a brief jerk of his head that begged her not to interfere. 'I'm sorry, Una. But Harriet needs to show her face and there's no better way.'

Una hung over the door of the stall and said, in a voice that throbbed with tragedy. 'How can you think of putting Harriet before me?'

Fergal bolted for the horsebox at the far end of the yard.

Harriet was transfixed by the virtual assault of the girl's outraged dark brown eyes. 'Are you dating him?' Una asked baldly.

Harriet was grateful to be in a position to utter a brisk negative.

'But he still chose you over me,' Una breathed in a wobbly voice, her eyes glassy with the threat of tears. But then you're an older woman.'

'He's thinking of business,' Harriet answered with determined lightness, while endeavouring not to picture herself as some sultry aging vamp given to charming toy boys off the straight and narrow. She remembered all too well how super-sensitive she had been to every perceived slight and rejection at Una's age, and could not decide whether the girl's startling prettiness was more of a blessing or a curse. 'Would you like some tea before we leave?'

'I'm not sure I'm coming any more,' the teenager mumbled chokily, half turning away. 'It's hardly worth my while, is it?'

'I'd really appreciate the company,' Harriet responded gently. 'Do you realise I know nothing about you yet?'

'Ask anyone in Ballyflynn. I'm Eilish Donnelly's little mistake. Always in trouble and no better than I ought to be, according to everyone!' Una shot at her in a tearful tirade. 'And when my big bully of a brother finds out I've been thrown out of another school he's going to kill me!'

Silence fell.

'I'll put the kettle on,' Harriet remarked prosaically, as if nothing out of the ordinary had been said.

'I suppose if I asked you if you fancied Fergal you'd tell me to mind my own business...' Una mumbled.

'I would.'

That instant comeback provoked an unexpected giggle from the temperamental teenager. 'At least you say what you think and don't talk down to me like I'm six years old—like *some* people I could mention!'

'Thanks…you saved my bacon,' Fergal muttered with real gratitude when he found Harriet alone in the kitchen. 'I am *really* glad you're around the yard now. Una can be a handful and no mistake. I don't know what's come over her.'

Harriet believed him. He was pale at the memory of Una's tearful emotional outburst, and practically shaking in his riding boots. Una was a strong-willed girl and she had Fergal in her sights. He probably did need to be very careful not to encourage her. Harriet could not help recalling how much more reserved and shy she had been with Luke, watching and loving from afar for so long, only revealing her feelings when it was safe to do so. Alice would have been much more open and extrovert and exciting. Perhaps that was yet another good reason why Luke had chosen to be with her sister rather than her.

'Don't get me wrong. Una's a good kid,' Fergal added hurriedly. 'She'll soon find someone more her age.'

Suspecting that Una was too passionate to quickly

forget her first love, Harriet said nothing. She struggled to shut Alice and Luke out of her thoughts again. The past was the past and she had to live with it.

In the horsebox, Una chattered pointedly to Harriet while shooting stony glances at a blissfully unaware Fergal as he drove. The fields where the Point-to-Point races were being held were accessed down a long rough lane. Marquee tents served as a weighing room for the jockeys and also provided a bar with one side walled off in a members only enclosure. The event was already thronged with people, most of whom were as sensibly and plainly garbed as Harriet, in anticipation of the muddy conditions.

As she waited for Tailwind to be unboxed, several men nearby in a huddle were talking nineteen to the dozen. As with Fergal, it took her a moment or two to be able to distinguish clear words in the colourful lilt and flow of the musical Kerry accent.

'So Martin the vet's trying to see to Flynn's mare that's in foal while the model woman is spreading herself across the stable wall like she's on one of those pop videos…you know, those ones they ban. And she's wearing a very short dress,' someone reported in an urgent whisper, 'And what does Flynn say? He only tells the hussy to go and get some clothes on before she frightens the horse! Isn't he the *man?*' was the conclusion, in a tone of deep envy and near reverence.

Her face hot, Harriet moved hurriedly out of ear-shot. Across the field she saw Rafael Flynn's girl-friend emerge from a big powerful four-wheel-drive. Garbed in a purely fashionable fitted tweed hacking jacket and pure white riding breeches that were skin tight, the leggy blonde moved as though she was on a catwalk, and looked so spectacular that everyone stopped dead to stare at her.

But Harriet's attention flew straight past her to the tall dark male striding towards the paddock: Rafael Flynn himself. His height and carriage picked him out from the crowd. The breeze had ruffled his lux-uriant hair into jet-black spikes. His lean, sculpted face was very bronzed against the light sweater he wore below an outdoor jacket so cool in cut it could only have been of Italian design.

Someone cannoned into Harriet and, caught un-prepared, she lurched backwards into the deep muddy tracks forged by some heavy vehicle and fell.

'I'm so sorry…I didn't see you. Are you hurt?' A burly older man was reaching down to help her up again.

Harriet glanced at the mud liberally staining her

jacket and jeans and then she laughed and shrugged. 'No, I'm fine…luckily I'm fully washable.'

From about thirty feet away Rafael watched the surprisingly good-natured exchange. Most of the women he knew would have been screaming the place down. Harriet's instant smile seemed designed to reassure the clumsy idiot who had sent her flying that being tipped into the mud had been a fun experience for her. Right on cue, Bianca approached him to lament the dirt now spattering her highly polished leather boots. The diamond choker he had given her as a farewell gift glittered at her swan-like throat. Within a few hours she would be boarding her flight home to Belgium. She dug out a little hand mirror to check her hair and the temptation was too much for her: she succumbed to studying herself from every angle. Crushing boredom assailed him and he walked away without her noticing.

'I wonder what Rafael Flynn is doing here,' Fergal mused as he accompanied Harriet over to the paddock with his gelding. 'He doesn't often appear at local meetings.'

Keen punters were lining the fence, eager for a look at the runners in the next race. Harriet took charge of Tailwind. Halfway through her first round of the paddock she connected with brilliant, dark and incisive eyes and her heart jumped as though she had hit an electric fence. Rafael Flynn. She looked away, colour warming her cheeks. Her copper hair blew in bright streamers across her face until she clawed it back with a self-conscious hand.

Once the jockey had mounted Tailwind, to warm him up before the race, Fergal ensured that she met a lot of people. He was popular and he knew everyone. Several locals spoke with warm regret about her cousin, Kathleen, and she was asked about the type of livery that she would be offering once she got the yard up and running again. Throughout it all she was conscious of an infuriating constant need to look around and see where Rafael Flynn was, but she fought that mortifying urge with every weapon in her armoury. For goodness' sake, she wasn't a schoolgirl any more and she wasn't about to behave like one!

Tailwind shot over the starting line like a bullet out of a gun. But he also ran out of the race at the second fence. Crestfallen by the poor showing, Fergal walked the gelding back to the horsebox. 'Where's Una disappeared to?'

Harriet noted the teenager ducking behind the sweet stall and moved with determination through the crowds to speak to her. 'What are you doing over here? Fergal's looking for you—'

Una peered nervously out at her. 'I'll be over in

a minute. My brother's over at the winners' enclo-sure…I don't want him to see me.'

'Is he that scary?'

'Scarier than scary.' For a moment Una looked very young and vulnerable. 'I'm never going to live up to his expectations. He wants me to be clever, like he is, and I'm not.'

'I bet you're a lot smarter than you think you are. Don't put yourself down,' Harriet told her squarely. 'Can't you talk to your mother about this?'

A thin shoulder jerked in an awkward shrug and Una veiled her eyes. 'My mum's not well a lot of the time. I don't like bothering her. I have my sister, but she has a husband and a baby too…that's why I hang out so much at the yard.'

Harriet resisted a sudden urge to hug the younger woman. 'You're always welcome there.'

An older woman intercepted her on the way back to the horsebox and questioned her closely about the livery yard facilities. Having expressed keen inter-est in a retirement package for her elderly horse, her first potential customer arranged to call and inspect the stables.

A smile of satisfaction on her lips, Harriet turned away and found Rafael Flynn striding towards her. Her tummy flipped like she was spinning on a merry-go-round.

'Is it true that you're planning to reopen the yard?' he enquired flatly.

'Yes…I don't think I'm enough of a gardener to make a living growing organic vegetables,' Harriet quipped, colliding with dark eyes that gleamed pure liquid gold in the sunlight.

Rafael Flynn braced a lean brown hand against a horsebox and gazed down at her. Instantly she was wildly aware of his size, and the raw charge of his potent presence. Forced to look up, she rested her attention momentarily on his impossibly long black lashes, which supplied the only softening influence to his lean, dark, overwhelmingly male features. She found it incredibly difficult to catch her breath.

'Business has no personal dimension for me. You may find the livery venture more of a challenge than you expect.'

'Don't tell me you're in the same line and that we're going to be competing!' Harriet breathed in unconcealed dismay.

A flash of momentary incomprehension tautened Rafael Flynn's stunning bone structure. Then he flung back his handsome dark head and laughed with rich appreciation, showing strong white teeth. 'No…I'm not in the livery line, Harriet.'

He had a dazzling smile. Rosy colour lit her fair skin, because his sexy accent did something almost intimate to the old-fashioned name that she had always hated. 'That's not a Kerry brogue, is it?'

He kept on smiling, and she tried to look away and couldn't. 'It is in part...but my ancestry is mixed.'

'Like mine,' she said breathlessly, fighting to think of something more interesting to say but finding her mind a horrific blank. Her eyes met his and a tight, hard knot of excitement spread a starburst of heat low in her tummy.

'Dine with me tonight?' Rafael murmured lazily, deciding to put his acquisition plans for her property on temporary hold.

With astonishing difficulty she recalled the Amazonian goddess, reputedly in current residence beneath his roof. 'Your girlfriend—'

He shrugged a shoulder in a fluid gesture of unconcern. 'Bianca's history.'

His complete indifference to the reality that the blonde was watching them from about twenty yards away chilled Harriet to the marrow. 'But she's *here*—'

'She knows it's over. She's leaving this afternoon. Dinner?' he prompted drily.

Harriet backed off a step from him. He embodied every warning she had ever heard or read about a man: arrogant and emotionally detached, he was a pure-bred predator—absolutely not her type. She could not overlook or excuse his attitude to the unfortunate Bianca. 'Sorry, but no thanks. I'm not thinking of dating anyone at the minute.'

'I haven't *dated* since I was fourteen.' Rafael was wondering whether she imagined that a brief pretence of uninterest would increase his ardour—because he could not credit that she could be saying no to him.

'I was engaged until quite recently, and I'm still getting over that.'

'I'll get you over it,' Rafael promised in a low, earthy tone.

'I'm also incredibly busy right now,' Harriet muttered uncomfortably, backing away another couple of steps, intimidated by the effect of that full-on charge of raw charisma.

Rafael watched her retreat with concealed disbelief. He could not understand what her game was. Of course it was a game: in his experience all women played games. But she was playing to weird rules he did not recognise.

'Nice talking to you,' Harriet mumbled, and bolted, wincing at her own awkwardness.

There he was: literally the man of her dreams. But he was not the sort of guy she would dare to begin seeing or risk feeling anything for. Goodness, he had just dumped a woman who was so gorgeous people stopped dead to marvel at her! Off with the old, on with the new. Although she was certain that he had to be looking on her as more of a snack than a full banquet. After all, she couldn't hold a candle to his ex-girlfriend. She couldn't quite accept that he truly had asked her out to dinner. Her—Harriet Carmichael—dressed in muddy jeans and wellies, with no make-up, and probably a few pounds heavier than she'd used to be when she was with Luke.

Luke… The wash of humiliating memory sobered her feverish reflections. Perhaps she took life too seriously. Perhaps she needed to learn how to be more casual when it came to the opposite sex. Apart from a couple of boyfriends in her teen years, she had only had Luke in her life. Now she was back being single, and, though she might be twenty-eight years old, she felt no more confident or knowledgeable about men than she had done at twenty.

Hadn't she just made the ridiculous error of trying to mentally measure up Rafael Flynn as a potential life partner? Were her nesting instincts sending her to the outer edge of craziness? He was fling material—*wild* fling material. He was racy, shameless and…exciting. If she was honest, he was more exciting than Luke had ever been. She should have had the courage to say yes to dinner and seduction.

It might have made her feel a little less inadequate when she thought about Alice and Luke as a couple.

'Harriet...' Una approached her, her expressive face full of concern. 'I think you should steer clear of Rafael Flynn.'

Although her own knee jerk reaction had been to run a mile from him, Harriet was already experiencing a certain amount of regret, self-doubt and confusion about that response. 'Why?'

'You're too nice for him—you're gentle and trusting. He'll think that's so dumb and he'll break your heart.'

'I haven't got one to break right now. Someone got there before Mr Flynn,' Harriet confided ruefully. 'But thanks for caring.'

'I'd hate to see you hurt—'

'Is he really that bad?' Harriet's plea for further explanation was unconsciously wistful in tone.

Una flushed. 'It's not that he's bad,' the teenager disclaimed hurriedly. 'Just from a different world. You'd be oil and water and he'd walk all over you.'

'No...he wouldn't do that,' Harriet countered with quiet but firm conviction.

Una did not look convinced. 'If an international supermodel can't hold him for five minutes, who can?'

A woman with the strength to be tough and subject him to a locked room and chains, Harriet thought abstractedly. Implanting a few basic standards in the midst of the smash and grab ethics that drove him might not go amiss either.

That evening, two prospective clients took a tour of the yard. Harriet had mapped out a business plan and drawn up a basic livery contract before she'd even arrived in Ballyflynn. Now she sat up late working out how many boarders she'd require to break even. She was also thinking of opening a tack shop that sold feed and basic supplies, as there was nowhere local meeting that demand. She didn't need to make a fortune, only a living, she reminded herself resolutely. She had downshifted to make a dream come true and enjoy a more simple life. And leading a successful simple life, she told herself censoriously, did not include any dealings whatsoever with the type of male who had affairs with fabulous fashion models.

On Monday morning Harriet received a call from the solicitor, Eugene McNally, and was surprised to be told that he was anxious to see her on a matter of some urgency.

The older man greeted Harriet at his office with perceptible discomfiture. 'I'm afraid that I've been notified of a substantial claim against Kathleen Gallagher's estate.'

CHAPTER THREE

HARRIET regarded the solicitor in surprise. 'Surely it's very late in the day for anything like that to surface?'

'It is. But it's only now I've been informed that three years ago Kathleen took out a large loan which now requires settlement in one way…' he hesitated '…or another.'

'Who's the loan with?' Harriet was struggling to remain calm and think clearly. She had funds in the bank, and there was no reason why she should not apply for a mortgage…although a mortgage would certainly raise her overheads, she thought anxiously.

'Flynn Enterprises.'

While Harriet digested that most disturbing news in astonishment, the silence stretched. 'How much did Kathleen borrow?'

'One hundred and fifty thousand euros…over a

hundred thousand pounds in sterling,' the solicitor advanced heavily. 'Believe me, I had no idea whatsoever.'

Harriet was shocked at the sheer size of the amount, but anger was already beginning to stir. 'Really?' she prompted, with a doubt she could not conceal. 'But you were my cousin's legal adviser and her executor.'

'Kathleen did not consult me when she signed the agreement with Flynn Enterprises, nor did I receive any papers relating to that transaction,' the older man revealed unhappily. 'Evidently your cousin was determined to keep the matter private. I would have cautioned her against borrowing at her age. It was most unwise.'

'But a very wise move from Rafael Flynn's point of view. My goodness, a hundred thousand pounds…' Her mouth had run dry. 'On what terms was the money advanced?'

'No repayments were required for three years. At the end of that period either the loan was to be repaid on demand—'

'On demand?' Harriet gasped in appalled interruption.

'Or Flynn Enterprises would be entitled to assume a full half-share in the property and the livery yard and to become Kathleen's legal partner. The company would also be entitled to first refusal in the event of a sale. The contract was drawn up by a clever lawyer and it would appear to be watertight.'

Harriet's lips parted in shock. 'Are you saying that I could end up with Rafael Flynn as a partner in a business that is pretty much non-existent at this moment in time?'

'Miss Carmichael…' Eugene McNally breathed tautly, passing a thick legal document across the desk for her perusal. 'Mr Flynn could move into your guestroom and you couldn't object.'

'So I'll pay off the loan…I'll get the money by taking out a mortgage!' Harriet exclaimed.

'While another party has an interest in half of the property that would be a challenge. You cannot define any one part of your inheritance as wholly yours. In those circumstances you will find it virtually impossible to persuade a financial institution to offer you a loan secured on the property. This contract leaves you with precious few options.'

Harriet was steadily turning paler. 'But why did my cousin borrow such a huge amount?'

'Trade took a downturn at the livery yard, and she had debts. I assume the bank refused to finance the improvements she wanted to make. She also thought she was on to a winner working with Fergal Gibson—though I know for a fact that two years back the pair of them took a heavy loss on a race-horse they bought together. But Kathleen was an eternal optimist.' The older man loosed a weary sigh. 'I'm betting she looked at the three-year holiday on the loan repayments and hoped for the best.'

'But surely she saw the risk of having Rafael Flynn foisted on her as a partner?'

'She might not even have read the small print. She was a horse fancier, not a businesswoman. At the time Mr Flynn did not own the Flynn Court estate. But he is a man of considerable stature and experi-ence in the bloodstock world, and Kathleen may well have…somewhat naively…thought that such a partner would be most advantageous to her.'

One hundred thousand pounds, Harriet reflected in growing horror. It was an enormous sum. Even if she took all the profit she had made on selling her London apartment she couldn't pay off a loan that size and still hope to rebuild the business. Settling the debt would destroy her prospects of making the livery yard pay. And if she couldn't settle the debt even if she did make money from the yard, *he* would be entitled to half of the proceeds! This was the guy who had dared to ask her to have dinner with him? No wonder he had suggested that she might find the livery business challenging!

'Why wasn't this contract mentioned sooner?'

Harriet asked tightly. 'I think it's inexcusable that I am only learning about it now.'

'Mr Flynn was apparently willing to overlook the contract's existence if you sold the property to him.'

'He offers a very generous tip for a man whose stately home appears to be falling down round him!'

'Mr Flynn only gained access to Flynn Court after his father, Valente Cavaliere, died some weeks ago. I believe that an extensive renovation project is being planned,' the solicitor explained, unaware of the bombshell that he was dropping.

Harriet stared at the solicitor with steadily rounding blue eyes of disbelief. 'Cavaliere? He's... Are you telling me that Rafael Flynn is actually Rafael *Cavaliere*?' she pressed, in a voice that was fading and breathless with shock. 'The first time I met him I thought there was something familiar about him, but I would never have made that connection in a hundred years!'

'My advice—and it's off the record—would be to sell to him and buy elsewhere in the area,' the older man suggested uncomfortably. 'He's a hard man if you cross him, but he has been extremely generous to this community and he has considerable local support. He's offering you a very fair price. You can't fight that amount of money and power—'

'Watch me, Mr McNally,' Harriet advised with

fighting fervour. The craven suggestion that she simply accept defeat filled her with raging resentment and a fierce determination to do exactly the opposite. 'Just watch me!'

She swept back out to her car in high dudgeon. Rafael rotten Cavaliere! What was an Italian tycoon doing in a tiny Irish village? And calling himself Flynn, of all things! It was like finding a barracuda in a goldfish bowl. She could not believe it was true. She could not credit that once again Rafael Cavaliere had contrived to cast the long dark shadow of misfortune across her path. She stopped her car in the lay-by next to the church because she was shaking with reaction. But the momentum of anger soon impelled her on to swing left through the crumbling stone entrance of Flynn Court. The long stately drive was full of potholes, but bounded on both sides by magnificent cypress trees, which gave occasional glimpses of the stunning view down to the bay and the sea. She brought her car to a halt right outside the imposing front door.

Tolly appeared in answer to the ancient bell she had pulled. 'Miss Carmichael…how may I assist you?' he enquired gravely.

In any other mood Harriet would have been tickled pink by the solemn manner which Joseph evidently assumed to carry out his official duties as butler. 'I'm here to see your boss.'

'I'll see if Mr Flynn is available. Please take a seat.'

Harriet preferred to stand. The hall was a vast semi-circular space, with walls ornamented with fantastic elaborate plasterwork. Even dirty and in need of decoration, it was a spectacular space.

'Miss Carmichael…bad news travels fast,' a lazy masculine drawl commented from behind her.

Her heart-shaped face tightening as though she was sucking on a lemon, Harriet spun round. Her tormentor was sheathed in a sleek black designer business suit. Staggeringly tall and vibrantly handsome, he also looked horribly intimidating. Every nerve in her tense body seemed to jump and her tummy flipped in concert. 'Allow me to tell you that you do business like a gangster.'

His lean, bronzed features remained impassive. 'My late father would be proud of me.'

'I'm not selling to you…I don't care what you do. I have a great dislike of being forced to do anything, Mr Cavaliere. But most of all I have a great dislike, not to mention complete contempt, for your methods. Why do you call yourself Flynn? To mislead people?' Harriet condemned with a heated sense of injustice. 'I mean, who the heck would expect to find an Italian billionaire slumming somewhere like this?'

'Let me answer you point by point,' Rafael murmured levelly. 'On my birth certificate it says Rafael Cavaliere Flynn, and I was born here. My mother named me. I am not concerned by the name that the press have allotted to me. Nor do I consider myself to be "slumming" in the house where many generations of Flynns have lived and died. I am proud of my ancestry.'

His immense self-assurance infuriated Harriet beyond bearing. All worked up as she was, she was already conscious that her face was hot with temper. Being rebuked for her bad manners was the last straw. She could have screamed for, ironically, she had never before dared to be that rude to anyone. 'Are you aware that you have blighted my life like the plague since I was fifteen?' she suddenly launched at him, half an octave higher.

Rafael quirked a mobile black brow.

'No, I haven't gone crazy. In the nineties you took over Benson Pharmaceuticals where my stepfather worked in the research lab and he lost his job. He was just one employee among four thousand. You shut the company down and sold off everything. The whole town died—'

'A business has to be in profit to be sustainable.'

'My stepfather had a nervous breakdown. He couldn't get another job, and he had to sell our house and just about everything we owned by the end of the year. Men like you destroy lives,' Harriet framed shakily.

'Benson Pharmaceuticals lost a major contract to an Asian company and crashed. I was in no way responsible for its demise.' Rafael watched her brow furrow in surprise.

He was standing below the cupola. The fall of light through the glass dome in the roof played over his superb bone structure and glinted in the dense black of his hair.

Registering that she was inadvertently staring, she tore her attention from him again, her cheeks burning. 'That may be so, but you make nothing. You simply tear things apart to make the most money you can.'

'You're wrong. In the case of Bensons, I refused a highly profitable offer to buy the site and redevelop it as a shopping outlet. I knew that the town would regenerate faster if the buildings became a base for an industrial estate where other businesses could be set up.'

Harriet had stiffened with discomfiture. 'I wasn't aware of those facts, and if I've misjudged you—'

'You have.'

'Then I'm sorry,' she framed between visibly clenched teeth. 'But I imagine that you usually put profit first.'

'Money is power. It can also be a great force for good as well as evil. I don't apologise for what I am. Did you think I would?'

'Two months ago you presided over the fall of Zenco. I was an account manager in charge of the Zenco marketing budget for my firm. The knock on effect of the Zenco crash was that the agency I worked for folded. Once again, you acted as a malign influence on my life. Please excuse me for not being one of your fans,' Harriet completed curtly.

'That is indeed quite a trail of curious coincidence. I'm not a superstitious man…' All his attention nailed to her, Rafael was conceding that he had never seen such flawless skin as hers and wondering if she was that pale creamy colour all over. 'But I do think you should take immediate action to avoid colliding with my influence a third time.'

'Is that really all you have to say?' Harriet shot at him wrathfully.

Rafael spread wide the door to one side of him. 'Let me show you something…'

Harriet stayed where she was, and folded her arms for good measure. He just left her standing there. The seconds ticked past until a sense of foolishness and the secret fear that she might be behaving childishly made her follow him into the room he had entered.

'This is the drawing room. Look out of the windows,' Rafael urged.

Arms still tightly folded, Harriet trod forward on stiff legs. His poise seemed to mock her awkwardness. Her gaze widened when she saw the ugly line of tumbledown buildings at the foot of the hill that destroyed what should have been a lovely view. The dilapidated sheds were the ones she had been planning to renovate as additional stables. He moved an eloquent lean brown hand, spreading his long fingers, and she saw his Italian genes in his fluid ability to express himself without speech. It struck her as an incredibly attractive trait that was fascinatingly at odds with the cool front he wore to the world. When he began speaking, she had to fight to regain her concentration.

'The house that you're living in was built as a cottage orne in the eighteenth century.'

Harriet could not hide her surprise. 'It's that old?'

'It was built as a folly, not as a house to be lived in. My great-great-great grandfather, Randal Flynn, planted the arboretum around it. You are, in effect, living in what used to be part of the garden belonging to the Court.'

Harriet lifted her chin. 'I didn't appreciate that.'

'The folly and the land surrounding it were sold out of financial necessity more than half a century ago, and were bought by your cousin's parents. But the folly is an historic building and, as such, should be conserved and reunited with the estate.'

'You can't have it,' Harriet told him succinctly, her fierce tension expressing the strength of her feelings on that subject.

Brilliant dark eyes shimmered in tawny challenge. 'I never lose.'

'You can't always have what you want. Yes, you can wheel and deal, and make things very difficult for me, but you can't force me to sell.' Harriet dealt him a truculent appraisal. 'My word, were you planning to break the news of this outrageous loan over dinner?'

'I'm not that crude.' His intonation was as even, calm and crisp as hers was argumentative. 'We could still discuss this over dinner, and reach a mutually beneficial resolution.'

Her eyes fired as bright a blue as gentians. 'When your only proposition is that I sell my home to you, we have nothing to discuss. I suggest you think in terms of a compromise.'

'There's room for negotiation, but not compromise.'

'OK…gloves off, then.' Harriet drew in a stark, sudden breath and dragged her gaze from the gleaming mesmeric hold of his, scolding herself for that momentary loss of focus. 'The contract my cousin signed with your company could be used in the public domain, to cause you considerable embarrassment. Before you assure me that public opinion means nothing to you, think of the local dimension.'

Rafael regarded her with cool impassivity. 'Is it possible that you are threatening me?'

'I'm merely telling you that I will fight back with whatever weapons I can muster.' Harriet was rigid. 'Do you want it said that you used your power, your cash and your cunning lawyers to hoodwink a woman of pensionable age into signing an unfair contract? And that you then used it to deprive me of my inheritance?'

'That would be a very false representation of the facts. Miss Gallagher made the first approach to Flynn Enterprises, and she was astute enough to use my desire to acquire her property as a bargaining tool to win preferential treatment. In addition, a solicitor was engaged at my company's expense to advise her.'

As he finished speaking a slow tide of guilty pink blossomed below Harriet's skin; she was painfully aware of the blackmail tactics she was utilising to fight her corner. Quite deliberately, however, she suppressed her finer sensibilities—which, she was convinced, were a distinct handicap in Rafael Cavaliere Flynn's radius.

'I take your point, but can you prove those facts?' she enquired, slamming the door fully shut on her sense of fair play and on her conscience. 'As I'm sure you're aware, newspaper stories do have a sad habit of concentrating only on the more scandalous angles. Even if a retraction is printed afterwards, people tend to remember what went before better.'

'And you say *I* do business like a gangster?' Rafael murmured in a silken tone of dark appreciation, for this confrontation was developing along lines that he could never have foreseen. She was neither crying nor pleading nor appealing to his better nature.

It was rare for someone to surprise Rafael's expectations, but Harriet Carmichael had succeeded. There she stood, all five foot four inches of her: her conservative black wool jacket and knee-length skirt were the last word in old-fashioned clothing to a male who had spent several weeks with a woman who displayed as much naked flesh as possible at every opportunity. Black lashes screening his reflective gaze, he viewed her with interest tinged with reluctant amusement, for he could barely credit that she had the nerve to threaten him. He wondered how long he would wait before he called her bluff. She thought the very worst of him and made no bones about that reality. Since he had few illusions about himself, and minimal concern about how the rest of the world viewed him that should not have bothered him. Yet, inexplicably, her automatic assumption that he would naturally sink to meet her lowest expectations annoyed the hell out of Rafael.

'I'm not giving up my home…I love it,' Harriet told him defiantly. 'I changed my whole way of life to come to Ireland and I'm staying put.'

'Then you're planning to repay the loan in full?' Rafael decided that it was time to bring her down to ground level again.

Harriet turned very pale. 'I presume I can have some time to explore my options?'

'Four weeks maximum—and that's a gift.' His response was swift. 'Try to be realistic. With what I'm prepared to pay for your inheritance you can pick a site, bring in an architect and rebuild a replica of your current home somewhere else in the neighbourhood.'

'But I treasure the family connection, and I very much doubt that I could hope to find anything that would equal the beauty of my present surroundings. I'll be in touch, Mr Cavaliere Flynn.'

Her slender back stiff, Harriet walked away.

'It's Rafael.'

'Fake bonhomie just irritates me.'

His beautiful mouth took on a ruthless curve as he strode past her to pull open the door for her exit. 'Bad manners do it for me.'

Her face flamed to her hairline; there was no denying that he excelled in the courtesy department. She tipped her head back and collided unwarily with glittering dark eyes that had enough of a charge to make her heart skip a startled beat. 'As you're planning to bankrupt me or make me homeless, the civilities seem rather superfluous.'

'Don't you think you're being a touch melodramatic about this?' Rafael slowed his long powerful stride to her pace as he accompanied her through the echoing entrance hall.

'I doubt very much that my home means as much to you as it does to me.'

'My late mother played in the folly as a child. Her father told her it was her duty to bring it back into the estate.' An almost imperceptible shadow tightened his lean strong face. 'That unattractive view was a constant reminder that she had failed.'

Harriet was mesmerised by the bleak, forbidding flash of emotion he could not conceal. His was a dark and dangerous temperament, she sensed, full of a passion rigorously controlled and rarely allowed expression. Yet that one fleeting glimpse of the powerful undercurrents that drove him gave her more of a flavour of his true nature than anything that had gone before.

'You're staring,' Rafael told her, his own attention sliding down to the peachy pouting softness of her lips.

The silence sizzled.

She was aware of nothing but him. 'So are you.'

'I like your mouth.' A smoky edge now emphasised the accented timbre of his dark drawl. 'It's very sexy.'

'Mr Flynn...may I have a moment of your attention?' A shrill female voice gushed in anticipation from about twenty feet away.

Slowly Harriet came back to the real world and shook her head as though to clear it. An older woman in an elegant suit had surged up to Rafael. Behind her trailed a little man, feverishly writing on a hand-held computer. 'I've decided that Etruscan blue is the colour of choice for the entrance hall.'

'Blue? But it's north-facing,' Harriet muttered, before she could think better of offering her un-asked-for opinion. 'A dull yellow would pick up the caramel tones in the faux marble pillars.'

Taken aback, Rafael shot a glance at Harriet that was tinged with new respect and appreciation. The slightest mention of the colour schemes to be selected for his ancestral home sent him straight out to the stables. 'Yellow sounds good. Go for it. Harriet, this is my interior designer.'

An introduction was performed but Harriet, bewildered and dismayed by her response to him, was eager to be gone. *I like your mouth.* A sinful quiver darted through her and she felt humiliated by her own susceptibility. A sudden wash of moisture stung the back of her eyes, for the insecure feeling that she had let herself down was too much on top of the experiences she had already had that morning.

'My private number…should you need to get in touch.' Rafael extended a card.

Her gaze screened by her lashes, she accepted the card while thinking that there was no way she would ever make use of that invitation. Like a timely knight on a white charger, Tolly glided forward out of nowhere to open the front door for her and usher her out.

'Thank you,' she muttered gratefully.

'Drive carefully…' the old man advised in a troubled whisper.

When Harriet walked back into the cottage, and Samson bounced forward in innocent welcome, she was gripped by an angry sense of frustration. It was only a week since she had arrived, convinced that she was on the brink of making her dreams come true. She had believed that for once she was going to hit the jackpot on the dream front. Suppressing the uncharacteristic surge of self-pity threatening to take her over, Harriet breathed in deep. Don't get mad, get even, she told herself bracingly.

A couple of hours later she was doing tough financial sums on various sheets of paper when a knock sounded on the door.

It was Tolly, with a basket of beautifully arranged fresh vegetables. 'From the kitchen garden. We always have too much.'

Harriet wasn't fooled by that excuse, for his worried eyes betrayed his concern for her. 'Your boss and I had a slight difference of opinion, and that's all I'm going to say.'

'Officially I don't even work for Rafael Flynn any more,' the old man explained in determined protest, scooping up Samson and petting the little animal to soothe him.

Her brow indented. 'I don't understand.'

'I've been retired for years. I have a comfortable home and a good pension, but I get very bored doing nothing,' Tolly admitted ruefully. 'That's why I still make myself useful round the Court and the estate. Anything you tell me will be treated as a matter of the strictest confidence.'

'There's nothing to tell.' Harriet was keen to turn the subject. 'I suppose I'm stressed because I have to go back to London to arrange for my possessions to be brought over. Are there any local kennels I could use for Samson?'

'He can come and stay with me. We'll be company for each other.'

'Are you sure you wouldn't mind?'

'Not at all. The late Mrs Flynn used to keep little dogs,' the old man remarked cheerfully.

Harriet went to the window to peer out at the large cattle trailer that had pulled noisily into the yard. 'I wonder who that is.'

'A customer?'

'No, my first boarders arrive next week, when I've got everything organised for them.'

A tall man of about thirty, with untidy black hair and shy blue eyes set in a thin attractive face, emerged from the battered four-wheel drive. His name was Patrick Flanagan and he was the kindly neighbour who had been housing Kathleen's live-stock. Harriet was grateful for the diversion, but only hoped that Fergal and Una would be able to look after the new inmates during her absence.

The hens were a tattered collection, but with Tolly's able assistance were soon happily installed back in their run. The rooster, Albert, a small white bird possessed of considerable self-importance, im-mediately took up a position on the hen coop roof and crowed with a volume and shrillness dispropor-tionate to his size.

'Fergal's bringing the mare over for you,' Patrick shared. 'But I've got Peanut in the back of the cab.'

'Who?'

Patrick grimaced and reached in to remove a very solid little pig from the front seat. 'She's a right problem. Kathleen kept her as a pet, and now she doesn't know how to be a porker. I had to put her in the barn for her own safety.'

Harriet watched in astonishment as Peanut the pig trotted at speed straight into the house. 'A pet?'

Patrick shook his head. 'She's a house pig. Kathleen used to say she was much brighter and cleaner than any dog.'

Harriet followed Peanut's eager path into the kitchen. With the pronounced aspect of a pig grateful to be reunited with the comforts of home, Peanut snuggled down on the old mat in front of the battered Aga and stretched out for a snooze. As astonished as a dog could be, Samson came out from below a chair with an aggressive flurry of warning barks. For all the world like another dog, Peanut rolled over playfully. Nonplussed, the chihuahua hovered, advancing and retreating while he got acquainted with the intruder. Finally they both pretended to go to sleep at opposite ends of the rug.

In no hurry to go home, Patrick accepted a cup of tea and with painstaking seriousness offered Harriet small helpful snippets of advice on animal husbandry. He also promised to bring round a book about chickens that had belonged to his mother.

Tolly took his leave only when the younger man did.

'I'm thinking you've made a conquest there,' Tolly remarked with an amused chuckle. 'I've never heard that quiet young fella talk so much. He's from a decent family, you know, and he has a tidy farm.'

Beneath the old man's meaningful appraisal, Harriet went pink. 'I'm not looking for a man, Tolly.'

'But sure love might be looking for you, and you'll hardly chase it away if it comes along.' He took his leave with an irrepressible smile.

Love, Harriet thought glumly. A laugh that rang hollow in the cosy kitchen fell from her lips. She had spent a good part of her adult life in love with a man who had replaced her apparently without a moment's thought or regret. Perhaps that lack of feeling and concern for her hurt most of all. Luke had grown out of their relationship and moved on. It was though she had been in love with a male who didn't really exist, for the man she had loved would never have been so cruelly indifferent to her suffering. There had been no evidence that Luke had agonised at any stage over whether or not to succumb to her younger sister's attractions.

Now Harriet found herself wondering if Luke had ever truly loved her. Or had she just been around for so long that she had become a habit in his life? Had he got bored with her? Had he felt trapped in their engagement? She remembered his unwillingness to name a day for their wedding and saw that reluctance in a new and humiliating light. It was possible that he had known for a long time that she might not be the one for him.

Fergal delivered Snowball, the elderly mare, who walked placidly into a vacant stall. Harriet saddled her up and took her for a ride. Snowball plodded down the back lane with an unshakeable good humour that was exactly right for Harriet's rusty prowess on a horse.

While Harriet was enjoying getting acquainted with Snowball, Tolly was serving his unofficial employer with a pre-dinner drink and the calm forecast that Harriet Carmichael would be married within the year.

Rafael frowned at the old man, and then decided to be amused by that prediction. 'Have you taken up reading crystal balls, Tolly?'

'I don't need to. Patrick Flanagan was making moony eyes at her, and the quiet ones are always the fastest movers when the right woman comes along,' Tolly opined with conviction. 'She'll be spoilt for choice, though.'

'Really?' Rafael dealt him an encouraging glance. 'The vultures are gathering, are they?'

'Fergal Gibson would probably like to be in the running...but he's got the mammy from hell, and she'd see off any girl who looked twice at her precious boy!'

'Quite a handicap,' Rafael conceded. 'But I have it on the best of authority that Harriet is not interested in men right now.'

'Sure, don't women always say that to the wrong 'uns until the *right* man comes along!' Tolly scoffed, with a conviction that set his employer's even white teeth on edge.

Ten days later, on the day before she was due to return from England to Ballyflynn, Harriet took stock of her situation.

Even before she'd left Ireland she had spent two days investigating the possibility of raising finance to pay off Kathleen's loan, and had been daunted by her singular lack of success. She'd taken legal advice about her position from a lawyer based in Dublin and had learned nothing that comforted her. But she'd been delighted when her mother had phoned her, to say that she would be visiting London at the same time. Bolstered by that cheering prospect, because she had not seen her mother for several months, Harriet had felt energised enough to deal with the transport firm she had hired to transport her furniture to Ballyflynn, and finally to hand over the keys of her London apartment to her solicitor.

In fact she'd come to terms with the reality that she could not raise anything like the amount of money that she needed to exclude Rafael Flynn from his interest in her home and business.

That afternoon she made use of the phone number he had given her and called him. 'Hello, this is Harriet Carmichael,' she explained carefully.

A slow smile curved Rafael's expressive mouth. Beyond the window a deep blue sky framed the ancient terracotta tiled rooftops of Rome. His keen dark gaze had taken on a reflective light, for she sounded so very earnest on the phone. Indifferent to the board meeting that had stopped dead the instant he chose to answer his mobile, he murmured smoothly, 'Harriet…how may I be of assistance?'

'I have a question to ask. Will you settle for fifty per cent of the loan being repaid now and a reduced stake in the livery yard?'

'No deal,' Rafael said without hesitation.

'Is *any* variation in the terms possible?'

'No.'

Harriet was not surprised by his intransigence. After all, as far as the loan was concerned he held the aces. But if she chose to settle for the alternative option the odds would become much more equal, and she rather thought that that possibility had not occurred to him. Breathing in deep and lifting her

chin, Harriet said brightly, 'Then it's a case of...
Hello, partner...'

Rafael found the surprise value of that comeback
highly entertaining. 'I'm afraid I don't do partner-
ships,' he confessed huskily.

'Oh, yes, you do. Read the small print,' Harriet
advised him briskly, determined to make the best of
the situation. 'Furthermore, as you are listed as the
CEO of Flynn Enterprises, I will deal with you and
only you. No lesser individuals, please. In the meantime, I've been thinking out of the box, and I believe
that with give and take—'

'I'm not a good candidate for that approach either.'

'With give and take, something can be done about
that ugly view you dislike,' Harriet informed him.
'Has anyone ever told you that you have a very negative outlook?'

His brilliant eyes glittered with reluctant appreciation. 'No, you're the first.'

'Believe me, this can work. I know it can work.
It may not be what either of us would have chosen—'

'As my partner, you'll have to dine with me,'
Rafael commented, with a single-minded purpose
that had nothing whatsoever to do with business.

'I doubt that I'll have the time. As I can't afford

to employ a groom now, I'll be much too busy mucking out and feeding the horses and drumming up new trade. Let me know when you can fit in a business meeting to discuss the yard.'

Harriet concluded the call with an unanticipated stab of satisfaction. Dine with him? He had to be joking! By the time he had finished rubber-stamping every minor decision she had to make she expected him to be heartily tired of being her partner and much more amenable to the value of sane and sensible compromise.

The next morning she visited her mother at her exclusive hotel. Clad in an exquisite suit that shrieked Parisian chic, Eva kissed her daughter on each cheek and then curled her impossibly slender fine-boned figure delicately back onto a sofa opposite. Although Eva was several inches taller, Harriet always felt like a total clodhopper beside her. She also wondered how Joseph Tolly could possibly have believed he saw a resemblance between them. The two women might share the same hair colour, but her parent's perfect features were so beautiful that even in her forties she still attracted a good deal of admiring attention.

'I have a wonderful surprise for you,' Eva announced brightly. 'As you must know, Gustav has some very useful contacts in the business world. A friend of his is opening an advertising agency in Paris, and all you have to do is call this number and arrange an interview.'

The older woman settled a business card down on the coffee table with a positive flourish.

'But I'm not looking for another job.' Harriet studied her mother in polite bewilderment. 'Of course I'm very grateful that your husband would go to the trouble of making enquiries on my behalf—'

'Gustav was delighted to be able to help. I don't think you have any idea how much concern you've been causing us all,' Eva countered, with a hint of censure in her light voice.

Harriet coloured and decided not to enquire into exactly who was included in the umbrella term of 'us'. 'Well, I certainly didn't mean to do that. A job in Paris too...my word, that would have done wonders for my schoolgirl French!'

Eva would have frowned had her forehead not been a wrinkle-free zone thanks to the Botox injections she swore by. 'The office will be bilingual. I'll be very disappointed if you don't give this opportunity serious consideration. You must get your life back on track.'

Harriet's discomfiture increased. It was most unlike her mother to interfere in her daughter's life to such an extent, and that troubled her. She linked her hands together and then glanced across the table with concerned but level blue eyes. 'Right now I feel my life is very much on track. I do appreciate what you've tried to do for me, but I could find another position in advertising if I wanted one. To be honest, I much prefer working with horses—'

'But you're throwing your life away,' Eva condemned thinly. 'Ballyflynn is at the end of the world! You'll never make your fortune there—'

'I'm not expecting to. Why are you still so upset about this?' Finally, Harriet asked that thorny question—for, even though the fact had not been openly acknowledged, she was painfully aware that her move to Ireland had thoroughly annoyed her volatile parent.

'I'm not upset.' But Eva could not hide the angry resentment in her accusing stare. 'But do tell me what Ballyflynn could possibly have to offer you.'

'A chance to live in the country and work with horses...and a sense of family connection—'

'What?' Eva snapped in scornful interruption. 'With a father you don't even know and should be glad not to know?'

A deathly silence fell. Harriet had lost colour at the rare reference to a man whom Eva preferred to pretend had not existed. Her heart was thumping very hard. 'Actually, I wasn't referring to my father.

I was referring to Kathleen Gallagher and to the fact that you grew up just outside the village. Why do you say that I should be glad not to know my father?'

Her expression irritable, Eva evaded her daughter's keen scrutiny. 'I didn't say that.'

'You did.' A stricken look in her gaze, Harriet asked in a taut undertone, 'Were you attacked? Am I the result of an assault? Date-rape? If that's why you won't tell me who my father is, I really would prefer to know.'

Eva raised a disdainful brow, her nose wrinkling with distaste at those suggestions. 'Of course I wasn't attacked.'

Harriet was very much relieved by that admission. On more than one occasion she had secretly wondered if Eva's determination to remain silent could be her way of concealing some deeply unpleasant truth. At the same time she had been equally aware that her mother tended to ignore or deny anything that made her feel uncomfortable. For that reason Alice and Luke's affair had never been discussed by mother and daughter. 'Then please tell me who my father is.'

Eva dealt her a furious look of reproach. 'Why do you keep on dragging this up when you know I'll refuse to discuss it? That's my right. I'm protecting my privacy. Believe me, it really doesn't matter who your father was.'

'I'm sorry to be so persistent. I don't want to upset you. But knowing who my father is *does* matter to me. All I want is a name,' Harriet confessed heavily. 'It means a lot to me, or I wouldn't raise a subject that I know you dislike. I would even be grateful if you could bring yourself to the point of giving me some idea of what happened back then, so that I could know something about my own history.'

Eva rolled her blue eyes heavenward. 'Why do you always spoil things, Harriet?' she condemned in a huffy tone. 'I invited you here because I thought I could talk some sense into you and do you a favour. Thanks to Gustav you have the chance of a terrific new job and the opportunity to make a fresh start in Paris.'

'Yes,' Harriet sighed, deeply hurt by the assurance that she had ruined their reunion. 'But unfortunately I don't want to live in Paris.'

'I thought it might help you to get over that silly business with Luke.'

'Silly?' The use of that particular word shocked Harriet, for it trivialised the betrayal that had almost torn her apart.

Her mother emanated a heavy sigh. 'Look, I don't know how to tell you this, and I don't mind admitting that I resent being landed with the responsibility…but there's nobody else to do it, so here goes. Alice and Luke are now engaged and have set a date for their wedding.'

The remaining blood slowly drained from below Harriet's skin. Her tummy heaved. She forced her mouth up into a very slight smile and struggled not to react in any way. But it wouldn't really have mattered how she reacted, for Eva was very careful not to look directly at her devastated daughter.

'When…is the wedding?' Harriet heard herself prompt, although in truth she did not want to know.

'August. Your sister would like you to be her bridesmaid.'

That suggestion hit Harriet like a cruelly triumphant kick after she had already been floored by a body-blow.

'You and Alice were close. She misses you. Naturally she doesn't want friends and relatives to think that there's still bad feeling between the three of you. You have to deal with this, Harriet.'

'I have dealt with it, but that does not mean that I'm prepared to walk down the aisle as Alice's bridesmaid. I think that might be a step too far for all of us.' As Harriet spoke she felt as though she was encased in ice from head to toe, for she dared not let her emotions react to what she had just learned. She did not want pity. She did not want to expose her feelings. But most of all she cringed at the mortifying threat of Eva revealing the extent of those feelings to Alice and Luke, as it was painfully clear where her mother's sympathies lay.

An hour later, having eaten not a morsel of the beautifully presented lunch that had been served, Harriet kissed Eva's cool, perfumed cheek and escaped. The older woman's apparent indifference to her pain had cut her to the quick. Was it inevitable that Alice should be the favoured daughter? Beautiful, confident and charming Alice, who, never having known separation from Eva, enjoyed a much closer bond with her mother. Harriet could not bear to think about Alice and Luke and engagement rings and weddings. Nor was it advisable to dwell on such distressing thoughts when she had promised to spend what remained of the afternoon at her stepfather's home.

The Carmichael household was busy and noisy, and at first glance always seemed to be bulging at the seams with lively children. It was only six years since Will Carmichael, having retrained, had embarked on a new career as a science teacher in a comprehensive school. There he had met Nicola, an art teacher, twenty-odd years his junior, and within a relatively short space of time he had become a newly married man with twins on the way. Josh and Jake were four years old now, and since then Emily, an adorable little girl of two, had been born.

Harriet had been grateful when the older man, whose self-esteem had been lacerated by her mother's infidelities, had finally found happiness and a new family with another woman. His first *proper* children, as Nicola had put it on the day her boys were born. Harriet had hidden her heartache, conscious that Nicola had not intended to cause pain, for she had always made her husband's stepdaughter very welcome in her home.

'You know I never liked Luke,' Nicola admitted abruptly as she passed Harriet a cup of coffee across the breakfast bar. Without skipping a beat the energetic blonde woman told Emily not to pull the cat's tail and warned the twins that if they did not stop fighting she would put them to bed early.

'You didn't?' Harriet struggled to hit a chatty note and concealed her dismay at the opening of that once controversial topic. Nicola had clearly decided that enough time had passed for extreme tact about Luke to be no longer necessary.

'No, Luke always thought he was something really special. Of course I've never met your half-sister, Alice. But from what Will says she seems to be quite fond of herself too. Couples like that don't stay together,' the other woman declared in a tone of consolation. 'Their egos clash.'

The desire to divulge Alice and Luke's wedding plans nagged at Harriet like an aching tooth, but she withstood the temptation. She shoved that devastating announcement back down into her subconscious and trembled at the amount of self-control that concealment demanded of her.

'You're very quiet,' Will Carmichael finally commented, when he was driving his stepdaughter to the airport for her flight. 'Either my rowdy children have drained you of energy or something's badly wrong.'

She thought of telling him about the financial complexities of her Irish inheritance and her very reluctant new business partner. But essentially that would have been a red herring, she acknowledged grittily. At that moment she didn't much care about any of that. Her entire being was consumed by what she had learned earlier that day from her mother.

'Luke and Alice are getting married in August.'

Her stepfather shot her an appalled glance and then focused his concentration studiously back on the road again. After a moment of uncomfortable silence, his hand reached for hers and he squeezed the life from her fingers. He said nothing. He didn't need to say anything. She knew he understood. She knew he was bleeding inside for her. Her eyes burned hot but she held the tears back with iron self-control. It would upset him if she cried, and he did not deserve that. He had been extremely supportive when her life had fallen apart more than two months earlier, and it was time she got over it… Only she didn't think she would ever get over Luke and Alice to the extent where she was willing to act as her sister's bridesmaid.

Harriet collected Samson on her way home from Kerry airport. The little dog gave her a rapturous greeting and Tolly seemed quite sad to see his canine visitor depart. It was well after eight when she got back to the cottage.

Peanut was snoozing in front of the range. The pig got up and wriggled all over in excited welcome, just like a dog. Even in the mood she was in Harriet laughed. She lifted a bottle of peach wine out of the glazed kitchen cupboard and poured a glass. Fergal had warned her that Kathleen's homemade wine was lethal, and she hoped it would help her sleep later, because that very night she was determined to burn everything that reminded her of Luke.

Una had left her a note on the table, but her writing and spelling skills were so poor that Harriet took several minutes to decipher the news that the livestock were fed, watered and bedded down for the night. Harriet was astonished that so bright a girl should barely be able to express herself on paper, and wondered vaguely if the teenager could be dyslexic—she remembered the similar struggles of a schoolfriend. Her mobile phone rang and she answered it.

'It's Boyce,' her younger brother announced in his usual quick, abrupt manner. 'Are you OK, kiddo?'

Her eyes prickled. 'Who are you calling kiddo? You're only twenty-one. Do you realise how long it is since I heard from you? You've got so big and famous I hardly see you any more.'

'You're nagging like a girlfriend,' Boyce complained.

Harriet grinned. 'Is the band still touring?'

'Yeah. But I'll be back in London soon, and I'm thinking of coming over to Ireland to visit you.'

'I'd really love to see you,' Harriet told him warmly. 'But I warn you…the cottage is pretty basic.'

'I just want somewhere quiet and private to chill. I'm exhausted,' Boyce confided.

It was barely three years since Boyce and three of his friends had formed 4Some, one of the most successful boy bands in the music business. Boyce was the lead singer. Mobbed by hysterical girls wherever they went, 4Some were on a global tour, playing to sell-out audiences and making mega-bucks, but her brother's schedule was a punishing one.

'Will you promise not to tell anyone that I'll be staying with you?' he pressed her anxiously. 'You can't trust people not to blab to the press, and I want total peace.'

'You'll find it here,' Harriet soothed.

'You still haven't said how you are.' Audible concern shaded Boyce's comment. 'If it's any comfort, I think Luke's a total freak show and I can't believe Alice has fallen for him too.'

'Does she really love him?' Harriet heard herself ask, before she could think better of it.

'She says so, but I'm not making excuses for her,' Boyce declared uneasily. 'Don't ask me to take sides.'

'I won't. Let's not talk about it.'

When Boyce rang off, Harriet's face was tight with restrained emotion. She went into her bedroom to retrieve the box that she had stowed below the bed on the day she'd first arrived. A box brimming with memorabilia far too precious to have been left behind even temporarily in London, she conceded with self-hatred. She should have dumped it after finding Luke in bed with Alice, not carried it all the way to Ireland with her! Did Alice really love him? What difference did that make? Grabbing her old portable CD-player and the bottle of wine, Harriet carried the box out to the field and emptied it, and then trekked doggedly back to the yard to fetch kindling to make a fire.

The sugary-sweet vocals of the song that had been a hit the night she first met Luke throbbed out of the CD-player. She knelt down and lit the fire with hands that trembled. She was in an agony of grief. Luke could never have loved her the way he loved Alice: it was obvious that he couldn't wait to get her sister to the altar. They had actually named the day. Harriet's heart felt like it was cracking right down the middle. Hot tears slid slowly down her cheeks. She hit 'replay' on the CD and helped herself to another swig of homemade wine. Luke was going to be her brother-in-law and she had to learn to live with that! But *how* did she learn to live with such pain?

'This is a strange time of day to start a bonfire,' a familiar accented drawl remarked, startling her out of her self-preoccupation. 'I saw the glow from the Court and decided I should check it out in case the stables were at risk.'

'I'm not that stupid.' With great reluctance, Harriet twisted her head round.

Rafael Flynn stood poised several feet away.

Silhouetted against the star-studded night sky, and seen from her vantage point at ground level, he looked unbelievably tall and authoritative.

'I appreciate your concern, but I'm not in the mood for company,' she added tightly.

'Is this emotive display designed to make me feel bad about our current business dealings?' Rafael enquired very drily.

Something inside Harriet just exploded. 'Hell's teeth…*men*!' she launched back at him with honest incredulity. 'Why are you all so blasted self-obsessed? My ex-fiancé accused me of leaving the country to make *him* feel bad. Now you think I'm putting on some melodramatic show for *your* benefit. Well, wake up and join the real world. Right at this minute I couldn't care less about that stupid partnership! I've got much more important things on my mind.'

Accustomed to women who expressed dissatisfaction in infinitely more devious ways, Rafael thought that she had a wonderfully straightforward way of expressing her feelings. 'Such as?'

'The man I love is marrying my sister in August!' Harriet bit out, and, snatching up one of the photos in the pile beside her, she chucked it into the flames. 'That's why I'm burning all this stuff.'

Rafael crouched down and scooped up a single large photo.

'What are you doing?' Harriet screeched, leaping upright and striving to retrieve it from his insensitive hold.

'Encouraging your pyromania… Is this him? The object of your affections?' Rafael extended the picture of Luke for her perusal but deliberately kept it out of her reach.

Deciding that a struggle lacked dignity, Harriet folded her arms and jerked her chin in a curt nod of affirmation.

'He'll be overweight by the age of forty. He's already losing his hair, and he's not very tall,' Rafael pronounced drily. 'Give your sister a badge for stealing him. She's picked a short, fat, balding guy!'

'Most women think Luke is very presentable.' Harriet was infuriated by his irreverence. Furthermore, while it was one thing to have told him she was still getting over a previous relationship, being caught in the act with the old photos, the cuddly toys and the sad music collection was distinctly embarrassing.

'Review him with a critical eye.' Rafael displayed the photograph for reappraisal. 'This is Mr Ordinary, not some mythical prince.'

Mr Ordinary? Oddly enough, she had not noticed before that Luke's hairline had begun to recede, or that his jawline was no longer crisp. He had definitely enjoyed her cooking. Whatever else had been a lie that at least had not been. Her throat closed over, for she was recalling cosy evenings when she had prepared meals while Luke talked about his day at work.

'Go away,' she told her tormentor in a jagged undertone.

'My aim is to accelerate the recovery process,' Rafael informed her, smooth as silk.

'But you're intruding. I'm trying to do my wallowing in grief bit, and nobody wants to do that with an audience!' Her head was spinning a little from the combination of night air and peach wine.

'I'll be an objective companion.'

'But you shouldn't *be* here…this is a girlie ritual…play the music, wallow and weep, and burn the photos!' Harriet slung at him shakily.

Rafael hunkered down beside the sizeable pile of memorabilia and surveyed it with a raised black brow of polite enquiry. 'How long were you with the little guy? A lifetime?'

Harriet flushed and hunkered down to say urgently, 'Look, he wasn't a little guy… Oh, for goodness' sake! I've known him for eight years. First we were friends, but we were a couple for five of those years.'

'All that time…' Rafael shook his arrogant dark

head in genuine wonderment at the longevity of her attachment. 'That's sick…almost obsessional in my terms.'

'I *loved* him!'

'You'll note that you are already using the past tense,' Rafael remarked with satisfaction.

'Do you think I don't know I have to get over this? But it's not that easy to get by without someone who was so much a part of my life. Haven't you ever been hurt?'

His gleaming dark eyes narrowed and caught the leaping gold of the flames. 'Once, when I was a teenager…never again.'

'Right, so here you are offering advice when really you're an emotionally damaged individual who doesn't fall in love like other people!' Harriet tossed back, unimpressed.

Taken aback, Rafael vented an abrupt laugh of disagreement. 'There's nothing damaged about me. I've seen the angst romantic nonsense causes, and I decided a long time ago that I would not repeat that mistake. May I?'

Harriet nodded in assent and watched him taste the wine direct from the bottle. She had to fight off a ridiculously guilty hostess-like urge to offer to go indoors and fetch him a proper glass from which to drink.

'Too sweet for my palate…but it's strong,' Rafael commented. 'I suspect it will give you a punishing hangover.'

In defiance of that uninvited warning, Harriet reclaimed the bottle for another rebellious swig. She rarely indulged in alcohol, but refused to worry about the morrow. She was sick and tried of always opting for the safe and sensible line. Alice had never played safe and sensible and she was the one Luke loved and was soon to walk down the aisle to the 'Wedding March'! Feeding another CD into the player, Harriet turned down the volume only because her companion winced.

'How did you manage not to fall in love again?' Harriet asked with helpless interest, for the mere thought of ever daring to risk her heart again was anathema to her. On the other hand the prospect of being alone for ever, with only Samson and Peanut for company, was not as attractive an option as she felt it ought to be.

'That's simple,' Rafael declared with absolute confidence. 'It's a question of self-discipline.'

Harriet was very impressed by that answer, for she had often suspected that the root cause of her biggest regrets was a lack of sufficient will-power. She needed more strength of mind, she told herself squarely. Having studied for a degree she hadn't really wanted to satisfy her stepfather's respect for academia, she had then settled for a high-pressured job she'd found less than fulfilling to make Luke happy. Time and time again other people's wishes had influenced her choices. Why did she have this awful urge to please others more than herself? But hadn't those other people been people she loved?

Now she tried to imagine having the self-discipline to enjoy a relationship without yielding to the dangerous desire to love that person and hold on to them for ever. That was definitely the way to go, she reflected painfully, studying a photo that depicted her with Luke at a university dinner and consigning it hurriedly to the flames. She had been so happy that night, so naïve, that she would have trusted Luke with her life. But she did not want visual memories of Alice's bridegroom. Nor did she wish to be tempted to retain keepsakes from a past that was better forgotten. After all, Luke had let her down very badly, and was quite unworthy of fond recollections and sad longings.

'A question of self-discipline?' Harriet allowed herself to look at Rafael properly for the first time since he had unceremoniously invaded her girlie grieving session.

She was immediately absorbed by her entrancing view of the long, lean, relaxed sprawl of his powerful body. No, there was no denying the obvious, Harriet reflected abstractedly: Rafael Cavaliere Flynn was completely gorgeous. In fact just looking, lingering to admire the striking charismatic potency of his lean bronzed features, could easily become an addictive habit. But an addictive habit of the most innocent kind, Harriet reasoned with confidence. After all, as long as she was still in love with Luke she was totally safe from making the even bigger error of falling for a male so out of reach he might as well have been an alien on a distant planet. A male, moreover, whom no sane woman would ever believe cherished even the smallest wish to settle down. Thus reassured by his essential unsuitability as even a possible life partner, Harriet went back to admiring the smouldering depths of his dark eyes, which were nothing short of spectacular.

'When did Luke take up with your sister?' Rafael was conscious that he finally had her full attention. He was carelessly amused by the reality that he could not recall when he had last had to make an effort to hold a woman's interest.

Harriet told him, and how she had found out, and how devastated she had been. In fact, after being encouraged to expand on several points, she told him the entire history of her relationship with Luke. From its inception to the bitter end, it erupted from her in a confessional, though any temptation to linger on ir-relevancies was ruthlessly suppressed by her interrogator. He refused to be impressed or shocked or even sympathetic—until she divulged the bridesmaid offer.

His steady gaze hardened. 'That's a joke…right?'

'No. I suspect that it's my mother and Alice's way of trying to pretend that Luke and I were never an item in the first place.' Sadness flooded Harriet and she tipped a whole pile of photos and a penguin soft toy emblazoned with 'Be My Valentine' across a red satin heart on the fire. 'I don't want her to marry him. That's so mean and selfish of me…'

Rafael tried not to smile while he surreptitiously set the wine bottle out of view and nudged the CD player behind his back before she could register that the whining tinny songs of heartbreak and betrayal had finally fallen silent. 'I don't think you have a handle on pure malice yet.'

'What would you know about it?'

'Probably more than you.' Rafael was thinking of the women he had known. Harriet was painfully honest, and in obvious daily contact with her conscience. Meeting enquiring eyes with the unspoilt clarity of bluebells, he decided not to shock her with tales of extreme female guile and greed. He lifted an assured hand to brush a silky straight strand of copper hair back from her cheekbone.

Her pupils dilated, her breath tripping in her throat. 'I'm supposed to be burning stuff…and I keep on talking instead…'

Helpfully he scooped up some more items and tossed them on the fire. 'Do you always do what you're supposed to do?'

The dark, husky timbre of his rich voice had an intimacy that skimmed down her taut spinal cord like a caress. She shivered, and slowly, as though she was afraid of breaking out of the spell she was under, moved her bright head in affirmation. 'Yes.'

'That's too predictable.'

'You mean boring.'

'Your slant on the word, not mine. You worry too much. You can't make every decision by some rigid rulebook,' Rafael censured, soft and low, his breath fanning her cheek. 'You need to learn how to enjoy yourself again.'

His stunning eyes burned tawny gold in the firelight. She dragged in another stark breath. 'Why aren't you doing what billionaires usually do on a Friday night?'

His lean, startlingly handsome face remained maddeningly deadpan. 'Which is?'

Harriet shifted slim shoulders to signify that she

had only the sketchiest idea of what billionaires did on their weekends. 'Something with a yacht or a private jet…at least a helicopter! You should be gambling at a casino…or waterskiing…or throwing a big party with loads and loads of beautiful women. Instead you're watching a bonfire in an Irish field—'

'I'm watching you…'

His intent gaze made her mouth run dry. He angled his proud dark head down and kissed her as if it was the most natural thing in the world. He tasted of woodsmoke and wine and sex. She shivered in response, shocked, excited, half terrified of what she was feeling. Even light-headed from the peach wine she had imbibed, she recognised that she was in the hands of a sensualist with a technique to die for.

As Rafael released Harriet she looked up at him with a flattering degree of appreciation and muttered without thinking, her words running together a little, 'You really are perfect fling material.'

Rafael went very still. 'Meaning?'

Harriet turned pink. 'My goodness—did I say that out loud?'

His strong jawline squared. 'You did…so explain.'

Harriet loosed an edgy laugh, and then concentrated on not slurring her speech. 'What's to explain? You're a guy with a wild, roving reputation—'

'And you're the "faithful unto death" type?'

'I was with Luke.'

A faint smile of amusement was playing over his firmly modelled mouth. 'You picked him for a lifetime, but you think I'm only good for a fling?'

As Harriet registered that his oddly chilling smile did not quite reach his eyes, she swallowed hard. Had she offended him? How could she possibly have offended him? He had a notorious reputation as a womaniser. He had already admitted that it was a lifestyle choice: not to love, not to be hurt. And she envied his detachment, longed to emulate it so that she could forget Luke and the pain of his betrayal and her sister's. Why should passion without strings be strictly a male preserve?

'Please don't be insulted,' she whispered wistfully, for at some stage she had begun to enjoy the stimulation of his presence.

Rafael shifted a dismissive shoulder in a fluid movement that was supremely Italian. 'How could I be insulted by such inspiring honesty?'

'You're a fabulous kisser,' she added, and then clamped a stricken hand to her parted lips and groaned out loud. 'Shouldn't have said that either. Close your ears…don't listen!'

Rafael studied the photos of her ex that still needed burning and pitched them onto the embers, prodding them into blazing destruction with a deft booted foot. She was in despair over a guy who could model for catalogues selling garden gnomes. She had drunk only the equivalent of two small glasses of wine but clearly had a low tolerance level for alcohol, since she was talking drivel. In vino veritas? It meant literally truth in wine. Perfect fling material? Was that how she saw him? As the male sexual equivalent of a bimbo? Suitable only for a one-night-stand? A casual encounter? He was outraged. There and then he decided that he had no intention of living down to her rock-bottom opinion of him.

As Harriet sat up her head swam, making her feel a touch dizzy. 'Oops…'

Springing upright to his full imposing height, Rafael reached down a lean hand and pulled her upright. 'I'll see you indoors before I leave.'

'You do have great manners. I like that,' she mumbled, swaying slightly until he braced an arm over her spine and managed to steady legs that seemed briefly to want to move in opposing directions.

'I'm thrilled that you noticed.'

Tugging free of his support, to be the new and brave independent woman she was determined to be, Harriet plotted a reasonably straight path through the rough grass on her own. But Rafael helped her over the fence, and vaulted over the same barrier with the intimidating ease of an athlete to escort her across the yard.

'I'd invite you in but I'm very sleepy,' Harriet confided. 'When are we going to have a business meeting?'

'I'm about to leave for New York,' Rafael divulged.

Stark disappointment swallowed Harriet alive. 'Oh…'

'We'll talk tomorrow afternoon at two. My place or yours?' he quipped.

'Here would be the better option.'

'In the meantime, I never did return your friendly salutation on the phone.' His dark eyes locked to her innocent puzzled face as he closed light hands over hers and drew her close to his tall, muscular frame. 'Hello, partner…'

He kissed her breathless. She wasn't prepared, and there was no time to muster her defences. She fell into that kiss and the heat of a passion that burned her from inside out. Gasping, trembling, suddenly painfully alive to the tingling reaction of every nerve ending she possessed, she was shaken by the seductive strength of her own pleasure. She didn't want to breathe, she didn't want him to stop, she just wanted to stay where she was, feeling what she was feeling for ever.

But Rafael pressed open the door behind her, eased her into the dim kitchen and said goodnight. In a daze she stood there for several minutes, not quite sure what had happened to her.

CHAPTER FOUR

THE NEXT MORNING, Harriet tried to avoid waking up:
a wheel of fire was turning inside her head. She em-
braced the pain with the masochistic conviction that
she thoroughly deserved to suffer for being so foolish with the wine.

At the same time, Rafael Flynn had kissed her—
and she couldn't quite credit that development.
Possibly the isolation of life in County Kerry had
driven him to lower his standards. From what she
had seen Ballyflynn wasn't exactly heaving with
young women. But he hadn't simply kissed her once,
she recalled. He had done the deed twice—and very
thoroughly. Of course there was a more obvious explanation for her sudden startling pulling power: she
was on the spot and single and he was over-sexed.
That made the best sense of all to her, for she felt that
it went without saying that a womaniser of interna-

tional acclaim would probably be *extremely* over-sexed.

The tentative knock that sounded on her bedroom door provoked a faint moan of self-pity from her. It creaked open. 'Harriet?' Una stage-whispered. 'Do you want your first plaiting lesson?'

Discomfiture ate Harriet alive. Ignoring her headache, she sat bolt upright. 'Yes...what a great idea.'

'I've been here for an hour. I let you have a lie-in,' the teenager told her chattily from the doorway.

Harriet lodged an anguished eye on the alarm clock, which confirmed that it was still only seven in the morning, and forced a valiant smile. 'Give me ten minutes.'

'It was so quiet here while you were away. I hardly saw Fergal,' Una lamented, while she demonstrated her failsafe methods on Snowball's somewhat thin mane. 'I'm starting to think he's avoiding me.'

'I expect he's very busy.' Harriet attempted without much success to make her fingers match the younger woman's nimble example. 'But I do have a couple of things to discuss with him. Do you know where I would be most likely to find him mid-morning?'

'In Dooleys Bar, of course.' Una was evidently surprised by what she considered to be an unnecessary question.

Harriet's eyes widened, but she made no comment and offered the teenager a lift home. It was a bright sunny morning. While she waited for Una to load her bike into the pick-up truck, she stood at the fence admiring the view down to the sea. The green fields stretched down to the deserted white strand and the sparkling sapphire blue of the Atlantic: it was so beautiful it almost hurt her eyes.

'There's a rumour going round the village that you've been fighting with Rafael Flynn. Obviously you're a lot cheekier than you look.' The teenager gave her a teasing glance.

Thinking of the kiss the night before, Harriet reddened, and to cover her blushes quipped, 'Don't you think I have to avoid him?'

'No. If you've got the nerve to fight with him, you could be just the woman for him!'

Harriet laughed. 'I don't think so.'

Una asked to be dropped off in the middle of Ballyflynn. It was market day and the village was busy. On the colourful main street Harriet bought fresh vegetables out of the back of an ancient lorry and fretted guiltily over the fact that she had still to pick a patch on which to grow her own. Dooleys Bar appeared to share space with the post office. She walked through the low green painted door into a cosy, impossibly crowded room floored with worn flagstones and warmed by a turf fire. The smell of burning peat made her think of lonely stretches of sweeping moorland. The bar was packed tight with farmers, who twisted round to look at her, and several offered a few pleasantries in greeting. It amused her that although she had not met one of them before they every one to a man knew exactly who she was.

'How you doing?' Fergal asked cheerfully

Harriet blushed at her uncharitable assumptions. He was not propping up the bar with a pint in his hand but serving drinks from behind it. 'There's been some developments at the yard, but we can catch up later.'

'Fergal…I'll mind the bar while you have a break.' A pale little woman with a tight perm and sharp eyes bustled out from behind the post office counter. 'Introduce me to your visitor.'

For some reason that request turned Fergal the colour of a beetroot. At the same time the noisy rise and fall of conversation in the busy room suddenly died. 'Ma…'

Marvelling that his mother's friendly welcome should have reduced Fergal to the level of an inarticulate schoolboy, and awakened so much apparent interest from the locals, Harriet stepped into the awkward silence. 'Mrs Gibson…I'm Harriet Carmichael.'

'Very pleased to meet you, I'm sure. Fergal…
don't keep the lady waiting!' the older woman urged
her son. 'Now, where would you like to sit?'

'Thanks, but we'll head over to the café!' Fergal
pulled open the door for Harriet with alacrity.

'If I'd known you were working I'd never have
come in,' Harriet was dismayed by the embarrassment she appeared to have caused him. 'Is the bar a
family business?'

'Dooleys belongs to my uncle. After my father
died we moved in with him. But I'd give anything
to train horses full time.' Fergal pulled out a chair for
her occupation in the cosy café across the street.
'But helping Ma run the bar is my bread and butter.'

Harriet unbuttoned her fleece jacket. 'I want to keep
you informed about what's happening at the yard.' She
gave him a brief rundown on what he needed to know.
'From here on in Rafael Flynn will be my partner.'

'I'm thinking it'll be a challenge for him to share
anything, for he's always the big boss. But he was
born knowing more about horseflesh than some
learn in a lifetime. He picks winners time and time
again,' Fergal volunteered with honest admiration.
'Do you reckon he'll want me out of the stables?'

'That's what I don't know as yet.' Distracted by
the sound of a car braking hard on the street outside,
Harriet glanced out of the window.

Across the street a big black Range Rover had come to a halt. Her attention sharpened as Rafael Flynn sprang out in an apparent attempt to intercept the girl hurrying with her head down in the opposite direction. His lean, strong face was hard as granite as he blocked her path.

'My goodness, that's Una!' Harriet exclaimed in astonishment. 'What on earth is he doing?'

When the teenager visibly broke down into tears of distress, Fergal looked miserably uncomfortable and averted his eyes. 'Well, her half-brother was certain to find out eventually that she wasn't safe in school, like he thought,' he sighed. 'She's been running round trying to avoid him. I felt guilty for not telling him. A few other people did too, but you don't like to get her in trouble.'

On the brink of racing outside to intercede on Una's behalf, Harriet froze halfway out of her chair. 'Her…half-brother? Una is Rafael Flynn's *half-sister*?'

'Sorry, I should've realised you wouldn't know. But it's an open secret round here because it was such a scandal when it happened. Her mother and his father—well…' Fergal frowned. 'Rafael's father didn't take responsibility, but when he found out about her Rafael *did*. Fair play to him, he's done his best for Una, but she fights him every step of the way.'

'She said her brother was scarier than scary,' Harriet groaned, watching the teenager slink into Rafael's car with the defeated aspect of a prisoner being taken into custody. 'I wish she'd confided in me.'

'He's only trying to keep her in school and out of trouble.'

'Does she live with her mother during the holidays?'

'With her married sister. But Philomena is too laid back to keep Una on a tight leash.'

Harriet called in to the newspaper shop to buy her favourite horse magazine. The owner chatted to her with the easy friendliness and unapologetic curiosity that was so characteristic of Ballyflynn. Although Harriet was worried about Una, she attempted to put what she had seen out of her mind. After all, Fergal had made it clear that Rafael had the teenager's best interests at heart, and it was not her place to interfere. But all she could think about was what a disaster Rafael and Una could easily be as siblings—for both of them were equally proud and stubborn and strong willed.

Just before she got back into the pick-up she noticed a display of handcrafted jewellery in the window of the exclusive gift shop and art gallery at the top of the street. A pair of flamboyant beaded drop earrings caught her eye; it would be Nicola's birthday in a couple of weeks. The shop was packed, though, and she decided she didn't have the time to queue. Before she could get back into her car, Fergal's mother came out to invite her over to supper on Sunday evening. Harriet was surprised, but accepted with a smile and rushed off. In a couple of hours she had her meeting with Rafael Flynn, and she wanted the yard to be spick and span for his visit.

At five minutes to two that afternoon Harriet was flat on the floor of her bedroom, trying to get the zip up on her favourite jeans. It was at the precise moment when success was within a half-inch of achievement that she heard a large vehicle pull up outside. In dismay, she released her breath, and the zip slid straight down again. While she was struggling to regain lost ground, a knock sounded on the front door. With an anguished moan, she tore off the jeans in a feverish surge of activity. As she had neglected to close the curtains, she scurried on her knees over to the chest of drawers to yank out a pair of mercifully stretchy riding breeches. Shimmying frantically into them, she scrambled upright, saw the glossy black Range Rover parked outside, and raced for the front door.

'Sorry—was I too punctual?' Rafael asked, wicked dark eyes glittering over her decidedly tousled appearance.

He looked effortlessly, classily stupendous, in a brown waxed jacket, breeches and leather riding boots. With the greatest difficulty Harriet fought the urge to smooth a tidying hand through her tumbled copper hair. 'No, I've been cleaning out the tack room,' she told him with studied casualness, reasoning that that *was* what she had been doing before she'd realised that she was running late and hurried indoors to wash and change. 'I lost track of the time. What would you like to look at first?'

'Been there, done that… Unless you've made sweeping changes?' A questioning ebony brow inclined. 'No, I didn't think so.'

Momentarily thrown by what she suspected had been an opening designed to deflate any pretensions she might have, Harriet decided to take the hint and get straight down to business. 'OK. Let's move on,' she suggested, pulling shut the door behind her to prevent Peanut and Samson galloping out and destroying her business credibility.

'Item one on our agenda,' Rafael drawled before she even got the chance to speak again, 'has to be this cottage. I want it restored.'

'I understand that, but—'

'Naturally I would cover all costs.'

Her pale smooth brow furrowed, her surprise patent. 'But this is where I live—'

'I now own half of it,' Rafael pointed out smoothly. 'At this point I'll settle for having the exterior restored. I'll bring in an architectural historian to do an appraisal, but I should imagine that one of the first steps will be re-thatching the roof.'

As the cottage was an historic building, his concern was reasonable, Harriet conceded reluctantly. Nor did she feel that she could raise an objection when he was offering to foot the bill. Yet by making so immediate a claim to his right to repair the very roof over her head he was striking right at the heart of her security. The reminder that he owned half her home could only be unwelcome.

'I'm making a logical request,' Rafael remarked.

'In theory I have no objection, as long as I don't find changes being imposed without my agreement. You have to respect the fact that this is my home. I'd also have to run this by a solicitor, to check that you couldn't later claim to have a right to a bigger share of the property because you covered the restoration costs.'

Dark eyes shaded by lush black lashes gleamed. 'Either you're my partner or you're not. Distrust will render any agreement between us unworkable.'

Harriet stiffened as if he had cracked a warning whip round her flanks—and in a sense he had, she reflected resentfully. If she did not meet his demands, he could quite easily make it impossible for her to get the yard up and running. 'Trust is a tall order.'

'One thing you should learn about me,' Rafael imparted in a light, conversational tone. 'I don't lie and I don't cheat. When I want something I'll tell you. When I don't like something you will find me equally to the point.'

It was an unnecessary admonition, for Harriet could not begin to imagine Rafael Cavaliere Flynn suffering annoyance in silence. His every move and his every word resonated with the unequivocal authority of someone accustomed to always getting their own way. Determined to seize back the initiative, Harriet said briskly, 'Now, with regard to the sheds that you believe spoil your outlook—'

Rafael spread lean brown hands in an elegant gesture of finality. 'They must be demolished. There is no other option.'

Exasperation gripped Harriet. 'Tell me, have you any plans to let me have my say?'

'But I don't want to talk business with you, Harriet,' Rafael confided huskily. 'I did have a much more entertaining agenda in mind for us. Unfortunately another obligation has to take precedence.'

Harriet dragged her sparkling blue gaze from him like a woman on a diet being taunted with a box of chocolates. 'That's irrelevant,' she said firmly. 'This is a business meeting because we have a partnership in this yard.'

'The concept of partnership is a learning experience for me.' Rafael was sending up her stern attitude like mad with his wickedly amused dark eyes.

Frustration and unwilling appreciation of his charisma warring within her, Harriet breathed in very deep and stared fixedly at the sheds. 'I'll let you demolish them if you build me a new set of eight stables in the rear yard.'

'Harriet…' Rafael sighed. 'That is out of the question—'

'Then you're stuck with the ugly view!' Harriet told him curtly. 'I can't have a viable livery yard without adequate stabling. I have to make a living here!'

'Naturally I will oppose any further development on this site—'

'In other words, *you* have a conflict of interest.'

'But you were well aware of that reality when you decided to go for the partnership rather than repayment,' Rafael reminded her levelly.

Harriet felt quite dizzy with anger, and she studied the ground while she endeavoured to suppress it. Her temper was in volcanic mode, and she was not accustomed to that. As a rule she was the most equable and tolerant of personalities, who could handle difficult people and situations with patience and commonsense. Yet Rafael could rouse her to wrath with a gesture as minimal as raising an aristocratic ebony brow.

'There is another possibility.'

'I can't imagine what that would be,' Harriet responded, in a tone of waspish discouragement.

Rafael shifted a broad shoulder with graceful calm. 'I would have discussed this option immediately, but you preferred to state your case first.'

Her cheeks rosily flushed, Harriet stared woodenly into space. She was vaguely surprised that she did not levitate with rage.

'Come on. Get in the car and I'll show you the alternative.' Rafael made the suggestion with colossal cool.

Harriet breathed in slow and deep and climbed into the leather passenger seat of the Range Rover. She suspected that she was about to be ceremoniously upstaged, and that he would prove to have enormous aptitude for that tactic. At the same time, however, it gave her the opportunity to say, as casually as she could manage, 'I saw you with Una in the village this morning.'

'And this afternoon I am personally escorting her back to her boarding school. I had no idea she had been suspended,' Rafael pronounced with grim clarity of diction, resting back in his seat to survey her. 'Various people, who should have known better, conspired to keep that information from me. Had her headmistress not sent me a second letter I would still be in the dark.'

'What's her mother's opinion of all this?'

'Her mother is an alcoholic who has repeatedly failed to complete rehab. I'm Una's legal guardian. I placed her in boarding school because her home environment was unacceptable. She spends the holidays with her sister.'

Harriet was shaken. 'I had no idea…she comes to the yard. She's mad about horses and really good with them. Why was she suspended?'

'Temper tantrums, impertinence, refusal to turn in the required work. In the past three years she has attended four different schools.'

'Perhaps she's fallen behind and she's finding the work too hard?'

'I doubt that very much.'

'Even so, it mightn't do any harm to have her tested.' Harriet was thinking uneasily about that ill-spelt note.

Rafael laughed out loud as he turned the Range Rover on to the road. 'What for? Being a teenager?'

Harriet went pink and scolded herself for suspecting that he might not be aware of his sister's difficulties with the written word. It was hardly surprising that he should prefer to keep that issue confidential. Having rustled frantically through her pockets, Harriet managed to print her phone numbers on to a scrap of paper. She set the note on the dash. 'Tell her the horses will really miss her attention, and that if she gets the time I'd love to hear from her.'

Without comment, Rafael turned into the Flynn Court estate by the entrance at the gate lodge where Tolly lived. Harriet *liked* Una? He was really surprised. *Was* Una good with horses? He had no idea. Getting even basic dialogue out of his half-sister was more pain than gain. He would demand an explanation of her latest offence, she would sulk or sob and refuse to speak, and he would pronounce judgement. He had given up talking about the value of education and the rewards of good behaviour in terms of privilege and respect. He ruled now by force of personality and threat. But that was not how he had intended it to be.

'Where on earth are you taking me?' Harriet asked.

'Have patience.'

The long drive looped round through a glorious avenue of vast spreading cedar trees and then back again before leading down a gentle sloping gradient to a vast walled building that was tucked completely out of view of the cottage.

'I didn't even know this existed,' Harriet admitted as Rafael drove below an ancient stone archway.

'It's only visible from the sea.'

As the car came to a halt on the cobbles in the vast enclosed space, Harriet's eyes were huge. 'Oh, my word…' she breathed in wonderment, levering the door open with an eager hand to spring out and take a closer look.

It was a magnificent stable yard in which time appeared to have stood miraculously still, for the ancient stonework and the stable doors were in immaculate order. There was not a weed to be seen, not so much as a cobblestone out of alignment. Fascinated, she wandered round below the classic arches lining three sides of the yard. The loose boxes had been renovated to modern standards, with water and drainage and smoke alarms. Of equal interest was the spacious room that lay behind the imposing Doric pillars at the furthest end. What a tack shop it would make, she thought instantly, peering through the windows.

'What do you think?'

Snatched from her reverie, Harriet whirled round. Rafael was lounging up against the bonnet of his four-wheel-drive, the beginnings of a smile playing over his devastatingly handsome mouth.

'What do I think?' Harriet was so knocked out by the sheer possibilities of the place that she was excited to death. 'How come it's in such incredibly good condition?'

'Unlike the Court?' Rafael followed her reasoning with ease. 'This place has belonged to me for a long time. About fifteen years ago I began buying back parts of the original estate whenever they came on the market. But the house belonged to my father until he died.'

Harriet was puzzled. 'Then why didn't he maintain it?'

'It was my mother's family home, and because she loved it he hated it. Valente always went with his gut reactions, and none of them were charitable.'

Harriet was taken aback by the complete casualness with which he implied that such unreasoning malice could only have been expected. 'I gather your parents didn't get on?'

'They were divorced.'

Surely only the most malign influence could have deliberately sentenced that exquisite house on the hill to neglect and ruin? Now Harriet could see the superb stable yard in another light. Rafael might betray little emotion, but the strength of his attachment to his mother's home, and possibly even her memory, was patent in the beautifully maintained buildings around her.

'Why did you bring me here to see this?'

'I thought you would already have worked that out. I get my view back, and in return you get an embarrassment of purpose built stables in which to operate. You also gain the services of a full-time groom. I only keep a couple of horses here, and Davis could do with more work.'

Harriet surveyed Rafael with dazed blue eyes. 'I can't believe you're serious. You're offering me the use of this huge, amazing yard in place of some tumbledown sheds? What's the catch?'

'There is no catch.' Strong dark features impassive, his lean powerful physique relaxed, he studied her with unruffled composure. 'Don't bite every hand that seeks to feed you.'

Yet his indolent calm unnerved her, for natural instinct warned that there had to be a lot more happening below that deceptively cool surface than he ever showed.

'But there *has* to be…I mean, for a start, basing the business here would be impractical.' Harriet attempted to voice the more obvious objections to such a proposal. 'I can't take care of horses that are stabled a couple of miles away by road!'

'That's not a problem. I'll reopen the lane that once linked with the one behind the cottage. You and your clientele can use it as a shortcut onto the estate. It'll also keep the traffic well away from the Court. The groom already lives in an apartment above the stables, which means he'll be on site to provide emergency cover.'

Harriet had expected Rafael to put obstacles in her way. Instead he appeared to be offering her a free, once-in-a-lifetime opportunity.

'I'd also like to discuss the possibility of exchanging the field you own in front of the cottage with one adjacent to the back lane. It would enable the re-planting of some of the trees that were cut down.'

Harriet drew in a quick breath. 'I could consider that.'

'Excellent.' Rafael strolled to the back of the car and reached in to emerge again with a bottle of vintage champagne and two glasses.

'We're celebrating?' Once again Harriet was thoroughly disconcerted. She was starting to appreciate the strong streak of unpredictability that made Rafael Flynn such a powerful competitor in the business world. In old-fashioned parlance he was a law unto himself, for he had not once reacted as she'd expected him to. It was, she reflected headily, an incredibly unsettling attribute.

Breaking open the champagne, Rafael sent the golden liquid foaming down into the delicate goblets. 'Let's drink to mixing business with pleasure.'

'But I *don't*...' Tiny bubbles burst and tickled Harriet's upper lip as she sipped.

'Neither do I, usually.' Setting down his glass, Rafael moved lazily closer. 'But I get a kick out of breaking rules.'

A tiny twist low in her tummy filled Harriet with restless heat.

'Are you game?' Without warning Rafael filched the glass from her hand. His eyes glittering with high-voltage energy, he eased her very slowly up against his lean, muscular physique.

Her heart started hammering like a clockwork toy that had been overwound. She knew she should match her words to her behaviour and break away, but her every urge fought that commonsense. 'Last night I had been drinking...'

'Don't be so serious,' Rafael censured with wry amusement.

Harriet flushed to the roots of her copper hair. 'I just think—we're partners—and then there's Luke—'

Rafael lifted and dropped a broad masculine shoulder with careless cool. 'That's up to you. You have two weeks to agonise about it.'

'Two weeks?' Harriet gasped involuntarily. 'You're planning to be away that long?'

A raw smile of appreciation lit his hard dark features. 'I'll meet you here on the Friday, at six in the morning…we'll go for a ride along the beach. I keep a mare here as company for my gelding. Try her out while I'm away.'

Rafael checked his watch and ran her straight back home. Indecision was cutting Harriet in two, and she felt foolish for having paraded it. To fling, or not to fling, she punned pathetically.

'By the way,' Rafael murmured levelly when she opened the passenger door to get out, 'I'm not into one-night-stands.'

Her face flamed, and she almost fell out of the car in her eagerness to escape. 'Neither am I.'

'You could have fooled me.'

CHAPTER FIVE

HARRIET had supper with Fergal's mother on Sunday evening. Treated like an honoured guest, it slowly sank in on Harriet that Mrs Gibson had decided that she would make a suitable girlfriend for her son. Cheerfully ignoring all the bossy older woman's coy and encouraging comments, Harriet managed to extract herself again without causing offence.

Patrick Flanagan had also called round that afternoon, and asked her out to Dooleys. She'd turned him down as tactfully as she could.

It was the following week before she finally got the chance to visit the village gift shop and buy the earrings she had seen for her stepfather's wife, Nicola.

Luckily for her the earrings were still unsold. While she waited for the sales assistant to remove them from the display, Harriet had the sensation that she was being watched, and turned her head. An elegant dark-haired woman rearranging shelves on the other side of the shop treated her to a stony-eyed stare. Harriet coloured, and then asked herself why she had somehow come to expect everyone local to greet her with a warm, welcoming smile.

'Robert…weren't you planning to set up the new exhibition in the gallery this morning?' the brunette enquired acidly of the overweight older man who had emerged from the back of the shop with his arms wrapped round a large unwieldy carton. 'You'll need to get a move on if you want it finished in time.'

As Harriet confirmed that she would take the earrings, the same woman took over from the assistant and ran the purchase through the till in silence. 'So, you're Agnes Gallagher's girl from England,' she remarked when she gave Harriet her change. 'Are you planning on staying here for long?'

'For good, I hope.' Harriet tucked the tiny package carefully into her bag and looked up with a smile. 'Did you know my mother?'

The brunette shot her a scornful look of dislike. 'Not as well as all the men knew her…if you know what I mean.'

Ludicrously unprepared for that unpleasant reply, Harriet stiffened with surprise and anger. 'I think I'll pretend I don't.'

'Do as you like.'

Her face burning, Harriet walked back out of the shop. That would be the last time she shopped there, she thought, appalled by the offensive crack. She wondered what, if anything, Eva had done to rouse such animosity. That woman could easily have gone to school with her mother. Eva freely admitted that she preferred male company to female, and often complained that her looks and her popularity with men made other women envious. The status and wealth her mother had acquired since she left Ballyflynn might also have provoked jealousy, Harriet reasoned ruefully.

'Miss Carmichael?' a gruff male voice called from behind her.

Harriet stilled and turned round to find a little man the shape of a tub with a round merry face and a beard struggling to catch up with her. 'Yes?'

'I'm Frank Kearney…'

Father Kearney, Harriet affixed inwardly, noting his clerical collar and shabby dark jacket.

'I couldn't help overhearing that exchange in the shop. Mrs Tolly must be having a very trying day,' the priest asserted in an anxious and valiant attempt to smooth matters over. 'I'm certain she could not have meant to say what she did—'

'Tolly…' Harriet frowned in surprise at that familiar name. 'You're referring to the woman in the gift shop? Is she related to Joseph Tolly?'

'Why, yes,' he confirmed. 'Sheila is married to Joseph's son, Robert.'

'Tolly didn't mention that he had a son.'

Father Kearney said only, 'Will I be seeing you soon at mass?'

'I wasn't raised a Catholic, Father.'

'Sure, you can't help that.' His round brown eyes twinkled. 'The chapel is always open here, and you'll be made very welcome.'

On the drive home Harriet stopped for a moment to admire the stylish sign below the chestnut tree which now advertised the Flynn Court Livery and pointed the way. The old lane that ran down to the back of cottage had already been opened up and freshly stoned. Mature beech trees lined the rough track, which curved round the base of the hill before reaching the superb stable yard. Parking outside the yard, she walked in through the first door past the entrance to where she had set up a convenient office, complete with computer and phone. The stone walls held on to the chill and she had already learned that it was wise to keep a little fire burning in the ancient iron grate. Peanut and Samson abandoned the rug there to subject her to a rapturous welcome.

The phone rang: it was Una, who had phoned Harriet almost every day since her return to boarding school. As usual the teenager was bubbling with questions about everything that was happening at the livery yard.

'How does the new sign look?' she demanded.

'Totally fantastic. You were right…that guy is a real artist,' Harriet enthused, since the teenager had given her the name of the signwriter. Asked, she then spelled several words for Una, who said she had lost her dictionary.

'Have you heard from Rafael yet?' Una asked eagerly.

'No.' Harriet smiled brightly, while wondering whom she was trying to impress with her chirpy show of indifference.

'Whatever you do, don't ring him,' Una warned her very seriously.

'If I was drowning I wouldn't ring him.' Harriet reddened at that less than cool comment and compressed her lips, hoping it had gone unnoticed.

'You should get yourself another fella and flash him around Ballyflynn…not Fergal, though.'

'Una…I don't know where you get the idea that I'm desperate for your half-brother to phone me. He's my business partner, and if he's content to stay in the background and let me get on with running the yard on my own, I'm all for it.'

'All right—pretend there's nothing else going on if it makes you feel better.' Una's chagrin at what she had interpreted as a snub was perceptible. 'Rafael's playing the same game.'

But there was no game, Harriet reflected ruefully, finally surrendering to Peanut's persistent blandishments and throwing a ball out on to the cobbles for the pig to chase. Rafael's silence simply spelled out the truth that he was not that interested in the livery business…or in her. On the other hand he had barely left the country before experts on eighteenth century follies, landscape and thatching started rolling up at her door to perform detailed surveys and squabble with each other. How was her self-esteem supposed to survive the truth that a thatched roof had more instant pulling power than she had? After all, every one of the experts must have heard from Rafael.

A piggy squeal of rage made Harriet fly upright. One of the elderly wolfhounds from the Court had run off with Peanut's ball. As the dog capered round the yard like a giant shaggy coat, Samson set off in enthusiastic and noisy pursuit. The wolfhound dropped the ball to lie down and play with the chihuahua. Little round eyes bright with superior porcine intelligence, Peanut trotted over and deftly recaptured her favourite toy.

A few minutes later the customer Harriet was expecting arrived, with her child's pony in a trailer.

Business was booming, and Harriet could not understand why she was feeling so edgy and unsettled…

Rafael strode out of the shower and snatched up a towel.

It was still dark. Would Harriet turn up? Or wouldn't she? For the first time in his adult life he could not be confident of immediate success with a woman. That singular sense of uncertainty fascinated him. He didn't even know why he had invited her to share a pleasure that he usually preferred to enjoy alone. Was the secret of her attraction her level of casual uninterest that he had never met with before? She was in love with someone else. No secret there, he thought with brooding exasperation.

Yet nothing else was so clear-cut. He had expected her to phone with regular updates on the livery yard. He had assumed that she would take advantage of his vast experience and ask for advice. He had been certain that she would play on their partnership connection to ensure that he didn't forget her while he was away. But she had done none of those things and he was intrigued.

At the foot of the hill Harriet lay in bed, stiff with tension and wide awake, telling herself that she would drop back to sleep again at any minute. She wasn't going. He wouldn't be there. It had been a very casual arrangement. Even if he was there, it would be madness. They had a business relationship and, unlike him, she had great respect for following the rules. In any case she had stayed in bed too long, and now there wasn't enough time for her to get ready.

A split second later something stronger than reason—indeed, something remarkably similar to an adrenalin charge—energised Harriet into a sudden frenzied leap out of bed. It was not a decision she consciously made. Her hair needed washing, and she endured a semi-cold shower before fleeing back to her bedroom to drag clean clothes over her still wet skin. If Rafael was a no-show she knew she would absolutely hate herself. She dragged a comb ruthlessly through her wet hair and slicked it back with an agonised grimace. Hauling on her riding boots, she hurtled out to catch and saddle Snowball, thanking her lucky stars that the elderly mare was so docile.

On the lane, her senses straining to pick up the slightest sound of other human activity, she heard the rattle of a bridle and the shifting of restive hooves ahead. Her heartbeat quickened and she pressed Snowball on round the last corner at greater speed.

A slow smile of acknowledgement illuminated Rafael's lean, bronzed features. He mounted his big black gelding with the athletic ease of a confident rider.

Harriet grinned at him and found it hard to stop, for suddenly she felt incredibly exhilarated. 'Sorry I'm late.'

'I was about to come down and tip you out of bed,' Rafael admitted. 'I was determined to have your company today. Would you like to see the estate before we hit the beach?'

'I'd like that.'

'I believe you chose not to try out the mare I offered you. Don't you like her?'

Harriet coloured up. Missy, the palomino mare he kept with his gelding, was really beautiful, and probably a dream to ride. Accepting endless favours, however, made her feel uncomfortable. 'She's lovely, but I just didn't have the time—'

'If you exercised her, I would consider it an act of kindness.'

'OK…' They rode past the walled kitchen garden which was Tolly's pride and joy. 'I've been in there to admire Tolly's vegetables,' Harriet confided, and then, having found that opening, tackled a subject that had been nagging at her all week. 'I didn't know that Tolly had a son in the village…I was surprised he hadn't mentioned him to me and I didn't like to ask him why he hadn't.'

'I can explain that. Tolly's lucky if he sees Robert once a year,' Rafael replied grimly. 'His wife died when Robert was a child, and her sister insisted on taking the boy into her home. Tolly was kept at a distance and Robert learned to look down on his father because he was in domestic service.'

Harriet winced in dismay. 'Poor Tolly…'

'He was grateful to the couple for being so good to his son. He hoped that things would change when Robert grew up.'

'But they didn't…?'

'No. Tolly still only sees his son if he runs into him in the village.'

'That's sad,' Harriet sighed. 'I'm getting very fond of Tolly.'

'He gave unstinting support and service to my mother long after all her relatives and friends had stopped calling.' The rare warmth with which Rafael spoke welded her attention to his darkly handsome profile.

Harriet frowned. 'Why did they do that?'

'She was addicted to prescription drugs and often incoherent and confused.' Rafael gave Harriet's shaken face a steady appraisal. 'Tolly kept the household together and ensured that she had regular medical attention. I could never repay all that he did for her.'

'How did she get in such a mess?'

'My father systematically destroyed her.' Rafael made that statement levelly, a chilling look in his eyes. 'He met her in Dublin when she was still recovering from the death of her first husband. He wore down her resistance and she married him within the year. '

'What went wrong?'

'Valente began to suspect that he came a poor second to his predecessor in her affections. After I was born he accused her of marrying him for the money to save Flynn Court from ruin.'

Harriet was engrossed in the story of his background. 'So what happened?'

'My father invited his mistresses home to humiliate her. When she tried to object he became violent, and she ended up on medication. He then divorced her and retained custody of me by revealing evidence in court that, when she was at her lowest, she had had a brief affair. She never recovered from the public disgrace. I was only allowed to visit her for six weeks every summer. She died when I was fourteen…long before I was in a position to do anything to help her. '

The flash of bitter pain she saw in his eyes touched Harriet to the heart. She understood how much his inability to help his fragile mother must have marked him. He had been powerless, as children so often were, and the guilt and regret were still with him, even though it was hard to see what he could have done. Without hesitation she reached across to touch his arm in a quiet expression of sympathy. 'I should think that your visits meant a great deal to her, so you did do something for her just by being there.'

Rafael was stunned by that gesture. For a split second his fierce pride threatened to make him react angrily, but the warm-hearted concern in her clear gaze was too open to cause offence.

Harriet, however, was thoroughly ashamed of her own blinkered vision. He was rich beyond avarice and she had naively assumed that he had always had everything he desired, and a wonderful childhood to boot. Now she could hardly credit that she could have been so superficial and prejudiced. She thought it very probable that his unhappy background had driven Rafael into becoming the high achiever and tough survivor that he was.

Eager to compensate, she matched his honesty with her own. 'There's another side to every coin. By the sound of it you didn't like your father very much, but at least you knew his identity. My mother ran away from Ballyflynn as a pregnant teenager and still won't tell me who my father is. But it seems obvious that he was nothing to write home about.'

That bracing observation, voiced in a wry tone of acceptance, almost made Rafael laugh out loud in appreciation. His own tension dissolved. Her lack of drama on the thorny issue of her parentage was refreshing. 'You must be very curious.'

'Yes, but I'm fast reaching the conclusion that I'll have to live with being curious and that there are more important things.'

The scent of lily-of-the-valley hung heavy in the air. They were following a winding bridle path through ancient oak woods, which lay in a hidden valley sheltered from the wind. The silence filled her with a sense of peace. The twisted tree trunks of oak and holly and the weathered rocks were covered with a velvet carpet of green moss and lichens. Lush ferns interspersed with wood sorrel and red campion grew below the light canopy of the trees. It was very beautiful and unspoilt.

'This is a wonderful place.' Harriet loosed a dreamy sigh. 'If you told me fairies lived here, I'd believe you.'

A few minutes later Rafael brought his gelding to a halt in a grassy glade and dismounted. He reached up to help her down from Snowball's back and murmured huskily, 'According to local legend, this is the heart of the wood, and the magic is strongest here where an oak, an ash and a hawthorn tree all grow together.'

She met his stunning eyes, and her heart raced so fast she felt dizzy. 'I definitely didn't expect you to know fairy lore.'

His mouth melded with hers and she believed in the magic. Intoxicated by the taste of him, she shivered, mesmerised by the fierce response he could awaken in her. She had never felt that way before, and exhilaration leapt through her in an energising surge. He lifted his head, his black hair tousled by her fingers, and a slow-burning smile illuminated his lean bronzed features. 'You enchant me, *a mhilis*.'

Harriet strove not to betray disappointment when he released her as casually as he had pulled her to him minutes before. 'Was that Irish? Do you actually speak the language?' she asked him.

'Like a native…it annoyed the hell out of Valente!' Brilliant eyes full of vibrant amusement, Rafael tightened a loose stirrup on Snowball and helped her mount again.

The woods petered out into the rough grazing land above the sand dunes. She could smell the sharp salty tang of the sea. The gelding broke into an enthusiastic trot, but Snowball picked a much more cautious path down on to the beach.

'Next time you ride my mare,' Rafael pronounced with finality.

'I'm no good at accepting favours.'

'It's not a problem…I'll find something for you to do for me in return.' His silken mockery whipped fresh colour into her cheeks.

The Atlantic was blue as the sky, but lively. Waves were hitting the rocks, sending up cascades of water droplets in the bright sunlight before crashing down on the sand and then washing in across the pale strand with a soft rushing hiss.

Harriet urged Snowball into a trot, enjoying the cooling breeze. Her mount could not keep up with his, and she watched him unleash the gelding's surplus energy in a gallop across the sands. He was a superb rider. When she slid off Snowball to investigate a rock pool he cantered back to join her.

'I'm a total child about these,' Harriet admitted cheerfully. 'The water is so clear it's like a tiny sea world in miniature.'

As she straightened, Rafael caught her to him and covered her parted lips with deep, devastating urgency. The earthy force of his passion startled and excited her. An arrow of white hot heat pierced low in her belly, setting up a chain reaction that made her shiver.

He framed her cheekbones with spread fingers

and stared down at her with unashamed desire. 'I want you so much it hurts.'

She felt hot, and unbearably tense. Her own wild response shocked her, but being separated by so much as an inch from him was a torment that over-powered other considerations. She squirmed closer, blindly seeking that contact that her body craved. With a roughened masculine groan he backed her up against the rocks behind her and hauled her to him, to crush her eager mouth beneath his while she clung to his hard-muscled shoulders.

He ran his fingers through the tumbled copper strands of her hair. He explored her trembling length with sure hands, roved below her jacket and loose T-shirt to toy with the outrageously sensitive rosy tip of one rounded breast. A moan breaking at the back of her convulsed throat, she snatched in an agonised gasp of air below his marauding mouth. She could not get enough of him. When her mobile phone started ringing, she stiffened in surprise.

'Ignore it,' Rafael instructed thickly, lifting his tousled dark head and shaping her swollen lower lip with a caressing thumb. With every nerve in her body still pulsing with reaction, the mesmerising sexiness of his smouldering golden eyes held her en-trapped. 'We're heading back to the Court to enjoy a long leisurely breakfast.'

But the pressing need to always answer a ringing phone was too engrained in Harriet to be ignored. It was Davis, calling to let her know that her presence was required back at the yard, and she finished the call in a rush. 'I'd no idea we'd been out so long. I'm going to have to run…I have a customer waiting.'

Rafael looked down at her with an attitude of profound disbelief that required no verbal expression to hit home.

Embarrassed by her own intense reluctance to leave him, Harriet added in a taut tone of apology, 'She's a new client and she's arrived early—'

'Then it's not your problem,' Rafael informed her.

'But it would be a problem if the lady chose to put her two horses in livery somewhere else.'

'Let Davis deal with her.'

Her clear eyes urged his understanding. 'I'm selling a service, and she's entitled to expect my personal attention on her first visit.'

'But this is insane.'

Having recaptured Snowball, Harriet broke the simmering silence. 'It's going to take a lot of effort on my part to build up a big enough customer base for the yard. That can't be helped.'

'I understood that you'd moved to Ireland to embrace the simple way of life.'

'The simple way of life became much more complicated when I took on a partner and the need to raise my profit margins,' Harriet pointed out ruefully.

'If that's all that's dragging you away, take the loss out of my side of the balance sheet,' Rafael advised smoothly.

The nature of that careless offer dismayed Harriet. 'Please don't make suggestions like that—'

With easy dexterity he captured her hand in his to hold her. 'You want to be with me. You think I don't know that?'

Harriet pulled her fingers free. 'But I don't want to be with you so much that I'd let you virtually pay for my time!'

Her mobile phone went off again just before she reached the yard and she dug it out.

'Forgive me…I'm hopelessly spoilt by always getting exactly what I want when I want,' Rafael admitted, without a flicker of embarrassment. 'Dinner tonight?'

At the sound of his dark, deep drawl the troubled light in her blue eyes vanished. 'OK…'

As excited as a teenager, and thoroughly embarrassed by that reality, Harriet finished her working day as early as she could and raced back to the cottage to rustle through her wardrobe and paint her nails. Right on the dot of eight Rafael hit his car horn to alert her to his arrival. She fled into the kitchen, for pride demanded that she did not respond to the blast of a horn. Two minutes passed, slowly and painfully. Now she wanted to go to the door, but felt she couldn't, and to distract her frantic nerves she threw Peanut's ball.

She was disconcerted when the back door opened as she had forgotten it was unlocked. Rafael appeared to a chorus of frantic barks from Samson, who then went into ingratiating mode. Tall, dark and extravagantly handsome in a casual dark pinstripe suit worn with a collarless silk shirt, Rafael studied her with tawny intensity, his impassive face unnerving her. 'I saw you vanish in here.'

Harriet blushed as hotly as a schoolgirl caught in the act of misbehaviour.

Rafael angled his arrogant dark head to one side and continued to survey her, all masculine control and cool. 'Is it possible that you are trying to train me?'

Harriet struggled to keep a straight face, but his astute guess was too much for her and a helpless laugh bubbled from her throat.

Peanut dropped her ball hopefully in front of him.

'Why do you have a pig in your kitchen?' Rafael enquired with commendable calm.

'Shush…Peanut doesn't know she's a pig. She thinks she's a dog.'

Peanut nosed the ball encouragingly right up to the toes of his Italian leather loafers. He pushed it back. Tiring of his intransigence, the little pig picked up the ball again and dropped it down right on top of his foot.

'I think the pig may be trying to train me too.' Brilliant eyes alive with amusement, Rafael sent the ball flying across the tiled floor.

With an exaggerated gallantry that made her smile, he tucked her into the fabulous sports car parked outside. She had to squint at the logo to appreciate that it was a Lamborghini, and she was suitably impressed. He took her to a tiny restaurant overlooking a rocky sea inlet with water so dazzlingly blue it might have been a tropical lagoon. They appeared to be the only diners, and the service was so silent and discreet that she never quite managed to see the person whose hand topped up her wine. Or perhaps it was the company that made it excessively hard for her to stay aware of what was happening beyond the charmed circle of their table. She ate her way appreciatively through a delicate salmon terrine, dallied over wafer-thin slices of lamb and baby vegetables that melted in her mouth, and savoured the thorough indulgence of being urged to enjoy two puddings instead of one.

Stunning golden eyes watched her with appreciation. 'It's so novel to be with a woman who eats.'

'Luke was happiest when I was starving and showing off my skeleton,' Harriet admitted, in a sudden rush of confidence over the Brazilian coffee that was served with liqueurs.

Rafael skimmed a sensual forefinger along the back of her hand in self-assured reproof. 'You are blessed with heavenly curves...don't lose them.'

Her gaze meshing with the tawny glow of his, she was suddenly as out of breath as if she had run up a steep hill. 'I can safely promise you that the curves are here to stay for the foreseeable future.'

'With me you can be yourself.'

Harriet let the sweet rich honey of the liqueur touch her tongue, and longed for the taste of his passionate mouth on hers. As if he could read her mind, he rose unhurriedly upright and escorted her back out to the car.

A mixture of panic, bewilderment and guilty excitement was now in control of her. She was no longer thinking about Luke every five minutes. In fact the painful memories of her former fiancé and his affair with Alice, she registered in surprise, had begun to fade from her conscious mind without her actually noticing the fact. Even so, there was not a smidgeon of commonsense in what she *was* feeling: she was as mad for Rafael Cavaliere Flynn as a reckless teenager. Yet wasn't that exactly what she had told herself she wanted and needed? A silly fling that counted no costs and looked for no future?

But in a moment of stark self-doubt Harriet feared that if she slept with Rafael she would still want him in the morning, and keep on wanting him for far longer than could be considered cool, controlled or casual. That knowledge scared the heck out of her, for Rafael would not offer her any form of commitment. He had been upfront about that, and she could not criticise him on that score. Yet the same male could make an art form out of creating a romantic ambience, she acknowledged ruefully. But that was only artifice, and she would be foolish to forget that reality. Her emotions still seemed to be all over the place. Was that why she felt so agonisingly vulnerable? Suddenly she was terribly afraid of being hurt again.

Rafael drew up outside the cottage, took the key from her nerveless fingers and sprang gracefully out to unlock the door for her.

Caught unprepared by the smooth dexterity and speed with which he carried out those manoeuvres, Harriet scrambled out less fluidly in his wake.

'I enjoyed myself very much.' Golden eyes veiled, Rafael bent his handsome dark head and pressed a non-committal kiss to her cheek, much as though she was a maiden aunt.

'Me too…' Watching him stroll back to the

Lamborghini, Harriet went very pink: she was mortified by the conviction that he was giving her the brush-off.

Just before Rafael swung back into the driver's seat, he paused to say casually, 'Next weekend I'll be at my stud farm in Kildare. I'll take you to the races at Leopardstown on Friday. I'll be in touch about the arrangements.'

Like a marionette with a stiffly wired neck, Harriet nodded and backed slowly indoors. When the door closed, he drove off. She wanted to punch the air and shout. Yet at the same time she felt weak and tremulous with relief, as though some great and terrifying danger had passed, leaving her unscathed. He could take her high and the very next minute send her spirits flying down into a sudden low. She had not a clue where she was with him. But wasn't that supposed to be part and parcel of the excitement that supposedly went with having a fling? So why had he made no attempt even to kiss her?

Even Rafael was surprised by his own restraint. Having sensed her doubts in her preoccupied silence, he had immediately wondered if she was thinking about her ex-fiancé. It was extraordinary how much that suspicion had annoyed him, for he was not a possessive lover. He had never cared whether or not a woman's thoughts were centred on him. After all, it was the passion he went for, not the emotional connection. But a stubbornly perverse part of him was determined that Harriet should want him so much that she had no reservations whatsoever, and no spare mental energy to waste on the past…

Determined to give Rafael no reason to regret his invitation, Harriet made an enormous effort to dress up for the races. She drove all the way down to Cork to visit an exclusive little boutique where she purchased a smart dress in tobacco-brown and pink, and a hat that flattered. In between times she worked endless hours preparing the tack shop for opening. Although she planned to initially sell only basic supplies, she was a touch dismayed by the amount of time that was swallowed up by the ordering, delivery and setting out of stock.

Una called her only once, and was so uncommunicative that Harriet became concerned and tried to find out if something was worrying the teenager. She was guiltily grateful that she had not yet mentioned her dinner date with Rafael, and relieved when Una finally grudgingly divulged that she had exams the following week. Ringing her back a couple of days later, Harriet did her best to cheer her up by reminding her that school would soon be breaking up for the summer.

On the day of the races a helicopter landed on the purpose-built pad at Flynn Court to pick up Harriet. Leopardstown racecourse was about six miles out of Dublin. Feeling like royalty, she boarded with Samson—Rafael had assured her that the little dog was allowed to come too. While she admired the breathtaking aerial views of the Irish countryside, she wondered a tad nervously if she was quite up to the challenge of seeing a guy who used air travel as casually as other people used buses. When she clambered out again, with Samson tucked in a capacious handbag from which only his bright eyes and perky ears showed, Rafael was waiting a few yards away with a limousine, and all of a sudden she felt as though the sun had risen inside her: all light and bright and shining.

In the limo she found it hard to drag her attention from his lean, darkly handsome face, and as a distraction she asked him about the racecourse. While Samson danced across the leather seat to introduce himself to their host with all the panache of a little dog who had regained his confidence, Rafael told her that Leopardstown had been modelled on the Sandown course in southern England, and built in 1880.

'I like the dress.' Although conservative in style, the garment enhanced her lush figure with a quiet good taste that impressed Rafael. The silk organza feathered hat was so feminine it charmed him. The colours she wore set off the glossy fall of her rich copper hair and creamy skin to perfection. 'I'll enjoy introducing you to the rest of my party.'

Her smile tensed a little, for she had not appreciated that she would be spending the day as one of a crowd. 'Business guests?'

'And society acquaintances. It was arranged weeks ago, to return the hospitality I have enjoyed abroad.'

Samson once again settled in her bag, Rafael took her into the Pavilion, a vast glass-fronted building, which offered a selection of entertainment venues as well as private suites for the use of the crème de la crème of racegoers. From the instant she emerged from the limo and stood by his side she was aware that she was attracting notice, in terms of downright stares and sidelong glances.

'Do you get photographed by the press at events like this?' she asked him abruptly.

'If one of my horses wins. Will you enjoy that?' Rafael spoke with an innate cynicism that expected a positive answer, for he had yet to meet a woman who did not relish seeing her face in the newspapers.

'No, I wouldn't. If you don't mind, I'd much prefer to stay in the background.' Harriet was very reluctant to risk attracting the interest of the paparazzi, because she knew they would not rest until they had identified the mystery redhead and her miniature dog on Rafael Cavaliere's arm. Unfortunately that could prove to be a very embarrassing development, she thought worriedly. Her broken engagement and her half-sister's part in it might well be dug up and aired to enliven her otherwise boring history; Alice was very photogenic, and did at least enjoy a public profile. Unfortunately, that kind of muck-raking publicity would offend and embarrass Harriet's entire family.

An ebony brow quirked. 'Ashamed of me?'

'Don't be silly!' Harriet laughed, and explained her concern. But for some reason what had seemed so simple appeared to become very complicated when voiced beneath the questioning onslaught of Rafael's cool, dark scrutiny.

'I can read you like a neon sign…and the message is sad.'

Harriet gave him a look of astonishment. 'I beg your pardon?'

'You are reluctant to be photographed in my company because you don't want Luke to know that you're with me now,' Rafael framed with icy derision.

'That's total nonsense!'

'I don't think so. You're still hoping to get your ex-fiancé back—'

'Of course I'm not!'

'I don't believe you, *a mhilis*,' Rafael admitted very drily. 'But let's leave it there. I see no need to involve myself with your private concerns.'

Squashed by that lofty assurance of uninterest, Harriet breathed in deep, annoyed that she had been denied the chance to rebut his suspicions, but concerned that a too robust defence would make her look very uncool and unduly keen to please. At the precise moment that she was inwardly wrestling with such uneasy concerns they entered the private suite he had hired to entertain his guests. Within twenty seconds of their entrance a crowd was jostling for his attention, with waves, loud greetings and a physical pushiness that saw Harriet elbowed out of the way so fast she found herself sidelined by the wall without quite knowing how she had got there. Resigned to being ignored, or at the very least overlooked in that excited melee, she was not the only person surprised when Rafael swung round in patent search of her and waited pointedly for her to move back to his side.

The crush around him slowly parted to allow her a clear return avenue of approach. Aware that the gesture on his part had made her very much the centre of attention, her face burned. But at the same time she was secretly pleased that in spite of that crazy difference of opinion minutes earlier he had immediately noticed her absence and set about remedying it.

Rafael then dealt her a wonderfully cool appraisal that ensured she was in little danger of his attention going to her head. Within an hour her mind was a whirl of extravagant impressions and slices of conversation in several different languages. He introduced her as, 'Harriet', but only when someone pushed for that information—and few took that strong a lead in the conversation. She talked happily about horses at every opportunity, and soon picked out the social butterflies from those to whom breeding, training and running horses was a source of all-absorbing interest. She got on with the latter section of the guest list like a house on fire, and several admirers spoilt Samson rotten.

For the first time since she had got to know Rafael, however, Harriet was hugely conscious of his vast wealth and status. In his radius people often talked in hushed, respectful tones. He was approached with extreme caution, exaggerated humility or a grandiose male jocularity that made her squirm. But Rafael remained impassive, and although his manners were flawless the depth of his reserve intimidated his guests. He was often silent. He did not try to entertain people. His guests instead worked hard at entertaining him.

She was also quite astonished by the manner in which some women blanked her while offering Rafael languorous looks of invitation, suggestive *double entendres* and flattering, flirtatious remarks. He did not respond. It was like it wasn't happening—as if he was so accustomed to those constant encouraging female signals that he no longer noticed them. Then she caught the glimmer of contempt in his screened gaze as yet another man's wife appraised his darkly handsome features with flagrant longing, and she blushed for her own sex.

After a leisurely sit-down lunch served by caterers, the guests left the table to mingle. Harriet was helping herself to coffee when she became aware of a conversational exchange taking place somewhere behind her.

'Now I think I know why Rafael doesn't even flirt with me. It's quite obvious that he goes for girls with generous hips,' a woman was saying, in a meaningful undertone that her very precise diction made clearly audible.

A wave of dismayed incredulity gripped Harriet. A couple of feet closer to that dialogue, but concealed by the door that opened on to the balcony, Rafael turned his handsome dark head with the efficacy of a laser beam locking on to its target.

'She's definitely not small, is she?' a second female voice remarked in answer to the first, and Harriet breathed in so hard she almost burst. 'Not shy about displaying her advantage either. That silk emphasises every voluptuous curve.'

'Rear cheek implants are all the rage in North America. It would certainly make me take a fresh look at my hip profile,' the first woman countered, with deadly seriousness.

Vibrant enjoyment burnishing his eyes, and an outrageous smile on his firm mouth, Rafael strolled back to Harriet's side. He was very much amused. Her face was a feverish shade of pink. He drew her back against him and lowered his head to murmur huskily, 'Is this the perfect moment to tell you that I *do* think that you have the most fantastic derrière?'

'When you say anything of that nature you're more likely to get told off!' Harriet warned him in a waspish whisper, trembling slightly in the strong circle of his arms, but determined to maintain as much dignity and composure as could be grasped after being forced to eavesdrop on such an embarrassing snatch of dialogue.

'Harriet…the secret of your attraction lies in the

truth that nothing about you is fake,' Rafael confided, angling her head back against him.

He let his lips drift down the vulnerable curve of her neck and she quivered in sensual shock, her entire body coming alive. He brushed her throat with the tip of his tongue in a contact so fleeting she almost thought she had imagined it when he straightened again. She blinked rapidly and registered that absolutely nobody had noticed, yet her every nerve was singing at high frequency, and her legs did not feel quite strong enough to support her.

'Let's go down to the track,' Rafael urged lazily. 'When I have a horse running I don't watch from the balcony. I like to be at the sharp end.'

Having released her from his hold with the same underplayed lightness of touch, Rafael directed her towards the exit.

CHAPTER SIX

RAFEAL'S HORSE, Fearless, was a handsome chestnut with a white star on his forehead, and the jockey engaged to ride him was a champion. While Rafael talked to his trainer, Harriet watched the horses break from the starting gate. In spite of every intention to the contrary, she got caught up in the thrill of the race, and when Fearless pulled ahead she surrendered to frantic excitement and cheered him on.

'Brilliant, brilliant horse…he was really flying there!' she carolled, starry-eyed with satisfaction when the chestnut romped over the finish line, a clear winner by several lengths.

Rafael reaped almost as much pleasure from Harriet's innocent enthusiasm as from seeing yet another of his thoroughbreds triumph. 'You really do appreciate a winner. I'll buy you something special to mark the occasion.'

Harriet flung him a dismayed glance. 'No, thanks. You don't need to buy me anything.'

'Need…no. But want—*yes*,' Rafael declared immovably.

'Rafael, I—'

'If you still don't want to be photographed with me, I would advise you to stay out of the winners' enclosure.' With that smooth warning, he concluded her protest with his own departure.

Watching from a discreet distance, Harriet received no satisfaction whatsoever from having excluded herself. A curvaceous blonde in a white suit so short and tight that it should have carried a government health warning flung herself at Rafael with giggling gusto. Harriet's eyes widened. Rafael did not push his beautiful assailant away. Indeed, he curved an arm round her while the cameras flashed like mad. Harriet gritted her teeth, wondered who the blonde was, and decided that she would not sink to the revealing level of asking that question.

Following victory there was great celebration in the private suite. The drinks flowed. A recording of Fearless's race was run and re-run, and every detail of his performance and that of his competitors eagerly dissected and discussed. When the party was at its height, Rafael took her to one side and suggested that they leave for his stud farm. Having recognised his increasing boredom as high spirits and alcohol loosened his guests' inhibitions, Harriet was not surprised.

'Don't you like parties?' she asked on the way out.

'When I was a child, Valente partied every night. I picked up a preference for sobriety and rational conversation,' he confided softly.

Harriet turned an embarrassed pink. 'I can imagine what you must've thought when you found me by that bonfire, swigging from a wine bottle and talking a lot of nonsense.'

Rafael studied her with intense amusement. 'That you're in a class of your own.'

He piloted the helicopter to Kildare, flying with the same assurance with which he drove. He landed the craft a hundred yards away from a gloriously symmetrical Queen Anne house set in formal gardens.

'You didn't tell me you had *two* stately homes!' Harriet exclaimed, with barely concealed incredulity at such a crucial oversight.

'This was the first Irish property I bought, and the house was secondary to the location and included with the land. It's not a stately home; it's tiny.'

Tiny? Harriet reckoned the house might well have a good ten bedrooms. She fed Samson, who was an instant hit with the housekeeper. Already exhausted by the surfeit of attention he had received from female fans at the racecourse, and with an appetite much impaired by the numerous titbits he had enjoyed, the tiny chihuahua settled down for a snooze.

Rafael offered Harriet a tour of the stud. It was a big operation, with orderly lines of neatly painted buildings, extensive all-weather gallops and beautifully tended lush green acres of land with smart fences and gates. She could not help being impressed to death. He appeared to employ a large staff, for the stables were spotless and the horses perfectly groomed. It took enormous wealth to maintain such high standards. She quite saw why he would find it a challenge to view the livery yard they shared as a serious business venture.

'Are you staying with me tonight?'

In the quiet of one of the barns that direct question took Harriet unawares. Her colour warming, she collided involuntarily with smouldering dark golden eyes.

Rafael closed lean brown hands slowly over hers and drew her to him with measured assurance. 'When Fearless crossed the finishing line I wanted to celebrate alone with you. Never has the role of host been less welcome.'

Her throat was tight with nerves and her breath was feathering in her throat. She wanted him to kiss her. She wanted him to kiss her so badly her body ached with ferocious tension. Driven by an impulse stronger than she was, she leant forward. He looked down at her with intoxicating intensity and then, without any further warning of his masculine intent, he hauled her close and tasted her readily parted lips with explicit urgency. She was breathless with surprise, but exhilarated by his unashamed passion. Her fingers sank into the springy depths of his luxuriant black hair, making it all the easier for him to swing her back against the wall. As always unpredictable in his approach, his initial fervour was abandoned for a deliciously provocative exploration that melted her like honey on a hot griddle.

Lifting his tousled dark head, stunning eyes glittering like diamonds in sunlight, Rafael vented a roughened laugh. Every time he touched her he was startled by the raw charge of lust she roused in him. 'We're acting like teenagers.'

Her hands, which had dropped of necessity to his shoulders, sank down to the lapels of his designer suit jacket and tugged him closer again.

Her silent rebellion made his sensual mouth quirk. He wanted her there and then. He didn't want to wait. But his innate self-discipline triumphed. He was exasperated by the very strangeness of that momentary desire to act on a foolish impulse. Closing one of her hands in his, he eased her away from the wall. 'The grooms are waiting in the staff room to celebrate Fearless's arrival home.'

Ready colour flared over her cheeks and for an instant she could not recognise herself in the bold woman who had recklessly attempted to pull him back to her. But then in more ways than one Rafael Cavaliere Flynn was a revelation to her, she conceded, still all of a quiver from that sensational kissing session. No man had ever made her feel that hot with just a kiss. She was tingling, crazily aware of every sensitised inch of her own body.

They walked back through the yard to the house in silence. The night breeze was cool on her flushed skin. The silence didn't bother her. She discovered that she had no doubts at all, and wondered if that was because she simply could not muster sufficient concentration to think straight. She wanted to laugh: she felt incredibly happy.

Rafael cupped her cheekbones and reclaimed her mouth to taste her again. Linking his fingers lightly with hers, he led her up the heavily carved staircase. Her heartbeat started to race. She tried hard to focus on her surroundings. Her bemused gaze registered majestic furniture, grand paintings and a treasure trove of *objets d'art*. Pushing open a door, he stood back for her to precede him.

They were in a bedroom, and she could not understand why that far from unexpected development should fill her with such immense self-consciousness.

'You're shy...' Rafael breathed in wonderment. 'I'm not accustomed to that quality in a woman.'

'I'm not shy,' Harriet asserted in a defensive rush. 'Just not used to this situation... I mean, you... I mean—'

'You can't be afraid of me.' Capturing her within the circle of his arms, Rafael kissed her absolutely breathless.

But his very ability to set her on fire with one kiss put him into a class of his own—and not one she had previously encountered.

'I wanted you the first moment I saw you,' he confided in a husky undertone.

'Watch it...you sound romantic,' she said breathlessly.

'I don't do romance. Reality is infinitely more exciting.' He turned her round and slowly, carefully, ran down the zip on her dress.

Cooler air feathered her spine. He brushed aside the parted edges and lifted her copper hair to let his expert mouth circle the sensitive skin at the nape of her neck. A tight knot of wicked anticipation formed low in her tummy. She drew in a shallow fast breath.

The dress slithered to her ankles with a soft silken swoosh. He turned her back to face him. His intent gaze roamed with unabashed masculine admiration from the swollen pout of her soft pink lips to the burgeoning fullness of creamy breasts cupped in apricot lace.

'You're gorgeous…'

Harriet was trembling. 'No, I'm not—'

'You're not listening…you're gorgeous, *a mhilis*.'

Emboldened by that compliment, she resisted the urge to wrap concealing arms over her lush curves and stepped out of her shoes instead. He lifted her up into his arms and settled her down on the side of the bed. Stepping back from her he shed his jacket and tie with careless grace and let them lie where they fell.

'You're untidy,' she said, half under her breath, only just managing to stop herself from picking up the discarded clothes that offended her ingrained preference for order.

An irreverent grin curved his handsome mouth. 'I was a very spoilt child.'

'I can imagine…servants to do everything.'

His frank smile of acknowledgement awakened the strangest sense of elation inside Harriet.

'But it's never too late to learn new habits,' she told him.

'You'll have to work on me.'

Her mouth ran dry when his unbuttoned shirt fell open to reveal a muscular expanse of bronzed chest. She was entrapped. He was, without a doubt, magnificent. Until that moment she had never appreciated that a man could be beautiful too, and she couldn't dredge her attention from him. The high-voltage charge of his sexuality enthralled her. Cheeks rosy pink, she snatched in a tremulous breath and finally forced herself to look away: there was nothing cool or sophisticated about gawping.

'So untidiness freaks you out…what else?' Rafael moved lazily towards her.

'I can't think…' And it was true: at that precise moment she couldn't.

His tongue tangled with hers in a taunting sensual invasion. His lips traced the delicate line of her jaw to the slender column of her throat, where a tiny nervous pulse flickered above her collarbone. 'I don't want you to think,' he told her thickly. 'I only want you to feel.'

She was all liquid anticipation and restive energy. Her remaining garments melted away without her registering their departure. He traced the lush swell of her breasts, buried his mouth in her sweet-scented skin with a hungry masculine enthusiasm that made her moan out loud in helpless response. He teased

the rosy crests of her pouting flesh until the sensitive peaks throbbed. Heat pooled low in her pelvis
while tiny tremors of tension ran through her straining length. Desire tightened like a silken rope, pulling into an impossibly taut knot inside her. She had
never known that desire could be a physical ache that
hurt.

When he let her surface momentarily she gasped
in oxygen in a great gulp, her entire body thrumming
with response.

'What is so surprising?' Rafael had an intuitive
grasp of her bemusement.

'Nothing…' But Harriet was in a state of amazement at the sheer strength of what she was experiencing. Embarrassment that she should have been so
ignorant made her hide the truth that nothing had
ever felt so good or so exciting as what he was doing
to her. To discover at the age of twenty-eight that she
had more capacity for enjoyment than she had ever
dreamt possible was an enormous shock.

'Was it just a line when you said you wanted me
the first time you saw me?' she asked him abruptly.

He dealt her an amused look. 'I don't do
lines…you have the most divine shape.'

'But I was wearing pyjamas with big flowers all
over them!' Harriet reminded him in helpless protest.

'They clung in all the right places. You looked in-

credibly sexy. Instantly I was hooked and hungry.'
Rafael ran a caressing forefinger very gently down
the valley between her breasts. Super-sensitive to his
every caress, she jerked in reaction, as though hot
wires were tightening below her skin.

She met shimmering golden eyes framed by black
spiky lashes and her heart jumped as though she had
had an electric shock He shifted against her, all sleek
bronzed muscle and lithe masculinity powered by
masses of self-confidence. She was pretty sure he
had never doubted himself in his entire life. He knew
exactly what he was doing, where he was going and
what he wanted and indeed expected when he got
there: he fascinated her.

'And Bianca?' she prompted, although she had
not planned to be so indiscreet.

'It had already run its course between us. Nothing
to do with you.' Astute eyes lingered on her. 'Your
conscience must carry the weight of the world in it.
You're too vulnerable.'

'I'm much tougher than I seem—'

'The pig ruling your kitchen knows different.'

Laughing, she gave way to temptation and
dragged him down to her again. She could not get
enough of his beautiful mouth. He traced the hidden
heart of her with an erotic skill that seduced her utterly. No more did she laugh or speak. More primi-

tive need had taken her over, and between one twisting, turning, frantic peak of arousal and the next she breathed in tight little gasps only when she could spare the energy.

'Please…'

At the height of a tormenting pleasure that had reached an unbearable edge he pulled her under him and plunged into her yielding depths with strong, sensual power. Delight roared through her quivering body in a scorching wave. Eroticism personified, his powerful length stilled for an instant. He caressed her reddened lips with provocative expertise, letting the tip of his tongue dip into the moist invitation of her tender mouth.

'You feel like you were made just for me, *a mhilis*,' Rafael growled with raw satisfaction.

He was a very powerful lover. His hard pagan rhythm exactly matched her deepest need. Excitement controlled her. Sensation took over. She was lost in the hot, sweet storm of endless pleasure. He carried her to a wild explosive climax of feeling. She reached a shattering peak of glory and, with a cry of rapture, plunged over the edge into ecstasy. Aftershocks of exquisite sensation rippled through her before she slowly sank into voluptuous abandon.

Suddenly, and for the very first time in her life, she understood why the world she lived in seemed

obsessed with sex. Sex was everywhere, she thought
in a daze, in every magazine and every film, a hot
topic of discussion that had never interested her before. Never in her life had she talked about sex. She
had concealed her prudishness as best she could
while secretly wondering what all the fuss was
about. Only now could she appreciate that until
Rafael had educated her by example she had had no
way of knowing what real passion was. True fulfilment had evaded her until that timeless, glorious instant of wondrous release from the earthly confines
of her own body. Yet she had never suspected that
there actually might be something more to discover.
How could she have guessed that there was another
entire dimension still to be explored when she had
never experienced that truth for herself?

Rafael surveyed her with heavily lidded dark eyes
almost screened by the density of his black lashes.
With her copper hair spilling across the pillow and
a slight flush on her cheeks she was amazingly
pretty. Her skin was so fine, her eyes so clear and
bright a blue. He liked her silence, the restful quality she always exuded, as if inviolable tranquillity sat
at the very heart of her like an anchor stone. Her dazzled smile of contentment gave him an unexpected
high. He knew he was good between the sheets, but
she looked at him as though he was a god come to

earth. He almost laughed at that absurd thought. At the point where he usually moved away from his lovers, with a perfunctory gesture of affection, he curved an arm round her and gathered her back to him again.

'I would say that a repeat encounter is definitely on the cards, *a thaisce*,' Rafael mused, his rich, dark drawl languorous with satisfaction.

'What does that mean?' she whispered, gazing up at him and deciding that she would never tire of looking at his lean, vibrantly handsome features. He had remarkable bone structure, eyelashes that were amusingly longer than her own, and eyes of quite extraordinary depth and colour. Once he had seemed so distant from her, she acknowledged absently, but now he felt familiar.

'That you're a treasure.'

'And the other?'

'That you're sweet. A most rare virtue in my experience.'

Harriet felt light-headed with happiness. She stretched with slow, newly sensual abandon, her limbs weighted with languor and contentment. She thought she could happily stay where she was for ever. Never had she been more relaxed or more in tune with the world. Feeling impossibly feminine, she rejoiced in every point of contact where her softer curves yielded to the taut, hard muscles of his lean, tough physique. The very scent of his damp bronzed skin enchanted her. Her fingers splayed in a possessive curve across the washboard-flat expanse of his stomach. 'Luke…' she whispered.

And the instant she said it she knew her mistake, and was so utterly appalled by what she had accidentally said that she was struck dumb. She could not comprehend where Luke's name had come from, or why it had leapt without prior thought from her tongue. In shock at her own indiscretion, she lay still as a statue, seized up by the horror and ghastly timing of her blunder. She felt Rafael tense against her, but the change in his body language was infinitesimal. Hope that he had somehow failed to pick up on her verbal bombshell surged through her. Perhaps her guardian angel had stepped in to distract Rafael's attention at just the right moment.

'I need a shower,' Rafael murmured softly.

There was nothing in his intonation to persuade her differently and he detached himself from her with unhurried grace. Yet she felt the cold in him pierce her with the deep inner chill of his reserve and knew immediately that he had noticed. Of course he had noticed, she raged at herself in disbelief. He was not hard of hearing! He could scarcely have missed being called by another's man's name at such a very personal moment.

'Rafael…I don't know how it happened!' she exclaimed, a sense of panic making words brim from her lips so fast that they almost ran together. 'You probably imagine now that I was thinking about Luke, but I swear that I wasn't! He hasn't once crossed my mind today…of course I wasn't thinking about him! Why would I be thinking about *him* when I'm with *you*?'

A broad bronzed shoulder shifted in the very slightest shrug of dismissal. His lean, strong face was impassive, his eyes dark as sloes and without a shade of gold. Cold fear spread inside her like an icy pool: she knew he wasn't listening to her excuses.

'Does it matter?' Rafael enquired silkily.

'Yes, it does matter—very much!' Harriet gasped. 'I've been clumsy and thoughtless, but please believe that it doesn't mean what you think it does.'

'Don't presume to know what I think.'

Every scrap of colour ebbed from below her fair complexion. Her skin turned clammy, her tummy queasy. He was untouched, indifferent. He moved with the same measured grace into the bathroom and an instant later she heard a shower running. Her teeth were chattering, until she realised and clamped them together to still that nervous reaction, but she still felt icy cold and bereft. She was in shock, could not comprehend how it all could have gone so wrong at such terrifying speed. One moment everything had been wonderful and the next it had been gone, like a mirage, leaving only a taunting memory behind...

His magnificent bronzed body rigid with raw, leaping tension, Rafael leant back against the limestone wall of the power shower area, which was big enough to host a party, and very slowly and carefully uncoiled his clenched fists. With absolute force of will he subdued his temper. Of course he was angry with her. That was only natural. After all, such a thing had never happened to him before. He had heard others tell tales of similar experiences and had felt secure in the belief that no woman would ever commit such an error of good taste in his radius. To be addressed by another man's name in his own bed was deeply offensive. Her even more tactless attempt to cover her tracks had increased his annoyance. He was not a fool. Of course she had been thinking about Luke, possibly even closing her eyes in *his* arms and trying to pretend that *he* was her ex-fiancé! Cold rage and disgust lanced through him afresh.

When Rafael emerged from the bathroom the phone was ringing. A towel wrapped round his lean angular hips, he swept up the receiver. He listened to the caller with a darkening brow, stated that he would deal with the situation, uttered a flat apology and concluded the call.

'Can you be ready to leave in fifteen minutes?' he asked Harriet grimly. 'I have to get back to Ballyflynn in a hurry. Una's bolted from school again.'

'Oh, no!' she exclaimed in dismay, rising from the dressing table where she had been brushing her hair. 'Have you to call at the school first?'

'I see no point in going to St Mary's at this hour of the day. If I know my sister, she'll already be halfway back home by now.' Even as he spoke Rafael was getting dressed in a series of quick, economical movements. 'Right now I need to call her mother and her sister to find out if either of them have heard from her. As usual I'll be treated to a load of time-wasting bull, because nobody has either the guts or the interest to tell me the truth!'

'I'm sorry—'

'No, this time Una is the one who will be sorry.'

Harriet could not conceal her concern. 'Rafael—'

'Have you any idea how much at risk Una is? Every time this happens I have to ask the police to check out that she hasn't been kidnapped. She's very young, and very stupid when it comes to her personal security,' Rafael framed with icy clarity. 'The last time she did this she hitched lifts halfway across Ireland to get home. Suppose she picks the wrong car and the wrong driver to trust?'

Harriet paled. 'I hadn't thought of that.'

Samson was rudely snatched from his comfortable doze in the kitchen. He let out a cross little growl of complaint. Harriet held the tiny animal aloft and studied him with rampant disbelief. 'What was that?'

His liquid dark eyes blinked and he squirmed, looking as ashamed of himself as a chihuahua could look. 'No more bad temper,' she warned, tucking him under her arm.

Harriet met up with Rafael again in the hall. 'Any news yet?' she asked.

'None.'

She had to almost run to keep up with his long impatient stride on the path to the helipad. 'Obviously Una is extremely unhappy at school—'

'Una is extremely unhappy at being forced to do anything she doesn't want to do. Until I entered her life she did exactly as she pleased and she played truant for weeks at a time.'

'She's sitting exams at the minute, and that has definitely put her under pressure,' Harriet persisted gently. 'I think she may be struggling to cope with her schoolwork.'

'Like Valente, Una is cleverer than a cartload of monkeys, and equally manipulative. She hopes that if she gets chucked out of yet another educational establishment I'll surrender and let her leave school for good this summer. I'm sorry, but you don't know what you're talking about,' Rafael concluded, in cool and cutting dismissal of that suggestion.

In the sensitive mood that Harriet was in, it was a painful snub. She was dismayed and annoyed to feel tears prickle the back of her eyes, for crying was not something she did easily. But the warmth and intimacy between them had gone as if it had never been. Did she blame him for that? She tried to imagine how she would have reacted to being called by another woman's name. It would have hammered her self-esteem. She would certainly have wondered if she was a second best substitute for some female whom he would have preferred to be with. Ultimately, however, being of a practical rather than melodramatic nature, she would have calmed down.

Rafael might have been offended, but he was certainly intelligent enough to accept that that kind of error could be a mere slip of the tongue and nothing more. On the other hand, it was perfectly possible that nothing she had said or done was responsible for creating the fresh detachment she now sensed in him. It was a mortifying thought but perhaps, having slept with her, his interest in her was simply at an end.

With her temper rising rapidly at that lowering suspicion, Harriet had to force herself to concentrate on Una's plight instead. She was very worried about the younger woman, and concerned that Rafael would be too tough on her. Although she was very wary of interfering in something that was none of her business, she felt that she ought to at least show Rafael that misspelt note from his sister. Incredible as it seemed to her, he did not appear aware of Una's low level of literacy, or of the difficulties that this had to be causing her at school. He seemed to believe that only wilful defiance lay behind the teenager's problems. He might be right too, she conceded ruefully. How well did she really know Una?

When they landed at Flynn Court, Rafael walked her over to the Lamborghini to run her home immediately.

'There's something I want to show you. It relates to Una,' she said awkwardly when he drew up outside the cottage. 'Will you wait for a moment?'

She was surprised to discover Peanut waiting for her in the house, rather than in the barn where Fergal had said he would leave her overnight. But in a rush Harriet rifled through the kitchen drawer to find the note and hurried back outside again. Standing out of the car, with his arms braced on the driver's door, Rafael treated her to a cool, measuring appraisal as she moved back to him to extend the note.

'What is this?' he asked drily, before he had even looked.

Annoyance and mortification made her stiffen. She wondered if he imagined that she might be using delaying tactics to keep him with her. 'Una wrote it to me a few weeks ago...I thought you should see it.'

Rafael stared down at the crumpled sheet in his hand and then strode out to the front of his car, where the outside lights shone down with greater clarity on the paper. 'Una wrote this? Is this a joke?' he demanded.

'She can't spell very well—'

Rafael shot her a look of raw incredulity. 'But this is like something a child in nursery would write!'

'I think she tries very hard to hide the problems she has, but could this explain her failure to meet work targets at school? Whenever she gets the chance she seems to use a computer spellchecker, but most of her schoolwork has to be handwritten. When I last spoke to her on the phone she was really unhappy...I suspect it was the stress of the exams she was about to sit.'

Rafael was an ashen colour below his vibrant

olive-toned skin. He looked devastated. 'I've never seen Una write or read anything. I had no idea there was a problem.'

'I'm sure that with the right help she'll be able to catch up, but you'll need to be careful how you discuss this with her,' Harriet warned him. 'She's ashamed of the difficulties she has, and she does seem to think of herself as stupid—'

'She's not stupid,' Rafael breathed in gruff interruption, long brown fingers crushing the note. 'She's probably dyslexic. Like me.'

It was Harriet's turn to be shocked, and she could think of nothing to say but a muttered, 'Oh…' that made her wince at her own lack of verbal dexterity.

'I have been so blind,' Rafael ground out in a driven undertone of regret, his lean, strong face bleak. 'I'm very grateful to you for bringing this to my attention.'

Harriet went back indoors. Well, she'd had the fling she'd thought she wanted, and got her fingers burnt with painful thoroughness, she acknowledged tautly. But if she had managed to do Una a good turn, then at least something positive had come out of the experience.

'Is Rafael gone?'

Harriet almost leapt right out of her skin, for Una was poised a few feet away in the kitchen doorway.

For once, the fifteen-year-old looked her age, and pretty pathetic at that, in her crumpled clothing with her eyes and her nose red and swollen from crying.

'You almost gave me a heart attack...' Harriet whispered shakily. 'Where were you when I came in a few minutes ago?'

'Trying to get to sleep in the guest room,' the teenager muttered, hanging her dark head. 'I know where Fergal leaves the spare key...'

'Well, I'm really glad that you're here and you're safe. Will you ring your brother...or will I?'

'No!' Una sobbed. 'Please don't ask me to do that!'

Harriet put a comforting arm round the distressed girl, fetched her a box of tissues and let the storm of tears run its natural course. 'Why did you come here?'

'I thought you'd be at home and we could talk, but you were out,' Una mumbled unevenly.

'Rafael is worried sick about you—'

'No, he's not...he doesn't care about me.'

'He *does*—'

'No, he doesn't. Do you know how Rafael found out about me? Mum was in a bad way, so Father Kewney went to Rafael and told him that I was his father's kid. Rafael didn't get a choice about taking me up as a charity case. I'm just a nuisance and an embarrassment to him.'

'My stepfather raised me alone. He didn't get a choice either, but even though he's not related to me by blood he genuinely loves me,' Harriet said quietly. 'You *are* related to Rafael, and he values that. You matter to him.'

Una lifted her head and studied her through puffy eyelids. 'Did he tell you that?'

'No. He's not the kind of guy who's comfortable talking about stuff like that. But I've seen his concern for you, and I think he probably understands more than you imagine he does. He didn't have a very happy home life either when he was growing up.'

The teenager could not hide her surprise at that news. 'Are you serious?'

'Perhaps you have more in common with your brother than you think.'

'Yeah, like I'm so rich and clever,' Una mumbled.

'He's very cynical too.'

'Is he raging with me?'

'He's more worried than angry. Please let me call him and let him know that you're safe.'

'No…I'll do it,' Una muttered tautly. 'Are you dating Rafael now?'

'No,' Harriet answered, feeling that that was the truth as matters stood. 'But he took me to the races at Leopardstown today.'

'So when is a date not a date?' Una hovered by

the phone as if it was an actively hostile object, likely to leap up and attack her at any minute.

When it's over before it's properly begun, Harriet reflected inwardly, suddenly taut and cold with misery. Why had she slept with him? How could that have seemed so right when it now felt so wrong in retrospect? How had she ever believed that she could handle a fling? What sort of a fool was she to know and understand so little about herself that she had believed she could abandon her principles with impunity? For now, in spite of her brave belief that she could enjoy passion without commitment, she felt cheap and silly and thoroughly unhappy. A few hours and it was over. She cringed at that awareness.

Una rang Rafael on his mobile. Determined not to intrude, Harriet stayed inside when the teenager went out to greet the arrival of his car. A few minutes later Rafael appeared at the front door on his own. 'Thank you.' His dark eyes were unusually level and open. 'This is the first time Una hasn't treated me like the enemy. I owe you for that.'

Harriet lifted her chin. 'You don't owe me anything.'

'Learn to accept compliments, gratitude and gifts with grace,' Rafael countered, smooth as silk. 'I won't change the habits of a lifetime.'

Hope leapt inside her and she crushed it back,

angry with herself. She was not going to start reading unintentional personal messages into his every stray remark. Nor was she planning to jump with painful anticipation every time the phone rang over the next week. 'Neither will I,' she traded, smothering a suggestive yawn in a hint that he was keeping her standing around on the doorstep.

After Luke, she told herself staunchly, she was as hardened and tough as old boots, and Rafael Cavaliere Flynn was already the equivalent of ancient history. He had cooled off and her pride had suffered a momentary pang. But that was all! And naturally there was a more positive angle to be considered. Now that she had lived through the proverbial rebound romance, popular report suggested that she would be in prime emotional condition to embrace a deeper and more lasting relationship with someone else. If right at that moment she felt that she would never in the longest day she lived look at another man again—well, no doubt that was only because she was feeling tired and battle-weary.

'Rafael...my sister and her husband will have gone to bed if you don't hurry up!' Una wailed from the Lamborghini. 'If we wake the baby Philomena will be furious!'

'Relax...I've told them that you'll be staying at Flynn Court tonight.'

Rafael continued to look at Harriet until she was rigid with nervous tension and the stress of avoiding a direct encounter with his all too knowing gaze. When he finally headed back to the sports car Harriet sagged and shut the door fast.

The phone rang. It was Boyce.

'I've been trying to get hold of you all day,' her brother complained. 'Guess what? I'm flying in to Kerry airport tomorrow afternoon.'

'Oh, that's wonderful!' Harriet was delighted at the news that she was about to have a house guest.

CHAPTER SEVEN

RAFAEL WAS RUDELY awakened by an infernal noise that in terms of annoyance fell somewhere between an animal shriek and chalk scraping down a blackboard.

A scraggy black and white rooster had taken up a perch on the worn statue of Neptune on the paved terrace below his bedroom. Rafael sprang out of bed and hauled up the nearest sash window. The bird loosed one more teeth-clenching screech before hopping niftily down and taking urgent flight over the fence to disappear into the long grass in the field.

'I can't believe that neither of you heard the hideous racket that bird was making this morning,' Rafael commented at the breakfast table.

'I sleep like the dead.' Una was loyally determined to protect Harriet's rooster, Albert, from being identified as the culprit.

'At over seventy I can't expect to have the hearing of a young man.' Tolly cast his amused blue eyes down.

Harriet's day had enjoyed an equally lively beginning. Having slept in late, she got up in panic mode. She had to skip breakfast and race straight up to the yard to help feed the horses, for she felt that it was only fair to take advantage of Davis's presence there when she was away from home. A large delivery arrived for the tack shop and she had to check the goods and set them out. After all, on Saturday next she would be open for business. To publicise that opening she had, with the help of several keen parents, organised a mini gymkhana for the same day, and had promised a substantial percentage of its profits to a children's charity. The attendance of the local radio station at the event was part and parcel of her determination to promote the Flynn Court Livery yard in every way possible.

By noon she was still running against the clock and had to flee back to the cottage in a mad rush to get changed. Dressed in the first things that met her frantic hand, she sprinted out to her car. She was halfway to the airport before she appreciated that she was wearing a white T-shirt with a short pink canvas skirt that was the biggest current mistake in her wardrobe but which she had been too stingy to dump.

Her brother's flight had already landed. Looking anything but anonymous, he was seated on a bench sporting large sunglasses and a Texan hat pulled down low over his spiky blond locks. If she had shaken him he would have rattled with exclusive designer tags.

'I'm so sorry I'm late!' she gasped.

With the ready warmth that made him so well loved by his entire family, as well as his fans, Boyce wrapped his arms round his sister in a bear hug.

Harriet stared at the small discreet dressing over his nose. 'My goodness—what happened to you? Have you been in an accident?'

'No…I got my nose straightened out a few days ago,' Boyce admitted, in a pronounced whisper that warned her that his venture into the realms of cosmetic surgery was a matter of extreme confidentiality.

She was astonished, but she swallowed back any adverse comment on his decision. After all, her brother worked in an industry that was highly looks-orientated. He had been born with a snub nose that turned up at the tip in a slightly elfish fashion, and perhaps he had been teased about it, she thought ruefully. It was, however, a family feature they had shared until he'd decided to dispense with it, and she had to resist a strong urge to shape her own offending nose with apologetic fingers.

Picking up his bag, Boyce ran his eyes over her and slowly shook his head. 'By the way, you look amazing. Getting shot of old Luke was obviously the best thing that ever happened to you!'

'Flatterer.' Harriet turned her head in reaction to an indefinable sense that she was being watched. Her attention sped over several clumps of passengers but nobody appeared to be looking in their direction.

'I'm not flattering you,' her brother argued. 'You're glowing because you've got your energy back. Last time I saw you, you were way too thin— and you were always exhausted. You've grown your hair and it suits you. Even the skirt's a big improvement. Luke liked you to dress like an old lady, in drab colours.'

Harriet blinked, and then released an involuntary laugh. 'Thanks for making me feel good!'

'Why do you always refuse to believe in the positive things that people say about you?'

Harriet went pink. 'Do I?'

'It's annoying,' he informed her with brotherly bluntness.

'You're the second person to tell me that in twenty-four hours. I suppose I've never been very confident about my looks.'

'You should be comfortable in your own skin,' Boyce declared impressively.

'That sounds good, coming from a bloke who's just had a nose job.'

'You've still got the knack of taking your little brother down a peg or two, haven't you?' Boyce shook his fair head with a rueful grin of appreciation, curving an arm round her to point her in the direction of the exit. 'Come on—let's get out of here. I don't want to run the risk of being recognised.'

'I shouldn't think you've got much to worry about around here,' she told him soothingly. 'The price of land and the cost of farm feed are of more interest to my neighbours.'

Boyce loved the lush wildness of the landscape, and the quiet, often wooded winding roads. He even thought it was a treat to get stuck behind an ancient tractor driven by an even more ancient little old man, who helpfully kept on waving them on at blind corners. The cottage, with its eccentric roof, struck him as amazingly small and appealing. Even the guest room, which she had brightened up with her own furniture and bedding, looked very presentable. The huge television she had put in the kitchen where the desk used to be made his eyes light up.

'I was scared you mightn't have one,' Boyce confided with a shudder. 'I couldn't live without the football.'

Harriet grinned and handed him the remote control. There was no need to tell him that she had only bought it the week before, in anticipation of his visit. She wanted him to feel at home and enjoy his stay.

Fergal knocked on the door when they were about to have the meal she had prepared the night before. Swearing under his breath, Boyce shot out of his seat and hurriedly backed out of the room. 'Do you think he saw me?'

'Of course he did… Look, Fergal's up here every day, seeing to his horses—'

'He has no need to know who I am…just say I'm a friend.'

'Sorry, I didn't realise you had company.' Fergal scanned the empty kitchen behind her in some surprise. His attention returned with strong curiosity to the table set for two, with a crisp white cloth, a bottle of wine and crystal glasses.

'I have a friend from London staying.' Harriet was uncomfortable, for skirting round the truth did not come naturally to her.

'Shy sort of bloke, is he?'

Harriet went pink. 'I suppose he is.'

'Right…I'll not interrupt you, then.'

'No, really, there's no need for you to rush off.'

Fergal gave her bemused look. 'But when you're

all dressed up and you've got the wine out even I can see that it's a special occasion. Can I mention this to my mother?'

'Your mother?' It was Harriet's turn to be bewildered.

He gave her a cheeky grin. 'She's decided you'll make me a good wife.'

Harriet winced. 'Oh, dear…'

'But hearing that you're entertaining another man will change her mind.'

'Sing like a canary,' she advised him.

Boyce reappeared as soon as Fergal had departed. 'Did you tell him?'

'No—with the result that he now thinks you're a boyfriend!'

'If he's interested, it'll fire him up. If he's not, it won't matter,' her brother countered with his happy-go-lucky grin. 'But as long as you're the only person who knows who I really am I'm safe from the paparazzi.'

'A lot of celebrities live on the west coast of Ireland. I honestly don't think you need to hide.'

'I'm just being discreet. I definitely didn't come here to hide. First on my agenda is a visit to the old place where Mum was born…have you been there yet?'

'No. When you said you were coming to visit I

decided that that was one trip we should make together. How *is* Mum?' she asked.

Her sibling grimaced. 'Not too pleased that I'm here instead of in Paris…and awash with wedding fever.'

Harriet gave him a wry smile. 'It's all right. That's pretty much what I expected. How are the happy couple?'

'How honest can I be?'

'I want you to be brutally honest.'

'Alice doesn't fit your shoes very well.'

'I had no idea she was trying to.'

'She's tripped up a few times, but I guess I shouldn't go into details.'

'You said you wouldn't take sides.' Harriet topped up his wine glass with a shamelessly encouraging hand. 'I'm over Luke, but I'm still very human and curious.'

'Alice cracked jokes at some legal dinner and offended some of his uptight colleagues, his friends all bore her to death, and after spending one weekend up North with his parents she flatly refuses to go back there. Luke went for the party girl and the forbidden thrills. She went for the clever-Dick lawyer. But I don't think either of them were prepared for the daily trials of living together.'

Boyce had always been extremely astute. That

skill had helped him avoid the most obvious pitfalls when he'd found fame at such a young age. Harriet was startled by his take on Alice and Luke's relationship, but impressed. She was also relieved to appreciate that her kid sister's betrayal now hurt her more than the recollection of her former fiancé's treachery. She had soon seen that Luke was not worth her grief, but she still missed the bond she had shared with Alice before Luke came between them and made her a rival to be scorned and deceived in her envious half-sibling's eyes.

'So, what about your love life?' Feeling that the past should now be left in its proper place, Harriet changed the subject.

Boyce looked surprisingly serious and compressed his lips. 'I got into something hot and heavy with a girl. It was hard to deal with at the time, but it's all done and dusted now. '

At that point, while Harriet was stifling her curiosity and wondering if she dared ask for more details, the doorbell sounded. It was a special delivery and she signed for a small parcel. The gift card bore Rafael's signature. Surprise gripped her, along with a surge of helpless anticipation and excitement. Carefully she removed a jewel case from the padded delivery pouch. Whatever it was, she was giving it right back.

She flipped open the lid to reveal an emerald and diamond-studded gold horseshoe brooch. The jewels were so bright they dazzled her. It was a truly gorgeous thing. Returning it was going to hurt, but she felt that to accept so costly a gift on so short an acquaintance was absolutely out of the question.

'Bling-bling!' Boyce decried, with a chuckle of amusement as he peered over her shoulder. 'A horsy brooch and, what's even worse, one chosen with a shocking lack of good taste. Fake jewels should never be so obviously bogus.'

'Yeah.' Harriet shut the case again fast, happy for him to continue in that assumption and save her from the humiliating necessity of explaining the whys and wherefores of her own recent behaviour.

'Still, I guess you're the type of woman who really goes in a big way for horsy brooches.' Sensitive as always, Boyce misunderstood his sister's tension and pulled a comical face of apology. 'Sorry. I didn't mean to be so tactless. I'm glad you've got a bloke in your life again.'

'I haven't…er…this is only a little friendly gift from someone who took me to the races the other day,' Harriet mumbled evasively.

Boyce spent most of the following day in bed, catching up on his sleep. Harriet had heard Rafael take off in the helicopter at eight that morning and it was very late that evening when she heard him return.

Monday dawned with the drenching sunlight of a hot summer day. Harriet withstood the strong urge to phone Rafael at an inexcusably early hour just to hear his voice as she explained that, while she very much appreciated the brooch and didn't want to offend him, she just couldn't accept it. She decided that a face-to-face meeting would be friendlier, and less open to misinterpretation than a phone call.

While Harriet was still agonising over the delicate matter of how best to approach Rafael without giving him the impression that he was being chased or encouraged in any way, he was picking up Una from her half-sister's home in the village. He should have been in Rome, but he had been forced to cancel his meetings. Una had panicked when he told her about the appointment he had arranged for her with an educational psychologist in Tralee. He had swiftly appreciated that if he did not want to risk the teenager going missing again she would need his personal support before she could face the prospect of sitting any type of test.

Una clumped into the Range Rover in big heavy boots. Rafael stared: she looked seriously scary. She was clad from head to toe in gothic black. Her eyes were heavily coloured in a variety of plum and purple shades, her lips were crimson against her pale skin. She was a dead ringer for a vampire from an old movie. He wanted to laugh, but was too shrewd to make the mistake.

'Did you know that Harriet's got back with her ex?' Una demanded.

Rafael went very still. 'Her ex?'

'Luke. A neighbour runs a taxi service to the airport and he saw Harriet picking up a blond bloke yesterday. She was hugging and kissing him…yeuk!' Una confided in a revolted tone. 'I called Fergal to ask him, and apparently he interrupted their big celebration meal at the cottage. So it's true. But I can't believe it. I thought she had more pride. Are you annoyed?'

'Why would I be?' Rafael fielded, and his half-sister subsided into silence.

He began to reverse the four-wheel-drive back on to the road. He felt nothing. He never felt anything. Messy reactions were for other people, and not something he could identify with either. He had still been a child when he had learned absolute control of his emotions. Forced to witness Valente's cruelty, and powerless to intervene, Rafael had switched off his human responses: it had been a simple matter of sanity and survival.

* * *

Harriet and Boyce enjoyed a hearty breakfast before making use of Tolly's hand drawn map to go and find the house where Eva and generations of Gallaghers before her had been born. The property was called Slieveross, and was every bit as remote in location as Tolly had warned. Although the land lay only a couple of miles out of Ballyflynn, they had to trek up a long steep lane across the lower slopes of a mountain. The hedgerows were bright with the lanterns of the fuchsia bushes that grew wild. They stopped several times to catch their breath and enjoy the spectacular panorama of the jagged coastline. Far below them the white foam of the Atlantic breakers battered the steep cliffs. The little farmhouse was a ruin in the lee of the hill.

'What a place this would be to get away from it all,' her brother breathed, in a tone of awe and longing that took her by surprise. 'Look at that view. It's out of this world. There's not a soul in sight. I can't even see the road. Can you hear that silence? I can't remember when I last *heard* silence. I'd pay a fortune for the chance to buy and restore this place.'

'But Mum would go mad!' Harriet was torn by simultaneous dismay and hope. She knew that she would get the blame if Boyce, who was Eva's pride and joy, put down roots in Ireland. Yet there was nothing that would please her more than the luxury of seeing a little more of him.

'Perhaps it's time she got over that. I don't see why it should influence me. I'd like a base where I could write music, unwind… Here I could just be an ordinary guy.'

Boyce had always been a mover and a shaker. On the way home he made her call in at the auctioneers in Ballyflynn, to see if she could find out who now owned Slieveross. That party's identity confirmed, and after a further visit to Mr McNally, the solicitor, Boyce returned to the cottage with plans to get his business manager on the phone to discuss the pros and cons of acquiring a home in Ireland.

'Did you make my bed for me before we went out?' Boyce called from the guest room while she was whipping up a quick lunch.

'No. I'm your sister, not your housekeeper!'

'Well, someone did,' he declared.

Harriet lodged in the doorway. 'You must have done it without realising it.'

Boyce spread emphatic hands in denial. 'I didn't!'

'Well, maybe we have fairies—and long may they stay under this roof if they like to tidy up!' Harriet teased.

'You don't know what the paparazzi are capable of,' her brother said worriedly. 'A paparazzo could have been in here taking photographs, or snooping in search of a good story.'

'Do paparazzi usually make beds for their victims?'

A reluctant grin wiped the unusual gravity from his boyishly handsome features. 'All right. I sound paranoid,' he conceded.

'Yes, you do. I honestly believe that while you're in Ballyflynn you won't be bothered by the press or anybody else.'

The day was flying past, and Harriet was determined to see Rafael. He would think that she had terrible manners because she had not immediately contacted him to thank him for his generous gift, she reflected guiltily. But she had just not known what to say. Leaving her brother happily discussing Irish property and investment values on the phone, she went into her room to freshen up.

There, she was visited without the slightest warning by the eerie suspicion that the perfume bottles on her dressing table had been moved. For some reason the room seemed indefinably different to her eyes, although there was not a single change that she could exactly identify. Had Samson sneaked up on the bed and rumpled the spread? It was perfectly possible. She did not allow the tiny dog to come into her bedroom, but he never gave up trying. My goodness—what was the matter with her? She was not a fanciful person by nature. Of course nobody had been in the cottage while she and her brother were exploring Slieveross! Things were almost certainly just as she had left them. Why on earth was she letting Boyce spook her? But, bearing in mind her brother's renown in the music business, perhaps it would be a good idea to be more cautious about locking up while he was staying. She went outside and removed the spare key from its rather obvious hiding place under a stone by the back door.

It was almost four by the time she reached Flynn Court. There was no sign of Tolly. A maid ushered her into the library. Harriet was astounded by the strength of her hunger to see Rafael again. That craving sprang on her without warning and filled her with the most unbearable shyness. As he strolled forward to greet her, the essence of sophistication in a silver-grey pinstripe suit, nervous tension rushed her straight into speech.

'I wanted to phone and ask what was happening with Una, but I knew you had a lot to sort out between you and I decided to wait for a day or two,' Harriet shared breathlessly, her attention welded to his lean, hard features, her mouth running dry. 'But when you sent the brooch—'

'Did you like it?' Rafael cut in, smooth as silk.

Her fingers knotted together as she sought for the right words. 'Very much… I mean, it's exquisite. But—'

'I'm glad you like it. We had a good time to-gether, and the Irish and Italian in my soul gives me quite a sentimental streak.' His deep dark drawl was casual, dismissive in tone, and could not have pro-vided a more cynical contrast to the emotional base he claimed. 'I like to say goodbye with style. Please don't try to return my gift.'

Shock made Harriet stop breathing. *Goodbye with style?* She did not move a muscle, did not trust herself to do so, for she was afraid that in the heat of the moment she might betray her hurt. When they had left his stud on the day of the races she had had no idea whether or not he planned to see her again. But when the gold, emerald and diamond horseshoe brooch had arrived, she had honestly believed that her worries had been misplaced. It had not once crossed her mind that a man might give such a care-fully chosen gift to mark the end of an affair. She could feel the blood draining out from below her skin. It was as though she had been forcibly woken from a dream to find herself walking a tightrope when she had a terrible fear of heights. And, worst of all, she was totally unprepared for the power of her own reaction.

'Una...?' In the humming silence, Harriet snatched at the teenager's name again with an edge of desperation.

His spectacular dark golden eyes rested on her with an impassivity that she found unnervingly distant. 'I've agreed to let her miss the last few days of term. The school doesn't want her back in any case. She's almost certainly dyslexic, and she's agreed to accept specialist tutoring. I've said that I'll look into more local possibilities on the education front, and make a decision by the end of the summer. However, I haven't made any promises.'

Harriet forced a valiant smile. 'It all sounds good... Obviously you're talking to each other and getting everything sorted. I'm pleased about that, but surprised that she hasn't called round even to see the yard. Though I expect she's very busy at present.'

'Perhaps.' Grim amusement assailed Rafael, for he was well aware that his surprisingly partisan half-sibling was furiously disappointed with Harriet, and would almost certainly speak her mind when she had got over her present desire to huff and sulk over the issue.

'Did I mention the opening I have planned for the tack shop next weekend? '

'I wasn't aware that you were planning to open a shop.'

'You did say that you weren't interested in details. But in future I'll put everything on paper to ensure that you're kept informed,' Harriet declared brightly, putting her all into maintaining a jolly front while she went on to tell him about the gymkhana. 'It'll provide good publicity.'

'Do you really think that you'll still be living in Ballyflynn in a year's time?'

That dry, sceptical note sent colour surging into her cheeks, banishing her strained pallor. His apparent conviction that the livery yard would fail within twelve months felt like the ultimate insult to Harriet, implying as it did a low opinion of her ability to keep the yard afloat.

'I'm well aware that most new businesses go bust in the first year, but the livery won't be one of them. The shop will stock only basic supplies, but it should generate enough trade to cover overheads, and it'll keep the customers calling. Perhaps you are not aware of it, but when you offered me a superb Georgian stable yard as a base, *and* a resident groom, you gave me a much better chance of surviving.'

The phone on the desk buzzed.

'Tell Una I said to call in whenever she gets the chance.' Harriet turned gratefully away, emptied of artificial good cheer, feeling much as though she had withstood ten rounds with a heavyweight boxer.

Rafael strode past the ringing phone to pull open the door for her. He wondered why even now he was so much better mannered with her than he had ever been with any other woman. He wondered what she would do if he simply used the fierce desire which had shattered her only days earlier to bring her back to him. That hunger had been very new to her. True love versus sexual passion. He was not convinced that she would be strong enough to resist temptation. In such circumstances Valente would not have hesitated to play dirty. Rafael was surprised to discover that, unlike his late father, he had scruples.

'Where's Tolly?' Harriet felt a need to fill the silence while she crossed the gracious hall with firm steps, her slim shoulders stiff with the effort of dignity.

'His brother in England has been taken ill. He went over to see him yesterday,' Rafael advanced.

She got into her car and drove off without looking back or doing a single dramatic thing. She felt hollow, shaken. Rafael had made her feel like a teenager on a rollercoaster of excitement. Like a silly kid, she had developed a crush on him. Everything about him had knocked her out: his incredible looks, his wickedly racy sexy reputation, his charismatic smile. No, she definitely didn't want to think about his smile. It had been a stupid transitory fling, a total and absolute mistake, and it was over…so what was the matter with her? Before she reached home again she pulled off the road because her face was wet with tears. Dragging in a steadying breath, she dashed away the tears, angry that she was upset.

Determined not to let her brother suspect anything was amiss, she drove round for a while with the car window wound down, praying the stiff breeze would blow away the evidence that she had been crying. For good measure she bought some groceries from the supermarket. At the checkout she noticed Tolly's daughter-in-law, Sheila, standing by the freezers, staring at her. What *was* that woman's problem? Irritated, Harriet felt like walking over and asking. But Sheila's husband, Robert, appeared behind her. His square face ruddy with colour, he hurried the older woman on.

She was driving back out of the village again when she saw Una. Harriet waved and looked frantically for a place to stop on the busy street, but by the time she found somewhere the leggy brunette had vanished from view. Her brow furrowed and she frowned, for she had been sure that the teenager had seen her and would wait. Had she been mistaken? Or was there something more behind Una's recent silence? Harriet thought about the badly spelt note she had shown to Rafael and paled. It was very possible that Una was annoyed about that, and regarded Harriet's interference as a betrayal of her trust.

When she got back to the cottage she was astonished to find Boyce and Fergal watching football together and generally behaving as though they had known each other all their lives. Nursing bottles of beer, they yelled and punched the air in unison as a goal was scored.

'So…you two have met?' Harriet stated the obvious as casually as she could.

'Yeah… Hey, look at that footwork,' Boyce groaned, his entire attention welded to the television screen.

She marvelled at the idea that she had worried that her brother might notice that she had been crying. Boyce would not have noticed had she turned cartwheels—unless, of course, she had interrupted his view of the match.

'Will the two of you be coming down tonight to the *ceilidh*?' she heard Fergal ask on his way out an hour later. 'It should be a good night of music.'

'I wouldn't miss it, mate.'

'What happened to your fear of being recognised?' Harriet asked Boyce.

Her brother gave her a look of satisfaction. 'I told Fergal my name. I even admitted that I was a musician. But he didn't show any reaction. He has no idea who I am. If someone in *his* age group doesn't recognise me, who will? And why didn't you mention that the village bar is well known for traditional music? I'm really into that sort of stuff.'

'Dooleys? Is it well known? I had no idea.'

'Fergal seems a good bloke. You could do worse,' Boyce declared, giving the young trainer his official stamp of bloke approval.

'We're just friends.'

Harriet discovered that the doors at the rear of the tiny bar she had visited opened into a very big low-ceilinged room with a smouldering turf fire, flagstones on the floor and seating arranged in convivial clumps. Initially tense at being in a public place, Boyce soon relaxed. A *ceilidh* band composed of a fiddler, an accordion player and a guy with a tin whistle entertained them. It was true toe-tapping stuff.

A couple of hours into the evening, when her smile was like set concrete on her weary face, Fergal brought the fiddler over to meet her brother. Technical talk of music batted back and forth across the table. In his schooldays Boyce had been an accomplished flautist, with plans for a classical career, and he was almost as proficient with a violin. Tunes were hummed, rhythms beaten out on the wood, old ballads discussed. Boyce was in his element.

Harriet did not sleep well, and when she awakened just after five the next morning she decided to take Snowball for a ride. She walked round the stable block to get into her car and stopped dead. Some sort of graffiti now marred the end wall of the stables. Disbelief made her throat tighten and her tummy clench hard.

LEAVE HIM ALONE, it said. The words had been picked out in white gloss paint. Someone had done it in a hurry, for the paint had dripped down from each letter. She was certain it had not been there when she'd gone out with Boyce the night before, but it had been dark when they got back and she had no memory of looking at the wall then.

She swallowed hard. Leave him alone? This was her home. It could only be a message meant for her eyes. Who was she supposed to leave alone? Rafael? And who would feel there was a need to warn her off him? Who was most insecure and likely to be possessive of Rafael's attention right now? Una, who was struggling to get through a bad patch? Yet she could not credit that Una would be at the foot of such an unpleasant act. An act designed to shock and scare. There was no denying that it was frightening to think that someone with malicious intent had visited her home and expressed their angry hostility in that painted warning. But, no matter how hard she sought to dismiss the idea that Una had been responsible, she remained painfully aware of the teenager's hot temper and impulsive nature.

Reaching a decision, Harriet hurried round to the

old shed, where various paint tins lurked. She levered open a can of white paint, poured some clumsily into a roller tray and got to work on the wall. Within a few minutes Harriet was liberally spattered with paint drops, but the scrawled words were obscured and no longer readable. She would lash on another coat later and she wouldn't mention the matter to anyone. It could only have been Una, and that saddened her. She had not realised until that moment just how fond she had become of the younger woman. Was Una under the impression that Rafael and Harriet were involved in some secret affair? Well, she would soon find out her mistake and learn that while Harriet might not be a rival for Rafael's attention, there was a world of very beautiful women out there, just waiting for him to snap his imperious fingers.

'I've been thinking.' Boyce leant back in his seat after lunch the following day. 'I'm going to talk to Mum and suggest that it's time she told you who your father is.'

Harriet would not have been surprised if that announcement had made her eyes shoot out on actual stalks of horror. 'No way, Boyce. Eva will never forgive me if you tackle her. She'll assume that I put pressure on you and—'

'I won't let Mum make that mistake. Maybe she's afraid of what Alice and I might think. I want her to understand that that certainly isn't an issue for me. She needs encouragement and support to speak up after all these years, but you don't need to apologise for wanting the information. It's your right, and when she realises that you have back-up it should help.'

Harriet worried at her lower lip with her teeth, her eyes troubled. Boyce was the apple of his mother's eye, and the older woman was a different person with him. How could he understand that she was afraid of damaging her relationship with Eva beyond repair?

Boyce patted her hand. 'Trust me,' he urged with confidence. 'I know Mum—*and* I know what I'm talking about.'

That evening, Harriet worked late at the yard. It was one of the groom's days off and there was a lot for her to do. Boyce had offered to help but she had turned him down, for he had never been keen on manual labour. When she had finished feeding the horses she went into the office to make a start on the monthly bills. Peanut was unusually restive, snuffling at the door and scratching at the stone floor. Samson barked a couple of times and trotted about. Had she not been so busy their fussing would have driven her mad. It was only when she heard a door slam in the yard that she went out to investigate.

She was surprised to see Rafael, striding into the feed store on the other side of the cobbled yard, in apparent search of her. 'Rafael?' she called.

Tall and commanding, he swung round in a fluid athletic arc, his lean, bronzed face grim, brilliant golden eyes zeroing in on her. 'The gate on the lower field was left open. Your horses are out!'

Harriet lost colour, but sprang straight into action. 'I'll call Fergal…we'll need his help!'

'Ask him to check the road first. I'll rouse Davis if he's at home.'

She raised Fergal on his mobile phone. He swore he'd be over in five minutes flat.

'I don't understand how this could have happened!' she gasped.

'Carelessness,' Rafael spelt out with ringing derision.

'Not mine. I check the gates every day—'

'How many horses were down there?' he incised, as Davis came clattering down the stairs from his apartment.

'Six…'

'An old mare is grazing by the gate. I cornered a grey gelding in the orchard and he's safe. That's two accounted for. You watch this end of the lane. Davis, come with me…we'll drive over the estate and try to locate the rest.' His dark drawl was cool, clipped and horribly impersonal.

'I'm not careless,' Harriet repeated tautly. 'I swear I checked—'

'I had to swerve off the lane when the grey ran out in front of the Range Rover. I have very fast reactions. Someone else might have been killed.'

'I'm sorry…really sorry,' she muttered wretchedly.

Rafael rested brooding dark-as-midnight eyes on her. In her shabby jodhpurs and sweatshirt, with her copper hair caught up in a schoolgirl's ponytail and her deep blue eyes shadowed with exhaustion, she scored nil in the grooming and vanity stakes. Yet the natural appeal of her delicate bone structure and fine porcelain skin was only enhanced by that edge of fragility. He did not want to think about which particular activities had deprived her of sleep to that extent. Without another word, he got into the four-wheel-drive.

Harriet used the pick-up as a barrier to block the lane. Six horses on the loose. By any standards that was a disaster. How had the gate come open? Had a rambler been responsible? But walkers were usually careful with livestock and gates, and few would choose to enter a field full of horses. The yard would be liable if any of the runaways sustained an injury, but accidents did happen and she was fully insured. But what would it do to the business if word of this escapade got out?

Fergal rang to tell her that he and Boyce were bringing two missing ponies up the lane.

'Thank goodness…I don't know how this has happened…'

'It's freakin' odd,' he agreed without hesitation. 'This pair are so docile they came to find us, so they did. They must have had a fright to run as far as the road.'

She collected the grey from the orchard, and put him and the placid old stager who had grazed the verge throughout all the excitement back in the field. Neither was injured. She could see nothing wrong with the stout bolt on the gate. From now on as an extra precaution she would tie the gate shut as well. Fergal and Boyce arrived, with her half-brother driving the car very slowly and Fergal on foot with the ponies.

'You look frazzled, sis,' Boyce remarked. 'But there's no harm done.'

'If we get the last two horses back unhurt, I'll agree with you,' Harriet sighed. 'As it is, Rafael is furious.'

'The horses must have stampeded down the lane

when they got out.' Fergal grimaced. 'I hate breaking bad news. But they've cut up the ground round
the driveway up to the Court, and the lawns there
may be damaged as well.'

Harriet groaned and winced.

'Who's Rafael?' her brother interposed.

Fergal looked at Harriet. Beneath his scrutiny,
which told her that Fergal noticed more that went on
around him than he ever let on, she went pink.
Digging her hands into her pockets, she contrived a
non-committal shrug that implied that Rafael was
nobody of any interest. 'Just a neighbour…'

'Young?' Boyce prompted.

'-ish…' Hooves sounded on the lane. The dulled
roar of a powerful car engine made her move forward
even before the glow of headlights pierced the soft
fading colours of dusk that had enveloped the landscape.

Davis led the last two horses back into the field.

'Are they all right?' she asked the groom worriedly.

The driver's door of the Range Rover opened.
Rafael sprang out with the lethal natural grace of a
panther. 'Unhurt, by the devil's own luck, and you
don't deserve it,' he told her icily. 'Those horses
have been loose for at least an hour.'

Boyce emerged into view from behind the hedge.
Rafael came to a sudden halt, ebony brows pleating.

A full head taller than Boyce, he was as dark and powerful in build as the other man was fair and slight.

'I don't think you should speak to Harriet like that,' Boyce told him stiffly.

'Honestly, I'm fine. Not one bit bothered. Plain speaking never hurt anyone that I know of. ' Harriet angled an apologetic glance at Boyce and spoke very fast, in an instinctive attempt to prevent Rafael from saying something cutting and hurtful to her half-sibling. 'I hadn't got around to mentioning it yet, but Rafael and I are actually partners in the livery yard.'

'Since when, sis?' Boyce queried in open astonishment. 'Why didn't you tell me? Why the secrecy?'

'It didn't seem important.' Harriet could not meet Boyce's scrutiny as she told that little white lie. She had concealed her difficulties because she had known that he would be offended that she had not approached *him* for financial help.

Having dismissed Davis with thanks, Rafael lounged almost indolently back up against the bonnet of the four-wheel-drive, his relaxation complete. He made no attempt whatsoever to join in the conversation. The blond guy staying with Harriet was not her ex, Luke. As soon as he'd seen the younger man he had realised that local gossip had got the facts wrong—for Harriet's guest bore no resemblance to the photographs Rafael had seen. In fact it was obvious that her visitor, who shared the same fair skin and fine features, was a relative.

Unexpectedly Fergal came to Harriet's rescue by reminding Boyce that his new friends would be waiting for him in the back room at Dooleys.

'Seamus has got hold of a flute for me, and I'm trying a reel or two with the boys tonight,' her half-brother volunteered. 'Will you be home in time? I'd like you to come.'

Tense as she was, she was touched by his desire for her to hear him play, and she watched him depart with Fergal.

Crazily conscious of Rafael's unusually silent presence, Harriet threw up her head, but still contrived to avoid his intent gaze. 'I've got nothing else to say about the gate, I'm afraid,' she stated, with an air of flat finality. 'When I saw it last it was firmly closed.'

Rafael strolled fluidly forward, his steps crunching softly on the lush grass of early summer. 'I don't give a damn about the gate.'

Harriet was bewildered by that blunt dismissal of the contentious subject. 'I'm sorry…I don't understand…'

Rafael reached for her clenched fingers and straightening them engulfed her hands in the sure grip of his own. 'For the past forty-eight hours I've

believed that you were celebrating a cosy reconcil-
iation with your ex at the cottage.'

'My ex? You mean Luke?' Harriet was astounded
by that statement. 'My only visitor right now is my
brother. Why on earth would you think I had got
back together with Luke?'

'Popular report suggested that your guest was a
lover. That I believed the story is really your fault.'
Stunning dark golden eyes liquid with teasing censure, he made that declaration smoother than silk.

It was hard to keep a grip on challenging dialogue with Rafael, Harriet acknowledged inwardly.
There he stood, spectacular in terms of sheer dark
good looks and raw charisma. He had the advantage
of taking her breath away while at the same time saying the most outrageous things.

'It isn't *my* fault that you decided to believe some
silly rumour about me!' As the sting of that arrogant
assurance sank in, Harriet pulled free of his hold.

His brilliant gaze narrowed with incisive cool.
'You called me by his name in bed. That's rather
more substantial than a silly rumour. Next I hear
you're wrapping yourself round some blond guy at
the airport and he's moved in with you. You can't
blame me for adding two and two.'

'I can blame you for a whole host of things!'
Harriet fielded in spirited disagreement. 'You didn't

trust me. You made no attempt to check out what you were told. You didn't even give me a chance to defend myself.'

'Why are you making such a great big production out of this?'

Believe it or not, she was tempted to hurl back, *being dumped is really not a fun experience.* His glorious indifference to the reality of the hurt he had inflicted with his rejection infuriated her. Indeed, she was shaken by the tide of rage that had come out of nowhere to fire her up to a pitch her even temperament rarely reached. The detachment of his unemotional calm only inflamed her.

'It *was* a big production for me. But I suppose I should be grateful that you showed your true nature so quickly.'

An ebony brow elevated. 'Which means?'

Harriet flung her copper head back, blue eyes defiant. 'You let me down.'

Rafael was incredulous at that accusation, and suddenly anger broke through his rigid self-discipline. No woman had ever accused him of such base behaviour. Men who let women down were cowardly, weak and untrustworthy, and he was proud of the fact that he was none of those things. 'Where do you get off, saying that to me?'

'I think it's scary that you didn't even *mention*

that you'd heard Luke was with me.' In spite of her attempt to match his cool, her voice shook slightly with the strength of her emotions.

His strong jawline clenched. 'It was a misunderstanding.'

'I'm too ordinary for you. You think fantastic dates, flash gifts and the bedroom stuff is all that matters. And, yes, you're right—all that *is* terribly exciting. But I would've been much more impressed if you had cared enough to ask me who my guest was. That you just ditched me says it all, really. Image was more important. Everything was more important than me or my feelings!'

Rafael gazed steadily back at her, only the raw glitter of his bright eyes telling her that she was not saying anything that he wished to hear. 'Whatever happened to your desire for a casual fling? That easy come, easy go attitude which you so admired?'

'You happened…you've put me right off flings,' she admitted with unhesitating honesty.

'But I don't do them…and I want you back.'

Her strained eyes veiled. She was shaken, for she had not been prepared for that immediate declaration. Violent confusion and uncertainty seized hold of her. When they had been together she had felt amazingly close to him, and wildly happy, but he had turned into the coldest of strangers, retreating behind a wall of reserve where he could not be reached. He had hurt her, and she saw that hurt as a warning slap on the wrist for her own foolishness. 'I'm not a toy you can chuck in the bin and get back out again when you feel like another game!'

His expressive mouth twisted, for that was a rather apt description of the usual dealings he had with women. 'That's not how I would treat you.'

'I'm sorry…it wouldn't work.' Harriet rested troubled blue eyes on him. His gorgeous, dark deep-set eyes held her fast. He seemed totally stunned by the idea that she would not fall back into his hands like a ripe plum.

Experiencing a horribly inappropriate desire to wrap her arms round him, Harriet clenched her hands by her sides and studied her booted feet with fixed attention. Where had her anger gone? She didn't know. He hadn't even apologised. She wasn't even sure that he knew *how* to apologise. Perhaps those eager to curry favour with a very rich man had always rescued him from that necessity. Say sorry, she mentally urged him. Say sorry… *Say sorry…*

'There's something else you should know about me, *a mhilis*.' Rafael regarded her with the ruthless resolve that was the backbone of his character. 'I don't retreat from a challenge.'

'I have to go…I need to change before I head

down to the pub,' she mumbled, slowly but surely backing away towards her vehicle.

'Harriet…'

'What?' Scarcely breathing, she hovered, her entire attention welded to him like top quality industrial glue.

'You're extraordinary…not ordinary.'

Pleased pink blossomed in her cheeks. She could feel decent resolution and restraint seeping out of her like water swirling round a bucket full of holes. She could feel temptation knocking louder than thunder on her heart. And it spooked her into beating a very fast retreat back to the pick-up. She could still walk away because she had not allowed herself to get attached to him in any way, she reminded herself staunchly. She wasn't out shopping for a broken heart, or a bored billionaire who would tire of her extraordinary ordinariness long before she tired of him.

At Dooleys, Boyce got up to play with the band. His talent with the flute was marked by the silence of an appreciative audience followed by prolonged applause. In high spirits, he came back to his sister. 'I can't believe I've only got a couple of days left in Ballyflynn,' he confessed. 'I want you to know that I've had a fantastic time and made some great new friends. Even if my offer to buy Slieveross is turned down, I'll be a regular visitor.'

'I've loved having you here.'

Suddenly her brother set his drink down with a stifled exclamation and began to rise.

'What's up?'

His frowning look of surprise evaporating, Boyce shook his head and resumed his seat again. 'I thought I saw a girl I used to know, but it must have been my imagination. The lighting's lousy in here.'

Harriet looked across the crowded room just as a tall familiar figure appeared in the doorway: it was Rafael. Several people hailed him when he strolled up to the bar to order. Long fingers wrapped round a pint of Guinness, he swung round to view the room and her heart literally jumped—so hard she almost pressed a hand to it. In a husky dark blue sweater and faded jeans, his strong jawline roughened by dark stubble, he looked stupendously sexy. As he glanced in her direction, she whipped round again, her face burning.

Rafael walked over and asked her with the utmost casualness to introduce him to her brother. She was astonished when he then sat down to engage Boyce in conversation. A ripple of perceptible interest passed round the room as attention centred on their table. His dark golden eyes amused by her wonder at his arrival, Rafael lounged back in his seat. A study in graceful indolence, he talked to her brother with sociable ease. Acquainted as she was with Rafael's reserve, she was impressed that he had made the effort to meet Boyce.

'You got some pulling power, girl!' Fergal bantered in a whisper on his way past. 'The man himself isn't a regular here.'

Boyce was invited back to the stage to play, but to Harriet's surprise he demurred, pleading tiredness. A moment later he angled an apologetic smile at Rafael and asked Harriet to take him back to the cottage.

'I'll be in touch.' Something that might have been amusement gleamed in Rafael's keen gaze.

Her brother turned to her in the car park and exclaimed, 'Rafael Cavaliere...*only* Rafael blasted Cavaliere! You weren't going to tell me either, were you?'

'Tell you what?' Harriet was astonished, for she had not realised that Rafael had been so up-front about his identity.

'That the biggest womaniser in the Western World is your neighbour and your partner in the stables!' Boyce snapped, tight-lipped with concern. 'I almost fell under the table when I realised who he was. Let me tell you, no brother worth the name would let his sister fall into the clutches of a guy with Cavaliere's reputation without saying something about it!'

Harriet got into the driver's seat. 'For goodness' sake, Boyce…I'm a woman, not a kid—'

'You couldn't handle him. He's into fast women. Don't you read the tabloids? He'll give you a fantastic time for a few weeks and then you'll be history. If he's hunting you, it can only be because there's a shortage of supermodels and actresses round here!'

Pain sliced through Harriet at that telling comment from her half-sibling. Boyce fell suddenly silent, as if he realised that he had been less than tactful. But Harriet could only acknowledge that it was true: she had no hope of ever falling into the supermodel category. Hadn't she too wondered if the secret of her attraction for Rafael was proximity and lack of competition?

'Harriet…I didn't mean it that way…'

'No offence taken.'

Boyce released a measured sigh. 'Luke really chewed you up, and you're vulnerable right now. The last thing you need is a super-wealthy tycoon running rings round you and then forgetting your name the minute he gets bored!'

'But I bet I'd enjoy myself…for a while anyway. Luke wasn't much fun. I didn't appreciate that until I'd got over him.' Harriet switched off the engine outside the cottage and lifted her chin. 'Life's too

short for regrets. Didn't you like anything about
Rafael?'

Her brother regarded her in frank surprise. 'When
did I say I disliked the bloke? He's clever, cool…a
touch intimidating, I have to admit. But I've got
nothing against him.'

Harriet could not help laughing. 'No?'

'No. I just don't want you to get hurt again. Let's
face it—you're into steady relationships and he
wouldn't know what one was…'

CHAPTER EIGHT

RAFAEL LAY in bed listening in resignation to Harriet's bedraggled rooster bring in the dawn at Flynn Court. Familiarity with the experience did not lessen the full effect of Albert in full flow. In spite of Tolly and Una's conspiracy of silence, he knew that the rooster belonged to Harriet's menagerie since Davis had spilled the beans. Apparently Albert visited the stable yard for a second chorus every morning, and Davis was definitely not a fan.

'I hear you're a fine shot, sir,' the groom had remarked hopefully. 'Sure, who would ever know if that pesky bird was just to disappear into thin air?'

'Albert is a pet,' Rafael had murmured in quiet warning. 'I want him to enjoy a long and healthy life.'

Harriet rose early. With the gymkhana taking place within twenty-four hours, she had a busy day ahead. The elderly farmer who owned Slieveross had agreed to meet Boyce, but had also intimated that he was not yet willing to discuss the possibility of selling it. The auctioneer had warned her brother that the old man would probably want to spend a few weeks, at the very least, mulling over whether or not he was prepared to part with any of the land.

'Such a quaint way to do business,' Boyce commented with immense appreciation over breakfast.

The two women organising the gymkhana arrived about nine, with helpers to put up the jumps and rope off separate sections in the field so that more than one event could take place at the same time. Harriet had just sat down to finish off the bills in the office when a knock sounded on the door. It opened slowly to reveal Una.

'It's me...I suppose you've been wondering where I've been,' the teenager said uncomfortably.

'Yes.'

Una reddened. 'I thought you'd gone back with your ex-fiancé and I was really annoyed with you.'

'But why did you think that?' Harriet asked gently.

Una hung her dark head and explained how she had reached that conclusion before saying, 'You're going to think I'm really sad...'

'I won't.'

'I just *so* wanted you to get off with Rafael.'

Harriet was surprised. 'You...*did?*'

'I like you. I thought you'd be good for him. Please don't tell him I said it, but left to himself he has really, *really* bad taste in women,' the slender brunette confided in a guilty whisper.

Harriet could barely keep her face straight. 'Is that so?'

'All they're interested in is his money, and they're dead fake and plastic. But you're into horses, like he is, and you're not always fussing about how you look. I knew he'd go for that. I was waiting on you two getting together and—'

'Giving me useful hints on how best to achieve that objective?'

Una nodded agreement, then got down on her knees to pet Samson and scratch Peanut at the back of the ear, in the precise spot that reduced the pig to an ecstatic porcine heap of contentment. 'So I was furious when I thought you preferred a guy who'd two-timed you,' the teenager admitted. 'Rafael said that that was none of my business, and that I shouldn't let it make a difference to me. I know that's true, but we were friends and I couldn't help being upset about it.'

'I can understand that.' But the faintest furrow still marred Harriet's brow, for she believed every word that Rafael's sister had said, and could not credit that the younger woman would have painted that warning on the stable wall.

'Are you very angry with me?' Una pressed tautly.

'No, but from now on I think it would be easier for you if you took a little less interest in who your brother sees,' she said quietly. 'Now, if you're here to stay I could really use an extra pair of hands around here today.'

At lunchtime Tolly appeared, with a large old-fashioned covered basket. 'I've brought you a picnic.'

'Have you?' Harriet smiled, delighted he had come to see her. 'Oh, I could hug you! I hope you're planning to join us?'

His blue eyes shone with pleasure at the warmth of his welcome. 'If you insist.'

'Of course, I do. Una, come on. We'll go and sit on the grass and enjoy the sunshine,' she suggested.

The meadow outside the stable yard was bright with wildflowers. Deep yellow cowslips, pretty pink lady's smock and oxeye daisies flourished in the undisturbed ground. On the other side of the lane the field bristled with brightly coloured jumps. She helped Tolly spread the rug on the grass. He opened the basket to reveal a mouthwatering selection of picnic delicacies.

'Delish,' Una pronounced happily, and munched her way rapidly through a handful of tiny bites. After reaching for a more substantial roll to keep her going, she got up again to throw Peanut's ball.

'How's your brother doing?' Harriet asked the older man. 'I heard he was ill.'

'Eamon has heart trouble, but he's making a good recovery. Rafael sent me over to Liverpool in his private jet and arranged for a consultant.' Tolly sighed. 'He's a very generous, but only those who have experienced that side of him appreciate that. He doesn't like to be thanked, and he doesn't like the help he gives to be talked about. But he's come to the rescue of many a needy family in this community.'

'Harriet!' Una shouted, loud enough and sharp enough in pitch to make Harriet flinch. 'I think you should come over here…'

The teenager was staring at Harriet's car.

'Don't tell me I've got a flat tyre,' Harriet groaned, crossing the lane to the gravelled parking area.

'Is that what I think it is?' Una queried with a revealing shudder.

A funeral wreath composed of pink and white chrysanthemums was resting against the front windscreen of her car. Harriet's tummy churned as if she had gone down too fast in a lift. The card had been turned out to display the time-honoured message: RIP. Handwritten in felt tip. Frozen to the spot, Harriet gazed at it in appalled disbelief. A creepy sensation of menace raised gooseflesh at the nape of her neck.

'What is it?' Tolly came to a halt beside her. The consternation on his kindly face was palpable.

'Do you think it's supposed to be a joke? It's really freaky!' Una exclaimed, backing off several steps. 'I think you should call the guards right away.'

'The guards?' Harriet echoed, wondering how the wreath could possibly look so pretty and so threatening at the same time.

'The *garda*...the police,' the teenager clarified. 'Wake up, Harriet! Someone must have come up here and left it while you were in the yard. You should ring those women who were doing the jumps and ask if they saw anyone acting strange up here.'

Tolly had already moved to a spot a few yards away to employ a mobile phone.

'No, don't call the police...' Harriet told him as he turned back to her. 'Look, give me a minute to think about this.'

'I'm afraid I've already called Rafael. He'll know what to do,' Tolly said soothingly. 'Let's not allow this to spoil our picnic.'

But Harriet had been badly shaken, and she had no appetite left for food. In any case, Rafael arrived within five minutes. He treated the wreath to a cursory appraisal, instructed Tolly and Una not to touch it or the car, and suggested that he and Harriet talk indoors.

Rafael pulled out her shabby office chair. 'Sit down…you look like you're in shock.'

'Maybe because this isn't the first thing that's happened.'

He leant back against the desk in a galling attitude of relaxation while she told him about the message on the stable wall. 'Why didn't you tell anyone about it?'

'I didn't take it seriously… Oh, for goodness' sake.' Harriet gave him a look of rueful appeal. 'You'll probably hate me for admitting it, but at the time I was worried it was Una, because I knew she was annoyed with me. And, *no,* I don't suspect her for one moment now, or think she's in any way involved with putting that wretched wreath on my car! She's not the type to sneak around behind backs.'

'I would agree—my sister is much more in-your-face than that. I don't think that we need to make a fuss about the wreath,' Rafael drawled with measured cool, his brilliant eyes veiled by dense black lashes, 'however, the *garda* should still be informed. I'll have the car checked over for you as well.'

'It's not like me, but I'm just a bit nervous,' Harriet muttered apologetically. 'Do you have any ex-girlfriend who is likely to qualify for the bunny-boiler stakes?'

'Anything's possible.' Rafael shrugged a broad shoulder in the same nonchalant fashion that suggested bunny boilers were no big deal, and she found that attitude wonderfully reassuring.

'I don't like knowing that someone was bold enough to plant that thing on my car in broad daylight,' she admitted.

'Davis says the yard now attracts a steady stream of callers, so one more car wouldn't attract attention.'

'Do you think it's all right to go ahead with the gymkhana tomorrow?'

'Of course it is!' he responded with emphasis. 'You worry too much. I'm sure this is a tasteless practical joke and nothing more.'

As soon as he had left Harriet, Rafael crossed the yard to warn Davis not to let Harriet out of his sight until his own security men were in place to watch over her. He called the head of his protection team, discussed events so far, with particular reference to his suspicion that the same malicious party had unbolted the gate and let out the horses the other night. He pointed out the need for discretion in Harriet's vicinity because he did not want her to be alarmed. He also organised extra security men to cover the gymkhana. At that point he drove down to the cottage and was just in time to catch Boyce before he went out. Some time later the two men parted, in full agreement on how to deal with the situation; Boyce's opinion of Rafael had rocketed…

* * *

Harriet's first surprise of the day took place when Boyce got out of bed at the crack of dawn and insisted on accompanying her. She was even more taken aback when he took the broom she lifted out of her hand and told her that he would make himself useful sweeping the yard into a state of perfect presentation.

A gorgeous arrangement of flowers awaited her in the tiny office. The card prominently displayed bore Rafael's distinctive signature, and she found herself smiling from ear to ear. After yesterday's unpleasant delivery, the bouquet was a happy thought on his part and she could not stop thinking about him. He hadn't said sorry but then she hadn't said as much as she should have done to excuse the hideous insult of her having addressed him by Luke's name. Over all, she decided ruefully, the odds were fairly even between them. If he had called her Bianca, and followed the offence up by taking in a fanciable house guest, she would have been equally suspicious and quick to cut her losses. Nor, after Luke's behaviour, would she have been eager to risk her pride in confrontation and a demand for an explanation.

Rafael called her on her mobile phone while she was helping to check the course for the obstacle race.

'I love the flowers!' she exclaimed, the instant she

recognised his dark drawl, and then she winced at her own lack of cool.

'I hoped you would. I've organised some helpers for you.'

'Oh, that's not necessary,' she hastened to tell him.

'Just occasionally you may wish to recall that I'm your partner,' Rafael murmured lazily. 'It's the holiday season and the sun is shining. You've publicised the gymkhana far and wide. The event is likely to be well attended.'

'I certainly hope so.'

'Large crowds require supervision and facilities. My staff have put some extra arrangements in place to cover all contingencies. You need do nothing but accept the discreet assistance of the expert event organisers I employ.'

'My goodness! Perhaps I gave you the wrong impression, but this is a very small meeting...I'll be lucky to scrape together a couple of hundred people! Are you planning to put in an appearance?'

'Yes.'

Two young women presented themselves soon after that call, and were followed by several well-built men. Soon the first keen competitive parent arrived, complete with trailer and child. When two horseboxes pulled up within minutes Harriet was very grateful when one of the men offered to take charge of the parking area and ensure that the access lanes were kept clear. It was not very long before she began to see that she had underestimated the potential appeal of a country day out; even though it was still early there was a regular flow of traffic. A *garda* car containing two uniformed officers had taken up position as well.

A queue had already formed in the tack shop. Boyce was manning the counter, doling out change and wrapping curry brushes.

'You know, you could make a bomb as one of them lookalikes,' an admiring teenage girl was telling him. 'You're the picture of that Boyce Taylor from 4Some. You're a lot smaller than he is, though.'

'Oh, well…can't have everything.' Boyce was hamming it up for all he was worth.

'I don't think you're half as cute as that guy in 4Some,' Harriet interposed deadpan, as she stepped in to take his place.

Her brother's eyes danced with merriment. 'Thanks a bundle.'

Mid-morning she went to watch the dressage competition in the paddock. She loved seeing the earnest children perform on their fat, well-groomed ponies. Fergal joined her, helpfully identifying the local kids and their parents for her benefit.

'When I found out Boyce was your brother I decided not to tell Una that he was that singer,' he shared rather abruptly. 'She knows you're related now, but I'm sure you've been wondering why I didn't put her right straight away.'

Until that point Harriet had not been aware that Una was still in the dark about anything, and she turned to study Fergal with dawning comprehension. 'Are you saying that you've known all along who Boyce really is?'

'Harriet…he's freakin' famous! But he's entitled to privacy if he wants it. Una would have been demanding his autograph and flirting like mad with him. I thought it was better that she didn't come round while he was staying. Not that I wouldn't have trusted him—or her. '

Ruddy self-conscious colour lay over his cheekbones and Harriet took pity on him, because she was amused by the extent of his protectiveness towards the younger woman. 'But you thought it was better not to take the risk. Who else knows Boyce is the lead singer of 4Some?'

'A good number.' Fergal grinned. 'He's pure magic on that flute. Sure, anyone watching him would guess he was a professional and a star.'

Harriet looked past him to where Rafael's customised and very distinctive Range Rover had purred to a halt. Her every nerve-ending sizzled into life and she left Fergal to head in that direction. But when she saw the gorgeous woman who had climbed out of Rafael's car it was like someone had closed a cruel hand round her windpipe. Unfortunately he had noticed her approach, and it was too late to practise avoidance tactics.

Exuding class and sleek good looks in his country casuals, Rafael glanced at the crowds milling round the field and remarked to Harriet, 'Give yourself a pat on the back. You must be a whiz at PR.'

'And you were right. I was wrong. We're being mobbed.'

Big brown eyes sparkling, the brunette flicked back her long black hair from her exquisite face and treated Harriet to an engaging smile. 'Hi…I'm Frankie. '

Harriet could not believe there was a red-blooded male within ten miles unaware of who Frankie Millar was. A former glamour model, Frankie had made a highly successful transfer into the world of television as a presenter. Popular and talented, she now interviewed the rich and famous on her own chat show. *He must have slept with her last night.* Try as she might, that was the only thought in

Harriet's head. She felt sick. But it was two days since Rafael had told her that he wanted her back, and she had turned him down and done a runner, so what had she expected? Guys that rich, handsome and in demand did not go solo for long.

'Rafael tells me you're his first business partner ever,' Frankie continued cheerfully. 'What's it like?'

'Interesting. There's not a lot of discussion about decisions, and there's a lot of the unexpected.' To avoid looking direct at Frankie, who was adding being warm and friendly to the unwelcome parade of her virtues, Harriet focused with a wooden smile on the rosettes being handed out to the winners in the obstacle race. 'But he has this very irritating habit of picking up on the things I miss, so I can't complain. Excuse me—I have some things to check on. Lovely meeting you, Frankie.'

As Harriet walked away, with an eagerness she could not hide, Frankie watched Rafael stare after the curvaceous redhead with the kind of acquisitive intensity he usually reserved for thoroughbred racehorses.

'You should've mentioned I was married to your best friend,' Frankie told him ruefully.

Rafael shot his companion a wickedly amused glance. 'It was a deliberate oversight.'

'You sneaky bastard!' the brunette gasped, as she

realised that she had been used to test the water. 'I hope she gives you hell!'

'She probably will. She's no push-over.'

'If you don't tell her I'm a mate, I will,' Frankie threatened.

Blinded by the raw surge of conflicting feelings surging up inside her, Harriet trudged slowly through the ranks of parked cars. Rafael had found a replacement for her and, what was even worse, a thinner, prettier and sexier lady, with a glamorous television career. She heard a shout and thought she recognised her half-brother's voice. Frowning, she glanced up from the ground. Boyce was racing across the lane as if he was chasing after someone. In fact several people from different locations seemed to be giving chase, and she spun round to see what was causing the commotion. Had there been an accident? Or a theft? Wheels were screaming over gravel too fast, and she only had an instant to register that a car with a sobbing woman at the wheel was bearing down on her.

Someone shouted at her. Suddenly there was a blur of movement and she was snatched off her feet and hauled clear of danger. Her shoulder caught a glancing blow off the wing of a parked van before she hit the ground in a tangle of limbs. Winded and shocked, she gasped and fought to fill her squashed lungs with oxygen again. She heard the horrible crunch of tearing metal as the car, which had missed her, took the corner too wide and too fast and cannoned into a stationary vehicle.

Rafael bent over her. His eyes were bright as the heart of a fire, his lean, dark face displaying a level of anxiety that she had never expected to see there. 'Are you hurt?' he demanded. 'Tell me you're OK.'

Her shoulder was throbbing and her whole body ached, for she had hit the ground hard when she fell, but in that moment the discomfort meant nothing to her. He had risked his own life to yank her out of the path of a car.

'Frankie's married to my oldest friend. I used her as bait to see if it bothered you to see me with another woman.' He grabbed up her hand and his own was not quite steady. He turned his beautiful mouth into her palm to press a kiss there before lifting his head again and muttering roughly, 'I'm a stupid smart-ass bastard. I might have killed you!'

'It's all right…' Her throat tightening with the onset of shock and strong emotion, she was blinking back tears. 'I like smart-asses.'

For a split second she thought he was about to kiss her. Then the raised voices and the tearing sound of a woman crying intruded. Rafael vaulted upright and helped her up. 'I think we've caught your stalker…I just hope she hasn't hurt anybody else.'

'Stalker?' Her attention locked in consternation to the tableau playing out thirty feet away.

Mercifully nobody appeared to have been hurt in the accident, but a youthful blonde woman was having noisy hysterics at the bonnet of the Porsche that had just missed hitting Harriet. For some reason she appeared to be surrounded by a good proportion of Rafael's events organizers, and a *garda* officer for good measure. But what drew Harriet's concerned scrutiny was the sight of her brother, lodged ten feet away. He was staring at the blonde with an unusually bleak expression, and then he swung away.

'Boyce!' the blonde called frantically after him. 'Help me…don't leave me here like this!'

Shoulders hunched, Boyce walked straight over to Harriet and put his arms round his sister. 'I'm so sorry…I'm really sorry about all of this. Are you all right? Thank God you're not hurt. If Gemma had run you over I don't think I could have lived with myself—'

'Why should you be sorry?' Harriet winced as the blonde began to sob with noisy abandon. 'Gemma? Do you know her?'

'Let's take this discussion elsewhere. We're beginning to attract attention.' An arm around Harriet's form, Rafael led the way over to his car, saying only loud enough for her to hear, 'The stalker is your brother's ex, Gemma Barton. She went overboard for him and he broke it off. But she made it tough for him to cut loose completely and he was glad to get away on tour. Evidently she followed him over to Ireland and assumed that you were his latest squeeze.'

'Oh, heck.' Harriet stole a glance at her half-sibling's pale, set profile, her heart going out to him as she let Rafael help her into the passenger seat. 'Why didn't it occur to me that *he* might be the "him" in that message on the stable wall?'

'I suspect you felt that I deserved a bunny-boiler more than he did.'

Harriet was shocked to feel her lip quiver at that deadpan response. 'How come you know so much more about this than I do?' she asked. 'Look, why am I getting into your car?'

'I put you in it,' Rafael pointed out equably.

'But I can't leave the gymkhana,' Harriet argued as Boyce climbed into the back seat.

'Yes, you can. My staff are more than capable of running what remains of the show. You need to be checked over by a doctor—'

'No—'

'And make a statement to the *garda* and a complaint against the stalker who's been harassing you.'

'Gemma…'

'Don't personalise a psycho who frightened the living daylights out of you,' Rafael incised with ruthless bite. 'Five minutes ago she almost ran you down!'

'But that was an accident: she didn't see me. I walked out in front of her car. I saw her face and she was distraught, not looking where she was going.'

'You think that makes me feel better? Excuse me…I'll be back in a few minutes. Boyce, make sure your sister stays where she is.'

'OK,' her half-brother answered, like an obedient schoolboy.

'Are you just going to let Rafael tell you what to do?'

'I really would prefer the media not to get hold of this particular story; the lid could blow off it so easily,' Boyce admitted heavily. 'It's only thanks to Rafael that the situation is under control. He's had his people keeping an eye on you since yesterday.'

'What are you talking about?'

'Events organisers aren't usually so muscular. Most of the staff he sent over to help you today work for him in the security field.'

'I had no idea. But before Rafael comes back tell

me about Gemma and what happened between you. For a start, who is she?'

'She's the daughter of a wealthy property developer. When I first started seeing her she was a lot of fun, but that didn't last long. She began listening in on my calls and throwing jealous scenes. She stole a key to my apartment, showed up uninvited all the time,' he recited wearily. 'I couldn't handle her, so I ended it. She threatened to top herself. I talked to her parents and they were very decent about it, but I felt guilty.'

'You mustn't.' Harriet was impressed that he had tried to help Gemma even after she had become a real headache in his life. 'How did she find out you were in Ireland?'

'That was my fault too. She phoned me to ask me to her twenty-first birthday party and I said I'd be over here. She seems to have got the details of when and where from a mutual friend, who wasn't aware she'd become a problem. I was shattered last night when Rafael told me what had been happening. I wish you'd told me about the threat painted on the wall. You see, I *did* think I'd seen Gemma in Dooleys, but just assumed I'd been mistaken...'

Her brow was furrowed. 'When did you see Rafael last night?'

She soon realised how deceptive Rafael's apparent unconcern had been. Once her brother had confided that it was possible that his ex-girlfriend might be behind the disturbing things that had been happening, Rafael had insisted on taking careful precautions.

'He said that his gut instinct was to cancel the gymkhana, but that in the long term you'd be safer if Gemma came out of the woodwork and got caught. His security team got a photo of her and circulated it. I called her parents last night, and they were able to confirm that she was in the area. They were making arrangements to fly over and bring her home.'

Rafael opened the rear door of the Range Rover and deposited Peanut in the luggage bay. Harriet heard the pig's signature snuffle and turned her head in surprise. 'You found Peanut?'

'I knew you'd have them with you.' Rafael opened the door beside her and produced Samson from the inside pocket of his Barbour. 'Real men don't carry chihuahuas in public, *a thaisce*.' He settled the little dog on her lap. 'Right, one pig and one dog on board. You don't want the rooster as well, do you?'

'Albert? How did you find out about Albert?' Harriet laughed.

Rafael lifted an aristocratic brow. 'His fame has spread.'

'He's a little home bird. He hangs out round the cottage. He wouldn't thank you for a trip in a car.'

Boyce's mobile phone rang and he answered it. With a muttered apology, he swung back out of the Range Rover and told them to go ahead without him.

'You're his sister. Tell him to steer clear of all further involvement with Gemma Barton's parents,' Rafael drawled in wry undertone. 'He can't be on both sides.'

'How do you know it's them he's speaking to?'

'ESP. He should back off. She'll be arrested and charged—'

'Not for anything she's done to me. I won't make an official complaint just because of that stupid message on the wall or that wreath.'

'Boyce believes she was inside the cottage as well. I'm fairly certain she also let the horses out.'

'You think she was behind *that*?' Harriet was aghast.

'You were lucky. One of those horses could have caused a serious accident in which someone was injured.'

'I know but Gemma Barton has problems. She needs help more than she needs punishment—'

'Then when she attacks Boyce's next girlfriend, let it be on your conscience that you were too much of a wimp to prosecute.'

Harriet flinched at that blunt warning.

Rafael drew up outside Flynn Court and she

blinked in surprise. 'I thought you were taking me home?'

'You were almost road-kill. I'm suffering from a very male old-fashioned need to keep tabs on you right now. In any case, the doctor should be here soon.'

Harriet was dismayed to notice that her hands were trembling. 'What's the matter with me?'

'Shock. You hate the idea that you might cause anyone the slightest concern, so you're trying very hard to act like nothing's happened. But you had a fright and you got hurt and you're shaken up. A re-action is normal.'

Astonished by how attuned he was to her, Harriet didn't argue, and concentrated on trying to stop her teeth from chattering. Without a word Rafael scooped her off her feet and carried her into a sitting room furnished in delicate faded blue. There he settled her gently down on a sofa. Lifting a mohair rug from the arm, he spread it over her. Samson jumped up on to the seat beside her and cuddled up. Peanut stretched out below a nearby chair, little beady eyes watchful in unfamiliar territory.

Rafael went to order tea, took a call from his head of security, which lasted some time, and returned to the library to discover that Harriet had dropped off to sleep. He made several phone calls. With scientific cool he studied her while she slept, and wondered exactly which qualities made her seem so different from all the other women he had ever known.

Obviously she hit the right spot physically, in every area, he conceded reflectively. Face, hair, shape, height, weight. Although he had never been attracted to anyone like her before, she was somehow a wonderfully precise and perfect match of what he liked most. He enjoyed looking at her. She was so natural, never striving to make an impression with anything she wore or said. There was a trusting innocence about her too, which he found appealing. Her desire to be compassionate towards the stalker had irritated the hell out of him. But at the same time he admired her ability to retain that generosity of spirit and compassion. Suddenly he frowned, disturbed by the depth and tenor of his own thoughts. He liked her, and it was very rare for him to truly *like* a lover, but so what?

The elderly doctor was brisk and frank. Harriet had bruises right down one side of her body and would be stiff and sore for a day or so. He added that she was also showing all the symptoms of stress and overwork and needed to take more rest. Rafael reappeared during that discussion.

'For a woman who came to Ireland to downshift to a less demanding lifestyle, you're not doing very well,' Rafael remarked when they were alone again.

'I still love what I'm doing, and I love my home.

But I may have somewhat underestimated the amount of work involved in setting up a new business.'

'How tactful you are. You're being forced to work twice as hard to balance the fact that I own half of the yard.'

'Never mind that. I'm happy,' Harriet countered cheerfully. 'I'm sorry I fell asleep on you.'

'You were on the sofa, not in my bed, so you're forgiven.'

Harriet went pink.

Rafael rested stunning dark eyes on her. 'I want to be with you somewhere where we can enjoy complete peace and privacy. I have a country house in Italy, which is in a very quiet location. I'd like to take you there.'

'I...I'm flattered—'

'Good. All you have to do is pack, and even that isn't a necessity. I would be delighted to buy you everything you need. We shall leave in a few hours.'

It took Harriet a good thirty seconds to absorb that staggering declaration. 'For goodness' sake—me go gallivanting off to Italy just like that? It's a wild and wonderful idea, but be sensible...I can't leave the livery yard!'

'Of course you can. As your partner, I have equal responsibility. You've worked so hard that you're exhausted, while I've done nothing until now. But that's changed: I've organised a manager to take charge while you're away, and Davis will bring in local help from the village. Tolly has volunteered to take care of your pets—'

Harriet viewed him in startled disbelief and frustration. 'Rafael…'

'You'll love Italy,' he breathed huskily. 'What's wrong with wild and wonderful? How do you define sensible? Saying no to anything that sounds like too much fun? You might have died today. We might never have got the chance to be together again.'

He tossed those dramatic lines at her with a vibrant amusement in his eyes that made her laugh. Yet on another level she could not help but appreciate the inescapable truth he had voiced. But for a few bruises, she was alive and well, and she ought to make the most of her second chance. Indeed, it seemed to her that to be too sensible to snatch at the opportunity to go to Italy with Rafael would be pitiful.

'It's quite simple. Do you want to be with me?' Rafael asked levelly. 'Or don't you?'

And he was right: it was that simple. In the space of a moment, Harriet decided what to do.

'What's my home here like?' A lazy smile formed on Rafael's darkly handsome face. 'I will leave you to form your own opinion.'

The jet had landed at Galileo Galilei soon after dawn, and they had driven out of Pisa in a four-wheel-drive that had awaited them at the airport. Harriet had slept through most of the flight and was still sleepily relaxed, turning her head to view him with a sense of intense pleasure. 'It'll be very old and very large and very luxurious,' she forecast.

'Wait and see.'

For a moment Harriet spared a thought for Gemma Barton. Having talked to Boyce, she had decided not to press charges against his former girlfriend. Gemma had admitted everything she had done, and had agreed to undergo a residential course of treatment at a psychiatric facility. Her parents had taken their troubled daughter back to England with them. Rafael had disagreed with that more sympathetic approach but, to do him justice, he had not interfered.

Having left the motorway behind, they were travelling on a winding rural road that curved round a snow-capped mountain in a series of tortuous bends. On one side the ground fell sharp as a blade into a deep ravine with thickly forested slopes. Looking down at that endless drop made Harriet's tummy flip, but Rafael was a true Italian, she thought ruefully, for he still drove with the speed and dexterity of a male on a straight road. Above, the sky was a clear continental blue so bright it made her blink.

'Do you know…you haven't even kissed me yet?' she heard herself say.

Rafael cast her a surprised glance and then laughed out loud. 'I was being considerate. You were so tired last night, and you're bruised all over—'

'Not *that* bruised,' she told him.

He needed no further encouragement. He shot the car to a halt at a viewpoint overlooking the valley, released her seat belt and reached for her. He did all of those things in what seemed like one smooth, continuous movement. Hungry eyes flared over her sparkling eyes and pink cheeks. 'You're coming on to me…I like that…'

'Do you?' She was so desperate to feel his mouth on hers that she was tingling with anticipation.

'There was another angle to my restraint,' Rafael murmured huskily. 'If I'd kissed you, I was scared that I might not be able to stop.'

A curl of heat flared low in her pelvis and she shifted tautly in her seat, making an infinitesimal move closer to him.

He flicked a strand of copper hair back from her white brow. 'You don't scare easy, do you?'

'No.' Gazing up into his lean, bronzed face, she felt her breath trip in her throat. She was almost

mesmerised by the raw sexual intensity of his smouldering appraisal and the hot pulse of her own response.

He brought his sensual mouth down on hers, and
a pang of such feverish longing gripped her that she
shivered. His kiss was so sweet and addictive she
wanted the next before the first was complete.
Breathing raggedly, he lifted his proud dark head
again. 'I want to continue this in the comfort of my
own bed.'

'Spoilsport,' she framed, through swollen lips.

'Hussy,' he growled, with a grin that revealed a
flash of perfect white teeth as he settled her very gently back into the passenger seat.

Harriet very much enjoyed her new feeling of
confidence around Rafael, but she would not have
let him know. After all, he might have forgotten what
he had admitted in the heat of the moment when he
had snatched her back from the threat of Gemma's
car wheels. She wasn't about to remind him that he
had confessed to flaunting Frankie Millar in front of
her to see whether or not she was jealous. However,
that revelation had done real wonders for her self-
esteem.

He turned the car on to the narrow unmade road
that threaded through the mountains, and finally
struck off on what appeared to be a grassy farm

track. Spreading chestnut trees dappled the lane with shade and sunshine. Crimson poppies, golden broom and cobalt-blue cornflowers flourished in the long grass. A very old lichen-covered red-tiled roof came into view, and she sat forward for a better look. Below the terracotta roof stretched a long, low building of ancient stone, with windows at different heights and in no set formation. The farmhouse had a mellow charm and appeal that was timeless.

'Is this it?' Harriet asked doubtfully.

'This is it—the Cavaliere *fattoria*, or home farm. What do you think?'

Harriet was already scrambling out of the car to get a closer look. 'It's like we've stepped back in time.'

'Valente was born here.'

She whirled round, blue eyes agog. 'On a farm? Your father, the hot-shot businessman? You're kidding me!'

'I kid you not. He was the youngest son, and he hated country life. He left here under a cloud and never came back.'

'From what you've said about him, he kind of took his cloud everywhere with him. What did he do?'

Rafael thrust open the weathered oak door. She looked around with interest. A few pieces of antique country furniture had been retained, but there was no clutter. The décor had been scraped back to the bare-boned beauty of old wood and rough walls.

'Valente made his initial fortune by cheating people with various business scams. He was clever enough to keep himself out of prison,' Rafael shared with quiet derision. 'Then he married a neighbour's daughter for her money and abandoned her in Rome when she was pregnant. She was too proud to return to her family, and she died in labour along with the child—alone and broke. My grandparents were so ashamed that they disowned their son.'

'But this is your house now, so you must have got to meet them.'

'I met my grandmother before she died, five years ago. Two of her sisters survive her, and a host of other relatives. Now…to practicalities,' Rafael remarked with amusement. 'The facilities are basic in this house. You have a free choice. We don't have to stay here. Are you willing to rough it with me?'

'Is there running water and a bathroom?'

'Of course.'

'Then stop being precious,' she urged him. 'We won't be roughing it. Whisk the average woman off to a sunny valley in Italy, show her a picture book farmhouse with all the necessities of life and she'll consider herself spoilt.'

'You're the first woman I've brought here, *a mhilis.*'

The pleasure of being the first was drowned out by her sudden awareness that she wanted to be the *only* woman he ever brought. Dismayed by that unwelcome knowledge, she tensed. As if he felt the distance in her, he pressed a kiss down on her parted lips, and she reached up to hold him to her, desire running like liquid fire through her taut frame.

He closed his hand over hers and walked her up the stairs. A gentle breeze cooled the wide landing. The shutters had been flung wide in the big front room. The big wooden bed was adorned with painted panels of pretty flowers and made up with plump pillows and crisp white linen sheets.

'It feels like a hundred years since I touched you. I was planning to go slow, but I'm too hungry for you to wait that long.' With that roughened admission Rafael hauled her to him with strong hands and devoured her mouth with fiery urgency.

Her heart leapt and her pulses raced like he had punched in a special code that set her alight. He reached below her T-shirt and battled with her bra to find the swollen peak of a sensitive nipple and make her moan in sensual shock below his marauding mouth. She shivered and knotted her fingers in his luxuriant black hair. Her hunger equalled his, and she could not hide it. She was wild for the sweet hot force of his body into hers.

'If we had stayed in the car I would have ended up on a charge of public indecency,' Rafael groaned, peeling off her clothes and his own with a masculine impatience that thrilled her. As each fresh expanse of pale skin was revealed he would pause to explore that part of her with the expertise and single-minded concentration of a highly sensual lover.

'If you make me wait any longer, I'll die,' she told him helplessly, breathless and squirming against the pale linen, tormented by the hunger he had roused and honed into an unbearably tight knot of need.

Through slumberous dark eyes, Rafael surveyed her. 'I want to give you endless pleasure.'

'Just pleasure will do.' Her hips shifted up to him in a tiny pleading movement. She was hot, aching.

He took her by surprise, entering her hard and fast. A shockwave of delight possessed her. Before she could recover he withdrew, and slammed back into her again. His fierce passion gave a raw edge to their lovemaking. Lost in that wild excitement, she reached a tumultuous climax of shattering pleasure. In the aftermath she experienced pure joy. Secure in his arms, she felt so happy that tears pricked below her eyelids.

Rafael kept her spread beneath him and shifted with earthy satisfaction against her damp responsive heat. Dazed with pleasure, she gave him a languorous smile. He pressed his mouth softly to her brow. The very smell of her skin intoxicated him. The feel of her, the way she fitted against him, was amazing. That fast he wanted her all over again, and he closed his hands over hers to hold her doubly imprisoned in his arms while he kissed her.

'Again?' she gasped in astonishment when he let her up for air.

'Again,' he said thickly.

Much later he slept, and she lay awake watching him. His black lashes almost hit his cheekbones. He looked fabulous from every angle, she decided. Against the white linen, his bronzed skin was rich as gold, a sleek covering for the lean, hard, muscular power of his masculine frame. She loved to look at him. She was on a high of satisfaction and self-discovery. She let her lips drift down to a broad shoulder in a whisper soft expression of affection. She couldn't keep her hands off him.

She wondered when she had fallen in love with him, and marvelled that she had been able to hide that truth even from herself. She knew she wanted to own him body and soul, and that that was a terrifying ambition pretty much destined to lead to disappointment when she hit ground level again at some time in the future. But she saw no reason why reality should intrude just then and spoil things. She intended to live the utmost out of every day she spent in Umbria.

CHAPTER NINE

MUNCHING A PIECE of bread fresh from the oven, and savouring the aromatic taste of herbs, Harriet lay back on the lounger and sipped her red wine. She wondered lazily what had happened to her earnest desire to work all the time, and to feeling horribly guilty when she enjoyed herself instead.

Above her an ancient cedar spread a wide arc of shade that protected her from the late afternoon sun. From the terrace beyond the infinity pool that shone like a mirror she could see the fields of ripening golden corn and tobacco on the far side of the valley and, nearer, the orchards and vines heavy with fruit and the silvery green groves of olive trees.

It was a moment of perfection and she knew it— a moment when happiness had no bounds and felt like the summer sun, captured inside her. Her body was heavy from the sweet pleasure of Rafael's lovemaking. A smile kept on sliding over her ripe pink mouth. One week had drifted into two. Two weeks, she thought absently. Where had it gone? It had passed by in an idyllic haze of endless drenching sunshine and a lover like no other.

Every day a glorious selection of freshly prepared dishes and newly baked bread appeared as if by magic in the homely farmhouse kitchen. A pair of sisters, Donata and Benedetta, took care of the house, and so scrupulously observed their privacy that Rafael and Harriet had scarcely seen them. Their brothers, who farmed the land, were equally discreet.

Rafael and Harriet had left the *fattoria* on only a few occasions. In the cool of the evening he had taken her to medieval hill towns, to wander through steep narrow streets and dine at tiny restaurants that catered to only a handful of customers. He knew all the special places to eat and to shop. If she looked at anything he wanted to buy it for her, so she had been forced to point out that that was rather inhibiting for someone who wasn't a gold-digger.

'But I like giving,' Rafael had complained without hesitation. 'You're inhibiting me.'

So she had accepted the gold necklace adorned with an exquisitely fashioned St Francis, which he'd given her to commemorate her only requested visit to Assisi and the basilica there, and a gold watch that had literally walked out of the jewellery shop into his pocket because it was so 'her', according to him. Told that there was an embargo on further expensive presents, he'd given her a hand-painted scarf so fine it could have passed through the proverbial wedding ring, a handbag of such exquisite workmanship it was a work of art and much too fancy for actual use, and a little carved crystal horse that her eyes had only lingered on for a split second in a shop window. *Enough*, she had groaned, and had persuaded him to concentrate his desire to give on his sister instead.

Tomorrow would be their last day—absolutely their last. And Rafael was as reluctant as Harriet to leave Italy. But it seemed appropriate that they would finally share a day with other people, as Rafael had accepted an invitation for both of them to attend the wedding of one of his cousins. Since her arrival, the only other person Harriet had spoken to had been Una. The teenager rang her every couple of days, and phoned Rafael on alternate days, making a cheeky game of never, ever asking a nosy question, or mentioning that they were actually in Umbria together.

That evening Rafael and Harriet strolled through the oak woods behind the house. 'I have a favour to ask,' Rafael murmured. 'As you know, Flynn Court is in the process of renovation. I have any number of professionals at my disposal, but I must confess that I was very disappointed with the results of a similar programme at my other house in Kildare.'

'But why? From what I saw of the interior, it was perfect.'

'Exactly. It was like a museum. I want the Court to remain a warm and welcoming place, rather than a showpiece. It's very much a private dwelling, where I will only ever entertain my closest friends. Would you be willing to act as an advisor on the redecoration?'

Taken aback, Harriet shot him a questioning glance. 'I'm not qualified to offer my opinions to a designer—'

Rafael turned her round to face him and trapped her hands in his to bring her closer. 'I think you are. I like the colours you wear. I like your taste. Don't be offended when I say that the folly looked like a hovel when your cousin lived there. You've somehow transformed it, with paint and cushions, into cosy and inviting.'

An involuntary laugh fell from her lips. 'Rafael… you can't do *cosy* in a Georgian mansion with fifteen bedrooms!'

'Why not? Possibly "advisor" wasn't the right label to employ. You would be the ultimate authority on colour schemes and so forth. I'm no good in that line.'

'You mean, you're not interested…'

An unashamed grin of acknowledgement slashed his lean, dark features. 'You know me so well. Are you worrying about the time factor?'

'Well, no, I hadn't got that far—'

'You needn't. I'd keep the current manager on at the yard, to ensure that you had more free time for the Court.'

'Stop trying to steamroller me into agreement. Why are you asking me to do this? There must be loads of more suitable choices.'

'No. I trust only a very select circle of people.' Dark golden eyes held hers levelly. 'This is a personal request, and as such unusual for me. I admit that I would hesitate to approach any other woman with it…'

Bewilderment made her frown. 'But why?'

'I know you'll accept it in the spirit it's intended, without imagining that it's a prelude to wedding bells,' he extended dryly.

Will-power kept her smile from freezing round the edges.

'I won't ever marry,' Rafael imparted flatly.

Hurt and embarrassment tipped into a momentarily powerful desire to slap him. Why was he talking in such a way? Had she seemed too keen? Too affectionate, too happy, too caring? Last night she had given way to temptation and picked up his discarded shirt. Did he sense love, like an earthquake warning, on the periphery of his precious single life? Had she spooked him into feeling that such an in-your-face warning was necessary?

'I think that's a very wise decision on your part,'

Harriet assured him, with all the warmth she could muster. 'You're just not marriage material.'

Rafael had always thought that too, but for some reason when Harriet agreed with his own view of himself he felt grossly insulted, and valued at far less than his deserved worth. 'Why not? How do I differ from other men?'

'You're very self-sufficient—'

'Next you'll be saying you go for guys that cry, and stuff like that,' Rafael derided. 'I wonder how enthralled you would be with some weak, needy character who always needed to lean on you for support!'

'Thankfully, I have no idea.' Harriet had nothing more to say. She had felt the urgency of her own hurt, stepped back from it, and resolved not to let her thoughts travel in forbidden directions.

'So what else is wrong with me?' Rafael asked with lethal cool.

'I didn't say anything was wrong with you. You are the one who told me that you don't do love or commitment.'

In the middle of the night he listened to the deep, even timbre of her breathing. She was enjoying the sure, sound and thoroughly irritating slumber of someone with an untroubled mind. In the moonlight, he punched his pillows and shifted position for the fiftieth time. He wanted to shake her awake and demand to know in what terms she saw their affair. He might not do love and commitment, but he did not do cheap, meaningless sexual flings either. He possessed deep emotions. He might not be in the habit of showing them, but the feelings existed nonetheless. He could be sensitive, considerate, caring. He could be anything he wanted to be. He made a real effort to please her too—although he was willing to admit that that was no sacrifice, as pleasing her invariably meant pleasing himself equally.

After all, what other woman could happily talk about horses all day? Search cheerfully through thoroughbred bloodlines and discuss breeding options with sincere interest? She might not have known much in that area to begin with, but she was a fast learner. What other woman would happily occupy herself while he worked, without a single whine of complaint or any attempt to regain his attention? She liked to read and go for long walks. Simple pleasures. And she seemed so straightforward, tranquil and undemanding… Yet here she was, sending him up the walls with frustration!

Harriet found a text waiting on her mobile the next morning. It was from Alice—her first communication after months of silence.

Must c u 2 talk. Wen?

Harriet was delighted, and messaged straight back to say she'd be in London within thirty-six hours.

Rafael made no comment, but he disapproved of Harriet's enthusiastic response and willingness to forgive the younger woman's betrayal. In his mind Alice was one link short of Luke, and as such a highly suspect element in Harriet's life, liable to cause grief.

The wedding celebrations of his third cousin, Teresina, and her bridegroom, Alfredo, began early, with a sumptuous buffet breakfast for the bride's relatives at her home. Harriet was overwhelmed by the friendliness of her welcome.

There was only room for close family in the tiny church where the ceremony was held. Teresina, a shy brunette, emerged on her new husband's arm to preside over the wedding banquet laid out on long trestle tables below the chestnut trees in the village square. Course after course was served, each dish seemingly more elaborate than the last. One of the guests got up to sing, several had brought musical instruments to play, and at one stage most of the children present formed into a choir to serenade the blushing bride and groom. The entertainment was delightfully informal and great fun.

'Una should be here,' Harriet whispered to Rafael. 'Do your Italian relations know that you have a half-sister?'

'Yes. I asked her to come on a visit last year, but she wasn't interested.'

'I bet she thought you were only asking out of politeness. She'd be scared she wouldn't be accepted. She's very insecure about being illegitimate.'

'You do realise that you're becoming the equivalent of a walking oracle on touchy teenage girls?'

'Rafael…right now I'm so stuffed with food I couldn't *walk* anywhere!' Harriet confided. 'You'll have to carry me back to the car.'

Glittering eyes rested on her teasing smile. Before she could guess his intention, he claimed a kiss, and there was a burst of laughter and hand-clapping, and amused comments were passed in Italian.

'What are they saying?'

Rafael shrugged and she reddened, guessing that the normal jokes that were made at weddings had been exercised on their behalf. She was enormously tempted to inform him that she wouldn't marry him if he got down on his knees and grovelled for a century, but she knew it would be cooler to leave that sentiment unvoiced.

They were waiting to board the jet at Pisa when Eva, who had clearly spoken to Alice, called and arranged to see Harriet while she was in London. Eva rarely chatted for long to Harriet on the phone, but on this occasion she was even briefer than was her wont, and gave her daughter no opportunity to share the news that she would be flying in from Italy.

In London, Rafael parted from her with a similar lack of fuss, booking her for dinner at his city apartment that evening before his departure for New York. 'You can stay there tonight, and fly back to Ireland in the morning.'

Alice opened the door of her flat abruptly. 'You'd better come in.'

Immediately Harriet noticed the changes the past few months had wrought in her sibling. Alice had lost weight and, as she had always been slender, the effect was not flattering: her lovely face looked pinched and her plain grey trouser suit was nothing like her usual young and adventurous style. Harriet recalled Boyce saying that Luke had liked *her* to dress like an old lady in drab colours too, and she almost winced.

Alice watched Harriet look around the lounge. 'Luke's in Manchester on business,' she declared. 'He doesn't even know I invited you here today, and if you tell him I'll deny it!'

'Why would I tell Luke anything?' The accusing note in Alice's voice took Harriet by surprise. 'I wasn't even aware you were both living here. I thought you were sharing his apartment. I haven't seen Luke since we broke up.'

'Have you really not seen Luke since then?' Alice

pinned strained brown eyes on Harriet. 'Or are you being clever with me? Maybe you think it's payback time, and Luke and you are chatting on the phone to each other every day! How would I know?'

Alice was on the brink of angry tears, and the raw state of her nerves was obvious. Reluctant pity filtered through Harriet's exasperation. 'I have had no contact with Luke at all.'

Her sister could not hide her relief at that confirmation, but just as quickly her eyes dulled again. 'Well, if you haven't heard from him yet, you soon will… He won't agree to the wedding invitations going out. The wedding's been postponed!'

'Oh…'

'Is that all you've got to say?'

Harriet thought about it, and then slowly nodded agreement. In the circumstances she could think of nothing to say that would not qualify as provocative. The wedding plans had struck her as premature, but she had believed that Luke had abandoned his usual caution because he was head over heels in love. Now it was clear that his relationship with Alice was troubled, and she wasn't surprised that he was backing away from the imminent prospect of marriage.

'We had a terrible row at the weekend.'

'Alice…I don't want to be involved in this,'

Harriet cut in hurriedly. 'But I am sorry that things aren't working out for you.'

Tears were streaming down her sister's distraught face. 'Of course you're not sorry. This is your moment—and you must be crowing!'

'I'm not. Why would I be? Luke and I broke up months ago.'

'He said I lured him away from you…he said I was too stupid for him,' Alice hiccupped in despair. 'I love him—I really love him—and I'm losing him!'

Dismay gripped Harriet. 'You mustn't let Luke speak to you like that. He can be very critical, but you have to stand up to him.'

'But I'm not clever like you!' Alice sobbed. 'I didn't go to university…I don't know how to talk about politics—and I couldn't care less about them either. But that's *all* Luke and his stuffy friends ever talk about!'

'What happened to skiing holidays, the cost of childcare and all those ghastly "in" legal jokes?'

Alice had been sorrowfully wiping her eyes, but at that unexpected comeback she stared wide-eyed. And then she started laughing—only unfortunately she couldn't stop. She laughed until she choked, and then she started sobbing again, as if her heart was breaking. Harriet abandoned her stance of dignified distance and put a hesitant arm round the younger woman to edge her over to the sofa. Alice sank down beside her and just wept and wept.

'I love him…I love him to bits,' Alice kept on gasping pitifully. 'I don't know what to do!'

Harriet felt guilty for reflecting that *she* would never have loved Luke enough to tolerate him telling her that she was too stupid for him. But the last remnants of her anger with Alice had melted away.

'At the beginning he was mad about me…he *was*!' Alice muttered painfully. 'He was always sending me cheeky texts. I thought he loved me. I thought you and he had been together so long he was bored, and that he was never going to marry you anyway.'

'You may well have been right.'

'No, I was telling myself what I wanted to believe. I certainly know different now.' Fresh tears welled up in her sibling's eyes. 'Luke never stops comparing me to you. You've been with him since you were students. How am I supposed to compete?'

'What's Eva got to say about all this?'

Alice loosed a tight, bitter laugh. 'Mum? What do you think? She doesn't want to know. She never does want to know when things go wrong. She's furious that the wedding is being postponed, and she says it'll never be on again. Last month she threw a big party for us in Paris, and introduced Luke as my fiancé. Now she's telling me that the wedding cancellation will embarrass her and that I need to learn how to hang on to a man!'

Her sister wailed the last sentence and then started crying again. Recognising that the tears were more half-hearted than serious this time around, Harriet passed her the box of tissues and went off to make tea. She had been planning to tell Alice about Rafael, but now felt that it really wasn't the right moment. She knew her sibling well enough to suspect that telling Alice about her own happiness would only make the younger woman feel more wretched than ever.

Over the tea, Alice gave her elder sister a discomfited appraisal. 'I've really missed having you to talk to. I never meant to hurt you…it just happened. I was mad about him, and so jealous of you for *so* long—'

'How long?'

Alice twisted a long strand of blonde hair round her finger and grimaced. 'I suppose it really started when I was seventeen. Luke used to tease me a lot. He knew I fancied him, and he liked it, so there was always this flirting thing going on between us. But I felt bad about that, so I began to act all snooty and superior when we met, and he hated that. It gave me a kick.'

Harriet was disturbed to appreciate just how young Alice had been when she'd first formed an interest in Luke. She could vaguely recall Luke teasing her little sister. She had thought nothing of it at the time, and had paid more heed to the seeming hostility that had eventually replaced the banter. Now it occurred to her that Luke had taken advantage of the girl.

'As for when the affair started... About six months before you caught us together I called round one evening to see you, but you were away on business.' Having begun, Alice could not stop confessing. 'Luke invited me in for a drink, and I had too much and he kissed me...and it went from there...'

Harriet didn't want the tacky details. 'We don't need to talk about that. But, whatever happens between you and Luke, you and I will still be sisters and we can stay close.'

'Not if Luke dumps me and goes back to you.'

'Alice...you're assuming that I want him back, and I don't, so please get that idea out of your mind.'

'I'm sorry...' Alice compressed tremulous lips and dropped her head.

Harriet thought it was unfortunate that she was not in a position to convince Alice that Luke was bad news for her. But the evidence was clear to see. Luke had stolen her sister's confidence and turned her into a nervous wreck, racked with self-doubt. All her life until now Alice had been a golden girl, who led a charmed existence. The experience did not appear to have taught Alice the survival skills she needed now.

'I'm at the other end of the phone whenever you need me,' Harriet told her gently. 'You're also welcome to come and stay with me in Ballyflynn.'

'That's kind of you.' Alice loosed a plaintive sigh. 'But it would be all mud and horses, and I'm not a country girl at heart.'

A couple of hours later, Harriet knocked on the door of her mother's hotel suite. She was surprised when Gustav let her in. A tall, spare man, with thinning blond hair, her mother's third husband rarely accompanied his wife to London, and as a result he was almost a stranger to Harriet.

'Eva is lying down…this has been a traumatic time for her,' the older man remarked stiffly.

Harriet felt that the postponement and possible cancellation of Luke and Alice's wedding had been rather more traumatic for Alice than for her mother. But she was also well-acquainted with Eva's ability to persuade people that she was an immensely fragile and sensitive individual, who had to be protected at all costs from every ill wind.

'I want you to promise that you will say nothing further to upset her,' Gustav added in an anxious undertone. 'I appreciate that this is very difficult for you as well…'

'How for me? Oh, sorry—you mean with me having once been engaged to Luke,' Harriet gathered wryly. 'I'm well over that. In fact, I'm even reaching the conclusion that Alice may have saved me from making the biggest mistake of my life.'

'Luke?' He studied her in visible bewilderment. 'Forgive me, but what do Luke and Alice have to do with this? It is Boyce's intrusion into what is a very confidential matter that has caused your mother such distress.'

'Boyce?' Belatedly Harriet understood what her mother's husband was trying to tell her. She froze. Evidently her half-brother had kept his promise to speak to Eva about Harriet's need to know who her father was. She was astonished, for their conversation on that issue had been brief, even casual, and she had not really expected Boyce to make good on his pledge to lend her his support.

'Yes, Boyce. It was fortunate that I overheard the discussion between your brother and my wife and realised what was happening. Quite understandably, Eva was distraught.' Gustav managed to lend more than a hint of reproach and censure to that statement. He gazed his fill at Harriet's pallor and, apparently satisfied that she was suitably impressed by his words of warning, then opened the door to let her enter the sitting room.

The blinds had been lowered to screen out the harsh sunlight, and it took a moment or two for Harriet's eyes to adjust to the comparative dimness. Eva was reclining on the sofa. Dressed in the ultimate little black dress, her mother looked very delicate and vulnerable.

'How are you?' Dry-mouthed, Harriet hovered, scarcely able to credit that finally she might be about to learn something about her paternal genes. 'I'm really sorry if Boyce upset you—'

'Do you think I don't know that you put him up to it?' her mother shot back at her accusingly.

'We have talked about this, my dear,' Gustav interposed, in the very mildest of tones. 'As it is natural for Harriet to be curious, so it is appropriate for you to satisfy that curiosity. After that has taken place, I am certain that Harriet will agree with me that the subject need never be referred to again.'

Harriet had been wishing the older man would practise tact and leave her alone with her parent. After that speech, however, she wondered if it was only thanks to *his* involvement that Eva had at last been persuaded to speak.

'Do you have to stand over me?' Eva enquired petulantly of her daughter.

'Sorry…' Harriet dropped down hurriedly on to the edge of the nearest armchair.

'Before I tell you anything at all, I want you to promise me that nothing I say will go further than this room,' Eva decreed.

Harriet's brow pleated. 'But why on earth—?'

'I believe that your mother's request for discretion is reasonable,' Gustav commented.

Harriet was so tense that she would have agreed to virtually anything, but she could not help thinking that that particular demand was unfair and perverse. Surely whatever information she received should be hers to do with as she liked?

'If you won't give me your word, I will refuse to tell you anything,' Eva declared.

Harriet breathed in deep and swore that she would treat any information that she was given with the utmost discretion. She was surprised when her mother became less tense, and wondered what the heck she was about to be told that could require such a mantle of confidentiality…

Gustav positioned himself carefully behind the sofa and leant over it to rest a supportive hand on his wife's narrow shoulder. Eva unfurled a minute lace handkerchief in one hand and whispered, 'Please remember how young I was when I fell pregnant with you.'

'Only seventeen years old,' Gustav chimed in, unnecessarily.

Faster than the speed of light, Harriet's usually stable nerves had rushed up the scale to over-wrought. She repressed a strong urge to point out that she was well aware of that fact, and had never demonstrated the smallest desire to be judgemental about the circumstances of her birth.

'I should first tell you that the man who got me into trouble…' Eva utilised that outdated phrase with a little *moue* of distaste '…is no longer alive.'

Harriet swallowed hard on a surge of piercing disappointment. It had never really occurred to her before that her birth father might be dead. Yet her conception had taken place nearly thirty years ago, she reminded herself.

'He was a great deal older than I was…more than twice my age,' Eva explained flatly. 'But a very handsome and sophisticated man. He knew exactly how to make an impression on the naive young woman I was in those days.'

The silence spread and spread.

'What happened?' Harriet pressed.

'I worked part-time in the village shop. Sometimes he came in to buy cigarettes, and we would laugh and chat. One day when it was raining he stopped to offer me a lift when I was walking home. I was flattered by his interest,' her mother divulged in a constricted voice, 'and when he asked me to meet him of course it had to be a secret, because my father was very strict. I should have known better—'

As Eva broke off her recitation with the hint of a stifled sob, Gustav swiftly abandoned his stance behind the sofa. Sitting down beside Harriet's slender mother, he grasped her hand in a gesture of encouragement. 'He was the type of man who preyed on young girls. How were you to recognise that?'

'I'm so glad that you understand.' Eva rested enormous blue eyes on her husband and spoke as though they were alone together. 'I'd heard whispers about how he'd treated his wife, but I paid no heed. Although the church didn't recognise his divorce from her, I did think of him as a single man.'

'Naturally you would.' Harriet was feeling rather superlative to the proceedings. She could not comprehend why her mother's husband was taking the leading role in a matter which she felt was really nothing to do with him.

Eva held on fast to Gustav's hand and looked across at her daughter, her eyes unexpectedly hard in her beautiful face. 'There's nothing new or exciting in my story, I'm afraid. Your father said he loved me. He said he wanted to marry me and I believed him. I was hopelessly infatuated with him. When I realised I was pregnant, I went straight to him. I was so innocent I believed that he would be pleased. Do you know what he said?'

Encountering her mother's cold, challenging gaze, Harriet felt most uncomfortable and shook her head. 'I have no idea.'

'He said that the baby I carried was nothing to do with him and suggested that I must have been intimate with other men.'

'Now perhaps you can understand why your mother wanted to forget what happened to her almost thirty years ago.' Gustav exuded the grave disapproval of a man with far from liberal views. 'It may be a cliché, but Eva was seduced with lies and deserted.'

'Horrible…' Harriet wondered if she was being super-sensitive in feeling that her unknown father's sins had somehow become hers.

'I never saw him or heard from him again. I ran away from home and caught the ferry to England.'

'When did he die?'

Eva pursed her lips and then shrugged a delicate shoulder. 'It was quite recent. In fact it was only a few months ago. But please don't get the idea that I deprived you of the chance of knowing him. He wouldn't have admitted you were his. He would have refused to have anything to do with you.'

'If anything, your mother was protecting you from the hurt of that knowledge and rejection,' Gustav opined. 'Regrettably, your father was not a pleasant character.'

Harriet studied the older man with an unease she tried to conceal. 'You seem to know a lot about my background.'

'I have no secrets from Gustav,' Eva proclaimed.

Harriet tried not to think of the secrets that had been kept from her. 'May I ask what my father's name was?'

'Cavaliere.' Eva tilted her chin as she said that name. 'Now perhaps you'll understand why I want your parentage to remain a secret.'

As still as a stone carving, Harriet stared with fixed attention at the older woman. She could not credit that she had heard a name she recognised and, of all names, that particular one which had such deep personal significance. 'Cavaliere?' She had to say it twice before sound actually emerged from her lips. 'Cavaliere?'

'Valente Cavaliere. I dare say you've never heard of him,' Eva contended brightly. 'But in his day he was a famous international tycoon. He married the daughter of the big house outside Ballyflynn and divorced her when she had an affair. She was always ill. He used to visit with his child.'

Gustav was frowning with distaste. 'Cavaliere was a notorious womaniser. In his lifetime he was involved in some very sordid scandals.'

Harriet was so rigid with tension that she was afraid a sudden movement might break her into a host of little pieces. Her mother had referred to Valente Cavaliere's fame in a bright, almost boastful tone that was horribly inappropriate. Tension pounded behind her brow. Unable to think straight, she sat as if she was frozen in time. *Cavaliere.* That name had gone into her mind and there it lodged, like a ship caught in a whirlpool. Round and round the name went inside her buzzing head, and her skin turned clammy, perspiration beading her short upper lip.

'You remind me of your father. You always have,' Eva said almost sweetly. 'You have the same problem with your weight.'

'Valente Cavaliere?' With pronounced care, Harriet vocalised every syllable of that name. 'You're saying that he was the man who got you pregnant….my father?'

'Haven't I just told you so?'

'There's a great deal for Harriet to take in, my dear,' Gustav said quietly.

Harriet parted numb lips. 'Yes. Are you absolutely sure that Valente was my father?'

'Now you're being horribly rude and insulting!
How dare you?' Two spots of feverish pink adorn-
ing her taut cheekbones, Eva rose up in a sudden
movement that took both her companions by surprise and stalked out of the room.

'You're very shocked. Eva can't have understood
that,' Gustav sighed. 'Perhaps you can now see why
your mother asked for discretion. She has a real
dread of her secret being exposed. Cavaliere had an
unsavoury reputation, and she can't face being as-
sociated with him in that way.'

Harriet said nothing. She did not trust her voice
or her temper. It seemed to her that there was no
proper acknowledgement of how she might feel. She
got up to leave.

The older man went through the polite motions of
offering her tea and suggesting she wait for her mother
to join them again. But Harriet sensed that he was
keen to close the chapter and the entire episode. He
wasn't comfortable with emotional scenes. She was
walking out of the hotel with no idea where she was
going when her mobile phone buzzed. It was Boyce.

'I tried to speak to Mum about your long-lost father,' her half-brother began. 'But it went pear-
shaped on me...'

'Did it?' she said dully.

'I had no idea that Gustav was working in the room next door and was able to hear every word I said. It was a bloodbath! Mum started crying, and Gustav came wading in, and I had to drop the subject.'

'Of course you did.'

'To be frank, I don't fancy tackling Mum again. She has Gustav wrapped round her little finger, and I would prefer not to have to tell him to mind his own business. I'm sorry.'

'Don't worry about it. It's really not that important.'

'Are you sure?'

'Totally.' She snatched in a deep, trembling breath. 'Did Mum tell you anything at all?'

'Nothing.'

'Did you mention Rafael to Mum?'

'No. You know what's she like. She didn't want me to go to Ireland, so she wasn't interested in hearing a word about what went on there.'

'That's good. Do me a favour—don't mention Rafael. It's...er...him and me...well, it's over,' she said jerkily.

'Is it? Was the two-week holiday the kiss of death? I have to admit I'm surprised. By the way, my offer to buy Slieveross has been accepted.'

'Oh, that's wonderful news…'

He soon rang off, and she put her phone back in her bag. Until someone passing by stared at her she did not realise that her face was wet with tears, and she worked hard at pulling herself back together. Her thoughts tried to travel straight to the heart of the agony growing at a steady rate inside her. But she was convinced that if she acknowledged that agony it would drive her off the edge of sanity. How could the world be so small? And how could fate be so horribly cruel that what she most valued and needed and loved had become what would ultimately destroy her? Feeling raw emotions starting to pull at her, she shut down that dangerous inner turbulence and made herself think instead in small, simple steps that only stretched a little way ahead.

She did not even need a plan of action. After all, she knew what had to be done, didn't she? Rafael would be waiting for her at his city apartment. She had to break off their relationship. Immediately. There was no need to tell him what her mother had told her. No need whatsoever. News like that he could definitely do without. It wouldn't change anything, or make the facts any more palatable. Valente Cavaliere had blighted his son's life practically from birth. Rafael could live without another score to add to Valente's considerable tally. She could protect

Rafael from knowing the unbearable truth and of having to live with it as she would have to. Wasn't that the best she could do for Rafael? Wasn't that the only way left to show her love?

A manservant let her into the penthouse apartment. It was as contemporary as Rafael's other properties were traditional: an imposing display of soaring ceilings and immense stretches of marble and limestone space. Rafael was talking in French on the phone and did not initially see her. He was propped up against the edge of a glass desk in a relaxed pose. His lean, bronzed profile was etched against the light spilling through the window behind him. He laughed, moving a lean brown hand in an expressive gesture of emphasis. For an instant she thought her heart might crack wide open; for an instant the agony she had suppressed leapt to the fore and threatened to destroy her.

'Harriet…' He framed her name softly and stretched out his hand with the unquestioning assurance of a lover who knew his every attention was welcome.

She lost colour, her fine skin tightening over her delicate bone structure. Numbly she compressed her lips, shook her head in urgent negative, and turned away to walk back out of the room in a silent indication that she would wait for him to finish his call.

Rafael watched her departure with a frown. Harriet had yet to utter a single critical word in relation to her mother or her sister. She had told no lies either. As a result, Rafael had wasted no time in reaching his own conclusions about Harriet's nearest and dearest. In his opinion Eva was shallow and neglectful, and Alice a spoilt and spiteful cheat; neither of them deserved Harriet. Now she had returned from visiting her relatives looking as though she had just staggered clear of a motorway pile-up, and Rafael knew exactly where to bestow the blame. Obviously there would have to be some changes, he reflected grimly. The next time he would be present when Harriet saw her relatives. That way he could ensure that she was treated with all due respect.

Harriet stumbled dizzily into the cloakroom, where she was overcome by nausea. In the aftermath, she leant up against the wall, rested her clammy brow on the cold, unyielding tiles and shivered uncontrollably. She felt like she was living a nightmare she could not wake up from. Please, please let me wake up, she thought wretchedly. For the first time in her life she could find nothing to be positive about, and that sense of black hopelessness was threatening to drown her. Struggling to get a grip on herself again, she freshened up. She examined the hollow blankness in her eyes in the mirror and glanced away. She had to do it and leave the apartment again. One small step at a time. But it was such a huge, terrifying step now she was actually facing it.

'I have something to say…'

Rafael inclined his proud dark head, the charismatic smile she adored tugging at the corners of his expressive mouth.

Her spine as stiff as a poker, Harriet contrived to look in his direction and yet not focus. 'I loved Italy. I had a great time. But I'd like us to just go back to being partners in the yard…and nothing more.'

'OK…' Rafael murmured, without any expression at all.

'I've been really happy, and I don't want you to think that I don't appreciate you.' Harriet hovered in desperate search of words that might remove the risk of her inflicting the smallest sting to his ego.

His lean, strong face was impassive. 'Why would I think that?'

'It's just that I thought you might, and I couldn't bear that,' she muttered frantically, letting her restive hands link in front of her and twist together. 'It's important to me that you know that I was really, really happy with you—'

'Only not right at this moment.'

Harriet blinked, misery choking her thoughts and responses. 'Sorry?'

'It would seem obvious that I am not making you really, *really* happy right now,' Rafael delineated, with cutting clarity of diction.

Harriet shot him a stricken look. 'But that's not your fault. Please don't think that it is. I hope we can still be friends.'

'No,' Rafael asserted, without hesitation.

Her lower lip wobbled and she studied the marble floor until she had a grip on her flailing emotions again. 'It's important to me.'

'Either you're in my life on my terms or out of it.'

'Out,' she mumbled sickly.

'Are you still planning to go straight back to the airport?' Rafael drawled.

'Yes.' She could hardly squeeze the word out.

He lifted the phone. 'My driver will take you.'

And she waited for him to say something else, but he didn't. The silence clawed at her, and she was afraid that she would fill it, that she would let the truth spill out to damage him as much as it had damaged her.

To guard against that risk, Harriet turned on her heel and walked back out into the echoing hall. A minute later the manservant appeared with her suitcase. No other sound disturbed the quiet until the buzzer on the intercom announced the arrival of the limo. She wanted to run back and say… What would she say to Rafael? What was there to say? Despair settling like a lump of concrete inside her, she let the lift carry her down to the basement car park.

CHAPTER TEN

UNA ALMOST FELL off her bicycle in her desperate eagerness to speak to Harriet. 'I think Fergal must be seeing that English tourist who's renting a room at Dooleys!'

Harriet glanced at the teenager's anguished face and hurriedly looked away again. 'So?'

'Don't you know how I feel about him?' Una gasped tearfully. 'I just saw him walking through the village with her!'

With effort, Harriet fought free of her preoccupation. She put an arm round the distressed girl and gave her a comforting hug. 'I'm sorry you're hurt.'

'I'm more than hurt…I love him. I can't stand to see him with someone else!'

Harriet breathed in deep but remained silent.

'Go on—say what you're thinking!' the teenager urged fiercely.

'You're too young for Fergal and I'm afraid that he has a life to get on with,' Harriet murmured, as gently as she could.

'You don't understand how I feel about him,' Una mumbled thickly. 'I told Rafael and he understands—because he didn't say anything like that... *he* just listened!'

Harriet stared a hole in the sack of feed she was opening. She was not as naive as Una, who seemed to have no suspicion of how protective her brother was. She was imagining Rafael listening. Rafael, who was too clever and too controlled to speak and reveal his thoughts. It was ten days since they had parted in London. He had been cold as ice. He had shown nothing, felt nothing. But what had she expected? Wasn't it better that way? On his terms it had been a casual affair that he, at least, would swiftly forget. Why should that hurt her even more? Her eyes were so heavy that she marvelled she didn't fall asleep standing up. But she knew that no matter how tired she was she would be tormented by nightmares. She would also wake up feeling distraught in the middle of the night, and then lie tossing and turning until dawn.

'Don't think I haven't noticed that Rafael and you are acting real weird. I just haven't said anything because Tolly said I shouldn't,' Una added, half under her breath, before she took off to park her bike and help in the morning routine of feeding, mucking out and exercising the horses.

Harriet wanted to chase after the younger woman and ask *how* Rafael had been acting. She craved information about him but would not allow herself to seek it. With every atom of her will-power she was attempting to suppress her longing for him and retrain her thoughts. Incest. The word and the meaning of it haunted Harriet. She had tried so hard to avoid it, but it crept up on her and attacked her countless times a day. A crime against the moral order of society. A crime in law. It was done and could not be undone.

Yet still she found it hard to believe that she had unwittingly made such a disastrous mistake—that in the whole wide world she had had to meet and fall madly in love with the only other man who was as closely related to her as Boyce was. But then it was quite natural for her to be reluctant to believe that, wasn't it? How could she trust her own misgivings about Eva's dramatic revelation? Why had some inner streak of unfamiliar cynicism noted that even at seventeen Eva had not sunk to the level of a Mr Ordinary? Even in a remote Irish village her mother had still managed to catch the eye of a very wealthy and newsworthy man. But then Eva was very beautiful, and why on earth would her mother choose to lie about such a thing?

If Valente Cavaliere had fathered Una, why should he not also have fathered Harriet thirteen years earlier? Rafael had acknowledged that his late father had been a womaniser without any sense of conscience or responsibility. Harriet had looked for pictures of Valente on the Internet and had sought in vain to find some point of similarity between her supposed father and herself. Rafael and Una had inherited Valente's height and colouring and his bone structure, whereas she bore not the slightest physical resemblance to the man. Yet that only meant that she had inherited her physical characteristics from the maternal side of the family.

Was it possible that on some deep level she had felt a strong affinity with both Rafael and Una right from the start because of the very existence of that blood relationship? That was a possibility she shrank from.

That evening she was running a bath when she heard the helicopter passing overhead. Before she could stop herself, she had run through to the back bedroom to watch the helicopter drop down over the trees and disappear from view as it went into land. Dressed in clean jodhpurs and a faded green shirt, she was feeding Samson and Peanut at the back door when she looked up and stilled in surprise. Rafael was out by the sand paddock beyond the stables, watching Fergal put Tailwind through his paces.

She feasted her attention on him, helpless before her overpowering need to stare. There was an aching familiarity now to his lean, dark profile and tall, powerful physique. But the instant she experienced that magnetic pull she was ashamed of herself, and she dredged her attention guiltily from him again. She no longer knew how to behave around him. Just ten days earlier she would have felt free to walk over and join the two men. Now she was constrained by a whole host of concerns and she went back indoors. Half an hour passed slowly and painfully before she heard a car engine start and a car move off into the distance. He was gone again, she reflected just as a knock sounded on the front door.

Her heart in her mouth, she answered it.

Rafael studied her with dark as midnight eyes full of keen enquiry. 'How are you?'

'I'm great,' she said weakly.

She was lying, Rafael decided: she looked as though she wasn't sleeping or eating properly. He had no idea what was going on, but he had every intention of getting to the bottom of the mystery.

'May I come in?'

Harriet hesitated, and then moved back to let him enter the cottage.

'Why didn't you warn me that my sister was infatuated with Fergal Gibson?'

Unprepared for that grimly voiced question,
Harriet frowned in dismay.

'Didn't it occur to you that she might be at risk?'

'Not with Fergal, no. He's decent and sensible, and
he's well aware of what age she is. He does nothing
to encourage her,' Harriet countered tautly. 'I hate to
say it, but he's probably at more risk from Una. '

Taken aback by that frank opinion, Rafael almost
laughed out loud. 'I get the picture. Your honesty on
that point is appreciated.'

'I just meant that she can be very determined.
But I don't think you need to worry. I gather Fergal's
dating some tourist at the moment.'

'Whitewash. Fergal is not as indifferent to my
sister as I would like him to be.'

'He's fond of Una…yes…'

'He may not even know it, but he's hooked. It's
a dangerous situation and I'll deal with it.' Rafael
leant back against the solid oak table with indolent
cool. 'Next on the agenda…us.'

Harriet stiffened. 'That's over.'

'But what I would like to know is…*why*?'

An electric silence fell. Her mind was blank. It
was the most simple question, and hardly unpredictable, and yet she could not think of an answer.

'There's no one else, is there?'

'No…' The admission had escaped her before she could think better of it.

'Then explain what happened with your sister and your mother.'

She froze. 'What do you mean?'

'When we flew back from Italy everything was fine. But then you went visiting for a few hours and came back the colour of a ghost, and suddenly all bets were off.'

'No, it wasn't like that—'

'It was, and I want to know what changed. Did someone warn you off me? Tell tales that made your blood run cold?' Rafael had his brilliant dark golden eyes pinned to her with penetrating force. 'I'm trying to understand what the problem is.'

'I didn't say there was a problem—'

'But there *is*… I've spent the last ten days without you. That's a problem.'

That statement shook Harriet. 'Is it?'

His dense lashes lowered over his intent gaze. 'The ten lonely nights were equally painful.'

Beneath his scrutiny, Harriet lost colour, her fine facial bones tightening as she spun away from him, saying, 'Don't!'

'Don't what? This is new to me, *a mhilis*. I haven't been in this position before. Usually I do the dumping. Full marks for taking me by surprise. Very few people have ever managed to do that to me.'

'Are you saying nobody ever dumped you before?' Suddenly, ridiculously, Harriet wanted to wrap her arms round him and cry.

'All I want is an explanation. What went wrong? I'm an alpha-male high achiever. If you tell me why, I will never mention it again.'

Her hands knotted into fists as she fought the tears burning the back of her eyes. 'It's not that simple—'

'It *is* that simple. Why do women always make things more complicated?'

The dark knowledge dammed up inside her weighted her down. 'You don't know everything… you wouldn't even want to know…'

Rafael picked up on that declaration straight away. 'What wouldn't I *want* to know?'

Too late she recognised her mistake. 'It was just a figure of speech.'

His hands came down on her rigid shoulders and slowly, carefully, turned her back round to face him. 'No, don't lie to me. Or, should I say, don't keep on lying to me. I respect your truthfulness. But from the minute you entered my London apartment I saw that you were hiding something from me.'

Harriet felt cornered, even though he had been

careful to drop his hands and step back from her again. 'No!'

Stunning dark golden eyes flared down into hers. 'Whatever it is, I need to know. Because *not* knowing is driving me crazy!'

Harriet sped back to the door and dragged it open. 'I think you should leave—'

'And you said you wanted to be friends?'

She didn't trust herself to look at him. 'I'll talk to you about Una or the yard, but not about anything more personal.'

Rafael strolled out through the door at his leisure. 'I won't quit until you tell me.'

'Just leave it,' she muttered in a feverish plea, half under her breath. 'Don't push me on this.'

She had not expected Rafael to tackle her and demand an explanation. She had not been prepared for him to drop his façade of fabled cool and impassivity to stage so open a confrontation. The only woman ever to dump him. A choked sob was wrenched from her and she rolled up in a tight ball, as if she was trying to contain her grief. The hot tears slid down her face in silence.

When she had believed that he was essentially indifferent to her she had been able to tell herself that she was only precipitating an ending that would have occurred anyway. She had consoled herself with the belief that their affair had had no future—that, in effect, she had lost nothing—for his interest would inevitably have waned before many more weeks had passed. But now Rafael had approached her, ten days after she'd walked out of his life, and asked her to tell him where things had gone wrong. He wasn't demonstrating indifference. He was reserved and he trusted few people. He was also very proud. Yet he had still been prepared to make that request, and ironically that made her feel more wretched than ever.

Rafael listened to Albert bring in the dawn on his new and unique middle-of-the-night timescale. It bothered him that for the first time he did not feel like strangling the rooster in mid flow. It bothered him that he had been lying awake for hours and that he had skipped dinner the night before. The uneasy rocking of his previously well-ordered world disturbed him.

He was a logical man. Illogical behaviour naturally unsettled him. Some men said women were illogical. But Rafael had from the outset of his acquaintance with Harriet appreciated her innate common sense. She had no inclination to make mountains out of molehills. At the *fattoria* she had glowed with contentment and happiness. Even when she had slept there had been a hint of a smile on her ripe mouth. Her good-natured tolerance had smoothed the edges off every tiny irritation. She drew him like an oasis of peace in a war zone.

Why, then, did such a woman suddenly begin acting out of character? Why would she suddenly finish a very satisfying affair? And contrive to look inconsolable at the same time? The more he devoted his powerful intellect to that conundrum the more impatient he became to get to the truth of the matter. Then he would be content, he reflected with confidence. Once she had given him a proper explanation he would be satisfied and he would put the matter behind him.

Harriet walked down through the ancient oak woods soon after six that morning, as she did most days. Usually she rode, but Snowball had been off-colour with a mild viral infection for a few days and the vet had recommended complete rest. She could have taken Missy out instead, since she had enjoyed exercising the young lively mare. But Una now rode Missy most days, and Harriet no longer liked to borrow her.

She always took a break at the heart of the wood, where the oak and the ash and the hawthorn grew. She would remember her first visit to the tranquil green bower with Rafael. Before she continued on to the beach she would shut her eyes tight and wish for happiness, as if she was still a child who believed in magical places and fairy spells.

Pale golden sand stretched in an unbroken arc all the way from the rocks at the lower end of the strand to the distant headland. On this particular day the sky was a moody almost purplish grey and the breeze was stiff. Head bent, she trudged down through the dunes.

'Harriet…'

Her head flew up, copper hair flaming back across her pale brow and a flash of dismay in her very blue eyes.

'How could you possibly not have seen me?' Rafael looked down at her from the back of his big black gelding. 'Why aren't you riding Missy?'

'Una adores her…'

He quirked a questioning brow and she understood his meaning completely.

'She wouldn't dream of commenting if I made equal use of Missy. But I remember how I felt about my first horse, and I think it's nice for Una to have her all to herself.'

Rafael winced. 'I can't believe that I didn't even think of buying her a horse of her own!'

Comfortable with the conversation, Harriet was

already losing her pronounced tension in his presence. 'Why should you have? As I recall, only a couple of months back you didn't know how fond Una was of horses.'

In a fluid movement he slid down off the gelding's back. His eyes sought hers and her mouth ran dry.

'I love looking at the flowers that grow down here,' she confided in a rush, nudging a pink lilac striped trumpet with her toe. 'This is so pretty.'

'That's bindweed…'

The dark, deep timbre of his accented drawl wrapped round her like a prison chain. She walked over the cushioned tufts of thrift and down on to the flat sand that bore the imprint of the gelding's hooves.

'When my mother was well enough she would walk along the beach with me, naming the wild flowers and the shells. Sea holly and samphire, scallops and whelks,' Rafael rhymed evenly. 'I still remember the names.'

Her throat was tight, as if a lump was lodged at the foot of it. 'Friends?'

'No way,' Rafael fielded. 'I'm only trying to persuade that you don't need to jump every time I come within six feet of you. You're not in any danger. In these politically correct times only a stupid man would risk physical contact without clear signs of encouragement.'

Involuntarily she clashed with a scorching gaze that challenged her. Painful colour washed up over her fair complexion.

'But the oddest thing is that you're putting out very mixed signals,' Rafael confided silkily.

'Please don't say that!' Harriet retreated from him with a negative shake of her head that denied that contention, her nerves leaping like jumping beans. 'You're mistaken.'

'If I was a very polite guy, I would agree that I was mistaken, but I won't lie to you. In fact I would go so far as to say that you are doing enough lying for both of us. Be straight with me.'

'Stop this now…just leave it alone!' Harriet spun away from him. 'I can't understand why you're keeping on at me!'

'Can't you?' Rafael fell into step beside her. 'Think of those long lazy evenings in Umbria when we talked over dinner and were still talking at dawn. Think of the fact that we never had a single argument—'

'Oh, yes, we did—'

'But only over complete trivialities. Remember when I brought you fresh cherries from the orchard and you said you had never been so happy.'

'The fact you were always feeding me was very appealing to a woman who used to live on an almost permanent diet. The wine helped too,' she put in shakily, memories bombarding her—memories she had refused to take out and examine on the grounds that it would be wrong to revel in what should never, ever have been allowed to happen between them in the first place.

'It wasn't the wine, it was the company. I didn't get bored with you either.'

Harriet laughed, but the sound had an almost hysterical edge, and she was walking so incredibly fast that her calves were aching. She had reached the rocks at the end of the strand and there was nowhere else to go. She spun round to face him, angry at the pressure he was putting on her and torn apart by the most bitter sense of injustice. 'What do you want me to say to you?'

'I only want to know what really happened that day.'

'*Only!*' she echoed hollowly.

Rafael gazed down at her, the entire force of his will bent on persuading her to speak. 'I deserve the truth.'

'Nobody deserves the truth I got!' Harriet almost yelled at him in her frustration, lack of sleep and misery combining to devastate her self-discipline.

Rafael kept up the pressure. 'Why? What truth was that?'

'That your father was my father as well!' Having been betrayed into that admission, Harriet went limp, her eyes blank with shock, for she had reached breaking point without realising it. The forbidden words had flowed from her almost without her volition.

Rafael continued to study her with dark-as-night eyes, only the very stillness of his bronzed features revealing that he had heard what she had said. 'What kind of nonsense is that?'

Her breath feathered in her throat. 'I only wish it were…'

'It's a disgusting idea!' Rafael reached down and closed both his hands squarely over hers. 'Of course it is nonsense. How could it be anything else?'

Stress had momentarily drained her of energy and resolve. Her fingers flexed weakly in his. 'That day I went to see my mother. She told me that Valente Cavaliere was my father.'

'Your mother…?'

'She has no idea that you live here, or that I know you or had got involved with you. In fact I don't even know if she's aware you exist. I've been asking her for quite a while to tell me who my father was…and finally she did, and she named Valente.'

'It's a filthy suggestion…' His hands almost crushed hers, and with a muttered apology he released her fingers. 'It is impossible.'

'Is it?' Harriet was clinging to his every word,

hypnotised by every fleeting expression that crossed his lean darkly handsome face. 'Is it impossible?'

'It must be… For my sanity, it must be impossible.' He swore vehemently. 'Without prejudice, I can tell you that it is an unlikely possibility. My mother was alive when you were conceived. I don't think Valente even came to Ireland during those years. He had nothing to do with my mother after the divorce. His staff brought me on my visits here—'

'But why would my mother lie now, when she has kept my father's identity a secret for almost thirty years?'

The healthy bronze of his skin was steadily retreating, to leave him ashen pale. But his eyes blazed. 'You weren't going to tell me.'

'I *shouldn't* have told you—'

'Why? Am I a little child to be protected?' Rafael raked back at her in raw condemnation, and it shook her because it was the first time she had seen him openly betray anger.

'No. But what is the point in both of us feeling as we do now?' Harriet whispered, in an agony of regret that she had failed to withstand his pressure. 'We can't change anything.'

Rafael stared down at her with fulminating intensity and then, without warning, he looked away from her again. He sucked in a stark, ragged breath. His stubborn jawline clenched hard; his beautifully moulded mouth flattened into a grim line. He was in severe shock. She recognised that. She could see him battening down the hatches and holding back on saying anything. She wanted to reach out and hold him, and knew she could not. In every fibre of her being she felt the pain that she had caused by failing to keep silent—and she despised her own weakness. He was as appalled and as utterly unprepared for that genetic bombshell as she had been.

'I have to deal with this…' Rafael breathed in a roughened undertone.

Jerkily she nodded, her eyes filled with tears, her hands clenched so tightly in on themselves that her fingers were numb. How could she have told him when there was no need for him to know?

'Are you OK?'

Again she jerked her head.

'Of course you're not.' He sprang back into the saddle and she swung away to gaze out to sea at the breakers rolling in, for she did not trust herself to watch him ride back across the sand.

His half-sister. Rafael asked himself how he could deal with the unimaginable. He had never allowed himself to hate Valente. Hatred, like most uncontrolled emotion, was anathema to Rafael. He had despised Valente, and from adulthood on had triumphed over his father with superior intellect and self-discipline. But it seemed that Valente might have the last laugh after all. For his father was dead and untouchable and the past was unalterable. Rafael had to ask himself why Harriet's mother would choose to tell such a lie after so many years. He discovered that he could not come up with one good reason.

The bottom line was simple: he could not have Harriet. He should never have had anything to do with Harriet, and he would never be able to be with Harriet again. Harriet was forbidden fruit. She could be his business partner only. How often would he see her in a business line? As a friend? Could he do the friend angle? If he had been the sort of guy who fell in love Harriet would have been the one, he acknowledged bleakly. He was so lucky he didn't do love. At that point he went down to the cellar and dug out a bottle of brandy. He felt seriously weird, and thinking was making him feel worse. He decided that he would feel much better when he had drunk enough to blot out all rational thought. It was the first and last decision he made for some time.

Tolly called on Harriet that evening. He wasted no time in getting to the point of what had etched the furrows deep in his brow. 'Rafael's drinking and he's a man who doesn't drink. Is there something I should be knowing?'

Harriet went white and bent her head. 'No.'

'But it's all off between you…?'

'Yes.'

'And obviously you're both very happy about that.'

'We have no choice,' she said chokily, for she could not bear the idea that Rafael was alone and upset.

'There's always a choice.'

'No. Sometimes it's made for you and it's very cruel!' she bit out, and, excusing herself, fled into the office to hide her distress.

On the third day Albert the rooster wakened Rafael with a more than usually loud chorus. Rafael groaned. The previous forty-eight hours were a blur of nightmares and desolation. Enough was enough. He hauled himself out of bed and into the shower. Harriet. The thought of her hit him like a punch in the gut. Strong black coffee awaited him when he returned to the bedroom. Tolly was always one step in advance, he thought ruefully, grimacing at the ache in his head.

'Breakfast…all your favourites,' the old man promised him from the back of the hall, treading softly, as though he knew that only fierce will-power was keeping Rafael from resorting back to the fleeting oblivion offered by alcohol.

Rafael stared out at the beautiful timeless view that now had the folly as a central focus. He wondered what Harriet was doing. He pushed away his plate, all appetite fading. 'After my parents divorced, how often did Valente visit Flynn Court?'

Tolly gave him a bemused look. 'He didn't.'

'I know I have no memory of him visiting. But perhaps he came to the village and stayed somewhere else?'

'Why would he have? As far as I know your father didn't set foot in Ireland again until months after your mother was buried. I remember that first visit well,' Joseph recalled with quiet assurance. 'It was the talk of the village. He had a special memorial mass said for your mother at St Patrick's. He had the house blessed. He was a superstitious man, and his conscience made him nervous. He came that once, and he was too uneasy to stay even one night below this roof. It was years more before he stayed again.'

'How good is your memory?' Rafael enquired.

'As good as yours—perhaps even better.'

Dark eyes flashing with renewed energy, Rafael drew his plate back and began to eat. The old man's memory tallied with what he himself had always believed to be fact. He could check it out. He could ask questions. But first and foremost he could bite the bullet and organise DNA tests. Harriet's mother might not have lied, but there was a chance that she could be mistaken, wasn't there? She would not be the first woman to make a false assumption.

'Were there any rumours linking Valente to any woman apart from Una's mother?' Rafael enquired as an afterthought.

Tolly's shrewd gaze narrowed. 'None that I ever heard.'

Rafael drove down to the little church on the out-skirts of the village. Although he had made liberal contributions to the restoration fund, he had not set foot there since his mother's funeral, more than twenty years earlier. He went inside. He breathed in deep and slow and moved forward. He reached for a candle, lit it, and said a prayer to St Jude, patron saint of impossible causes. He needed a heavy-duty saint up to a major challenge.

'Rafael…' Father Kearney had come to a startled halt just inside the entrance. The little priest was striving to conceal his shock at finding the most stubborn black sheep in the parish on holy ground.

Harriet was discussing holistic schooling methods with a client when Rafael strolled into the stable yard. Inclining his handsome dark head in polite acknowledgement, he went into the office to wait for her.

Her client, the sensible mother of three little girls, expelled an ecstatic sigh and shot Harriet a comical grin of apology. 'He looks just like a movie star. I know it's rude to stare, but I always do.'

Harriet walked slowly past the loose boxes. Rafael made her want to stare as well. In Italy, every morning that she had wakened beside him she had looked at him with fresh appreciation. But now looking at Rafael with pleasure was yet another prohibited act. That admission made her feel more wretched than ever. Peanut pelted out of the office and across the cobbles in ecstatic pursuit of her ball. She was touched that Rafael had given way to the pig, and her eyes prickled with stupid tears.

Rafael straightened as she walked in. 'OK…I want you to listen. I'm still not convinced we're blood relations. The facts don't tally enough to satisfy me yet—'

'But—'

'Exactly what did your mother tell you?'

Harriet shared the few facts that she had been told.

'Valente didn't smoke. It may well be the only vice he didn't have,' Rafael remarked drily. 'And if he had been a smoker he would have sent his chauffeur to buy the cigarettes. He never did anything for himself that he could pay an employee to do for him.'

Harriet frowned uncomfortably. 'Those are only small points.'

Level dark golden eyes rested on her. 'I accept that. But we need to know if he was your father, and we need to know beyond all possible doubt. The only way of achieving that is by utilising DNA testing.'

'No...I've spent two weeks struggling to come to terms with this, and chasing rainbows at this stage is pointless,' she argued heavily. 'I don't like what my mother told me, but I'm not going to fight it. I'm accepting it.'

'I don't have an accepting attitude to very bad news. It will take DNA tests to convince me.' Rafael banded an arm round her before she could guess his intention, and for an instant their reflections twinned in the age-spotted glass of the mirror above the fireplace. 'Looks-wise, we could not be more different. I know that it's possible for siblings to be dissimilar, but it's rarely so pronounced. I'm into science, not chasing rainbows.'

Harriet tore her attention from the mirror. 'I prefer just to close the book on what we've found out and live with it.'

'But I require scientific confirmation. Valente left a sample of his DNA in store. Don't laugh…my father hoped that one day he would be cloned. I will be DNA-tested too. It's only a saliva swab. You may not want to take the test, but for my sake you must. Your identity should be fully established. After all, if you're Valente's kid too, your days of travelling economy class are over for ever.'

Harriet took an angry step back from him. 'Don't you dare say that!' she told him in fierce repudiation. 'I don't want anything—least of all money. That's the very last thing I'd be interested in. If I'd realised what my stupid questions were likely to dig up, I'd have happily lived a lifetime without knowing what I know now!'

'Do you think that I feel any different? 'The bleakness in his lustrous dark gaze swallowed her anger alive and pierced her deep.

Eaten alive by guilt, Harriet twisted away. 'I'm so sorry…I should never have told you.'

'You're the only person I've ever met who thinks that she needs to protect me.' Rafael vented a roughened laugh. 'I'm not at all breakable.'

Harriet compressed her lips and tactfully passed no comment. But, after all, *she* wasn't the one who had spent three days on an alcoholic binge! Under pressure, Tolly had kept her informed, and she had worried day and night about Rafael. She had been desperate to go to him and offer support, but the unhappy fact was that she had to be the last person he needed in such a role. Yet she was painfully aware that just seeing Rafael in any capacity lifted her spirits and made the day a little more bearable. In turn that made her feel guilty and ashamed and horribly weak.

'Will you agree to the tests?'

'Yes…if it makes you happier,' she conceded.

'Excellent. It's organised for four this afternoon at the Court.'

Her eyes widened. *'Today?'*

'I want the testing done quickly and discreetly. The results will take a few days to come back.'

The tests were done within minutes of her arrival at the Court. The bespectacled chemist who performed the simple procedure behaved as though there was nothing out of the ordinary about it. Rafael accompanied Harriet back out to her car. 'Do you ever wear the brooch I gave you?'

Harriet swallowed hard. 'I look at it.'

'However the tests go, I'd like to see you wearing it.'

Harriet bent her head to hide the shimmer of tears in her strained gaze. 'OK.'

She had complete faith in the fact that the tests

would fully confirm her mother's claim. What would happen when Rafael was forced to accept the inevitable? Would he start trying to think of her as a half-sister? Or would he distance himself? When she found herself thinking that she was lucky that he owned fifty per cent of the livery yard, she knew she had sunk low indeed.

The following morning, Fergal called in to see her at breakfast time. Accepting the mug of tea that she automatically offered, he gave her a huge grin. 'Rafael Flynn has offered me a job on his stud farm. Assistant trainer, no less… Well, I'll be one of four, but it's a fantastic opportunity!'

Harriet was amazed. 'I had no idea you were looking for a job.'

'I wasn't.' Fergal laughed, his excitement making her want to smile too. 'But, sure, working with the horses is what I always dreamt of doing. When Mr Flynn came to watch me schooling Tailwind last week I thought he was interested in the gelding. Instead he was considering me for the vacancy he had!'

'So you'll be moving to Kildare. Will your mother mind very much?'

'She knows my heart isn't in Dooleys. She'll keep up the post office, but my uncle will hire a bar manager. I'll be earning good money, and sharing a flat at the stud, so I'll be able to send cash home to help out,' the young blond man said earnestly.

'I'm really happy for you.'

'The one drawback is that I have to leave almost immediately. I've made arrangements to sell my horses. It wouldn't make sense to try and keep them.'

'When do you have to go?'

'Day after tomorrow. I won't get the chance to say goodbye to Una, so I was hoping you would pass on my good wishes and stuff,' Fergal said gruffly, studying his oversized feet. 'I'm hoping to get home once a month.'

'Be sure to come and tell me how you're getting on.'

Harriet was appalled at how ruthlessly efficient Rafael was at attaining his own ends. He had said he would deal with his sister's infatuation with Fergal and he had not been joking. Una and Philomena had just gone off on a three-day trip to Dublin, which had been a gift from Rafael. Una would come home to Ballyflynn and Fergal would already have gone to live on the other side of the country. The teenager would be shattered by that development.

Harriet invited Tolly over for lunch the next day. He was always bringing her fresh vegetables and fruit, not to mention flowers and cakes, and she loved having his company. Indeed, if her mother's revela-

tion had not been of such a sensitive nature she would
have confided in Tolly. The doorbell went when they
had finished eating and were discussing possible sites
for the vegetable patch she had planned for the au-
tumn.

'I only want to grow easy things to start with…
lettuce, peas…' she was saying to Tolly as she
opened the front door.

'I would've phoned, but I was afraid that you
would put me off. I really do need to talk to you,'
Luke stated flatly.

Harriet was stunned into silence by the sight of
her onetime fiancé.

Tolly lodged in the kitchen doorway. 'If you have
company, I'll nip down to the kitchen garden to get
in a couple of hours before the sun goes in.' He
walked forward to extend his hand to the younger
man. 'I'm Harriet's neighbour—Joseph Tolly.'

'Luke Jarvis.'

The old man's welcoming smile died round the
edges, and he took his leave with clear reluctance.

Harriet turned back to Luke to say, 'What on earth
are you doing here?'

'Alice and I are finished.'

Harriet studied him, looking in vain for the man
she had once loved. He was not as tall as she recalled, and he was a touch heavy round the jowls.

She no longer found him attractive. Eight years, she thought with regret. Eight years that had been wasted in many ways—for she had never loved Luke as she loved Rafael. That undeniable fact made her feel oddly guilty, and a touch less ready to condemn Luke for his infidelity. But she could have borne his betrayal a good deal better had he strayed with someone other than her own sister.

'You've made quite a mess of my family circle,' she told him flatly.

'I do owe you an explanation.'

'You didn't feel you owed me one when it mattered, so don't waste your breath now.'

Stubbornly determined not to be deflected from his purpose, Luke stood his ground. 'I still have a lot of feelings for you, Harriet. In fact I don't think I ever stopped loving you. Alice was the biggest mistake of my life. I'm here to ask you to give me a second chance.'

Harriet surveyed him with incredulous eyes. 'Even *you* can't imagine I'd consider taking you back after you slept with my sister! Or accept a nonsensical claim that you still loved me while you were planning to marry her!'

'You and I were meant to be together for ever…but it got too comfortable. I didn't want to marry Alice, but once I'd lost you I couldn't face the truth that your sister and I were a disaster together. I should have married you a couple of years ago. It's my fault that we stood still and got stale.'

'We didn't have the passion anyway.'

'I would much rather have a woman with a brain and a work ethic,' Luke argued. 'Alice and I were only good for an affair, and it was never meant to be anything more. What I had with her wasn't real…it was a fantasy.'

'Maybe so, but I'm still not interested. I found my fantasy with someone else…and it *was* real—very real—I assure you.' Her throat thickened as she made that declaration, but she was no longer ashamed of it. It might not be possible for her to be with Rafael any more, but with him she had learned what it was to really love. Nobody could ever take the knowledge of the joy and fulfilment she had briefly found away from her.

Luke frowned. 'You've always loved *me,* Harriet. I may not offer fantasy, but we make a very good team—'

'I can't believe you think that I still might care about you…I *don't*!' Harriet declared in exasperation.

'My firm is opening a branch in New York and I'm transferring there to make a fresh start. We could go together.' His mouth tightened. 'We could even get married before we go.'

Harriet almost burst out laughing when he offered that ultimate sacrifice. Instead she opened the door again on the summer sunshine. 'Go home, Luke,' she advised ruefully, embarrassed for him. 'Don't be so lazy that you can't be bothered looking for a new woman!'

'But you were so much a part of my life…it doesn't feel right without you!' he ground out accusingly.

Harriet saw that he did still have some genuine feelings for her, but he had caused too much pain and too much damage for her to pity him.

When he was gone she went out to the barn to start going through the crates of miscellaneous items that had been removed from the old sheds before they were demolished. While she sorted the stuff out into various piles she put on the radio for company.

When the music went off suddenly, her ears rang in the silence.

'Harriet…'

She whirled round: Rafael was straightening, his hand dropping back from the radio. The last word in designer elegance, his pale grey silk business suit looked incongruous in the dusty untidy confines of the barn.

'I'm filthy,' she mumbled.

'So…' Stunning dark golden eyes glittered over her and then veiled. 'Your ex visited you.'

Harriet blinked. 'Does Tolly tell you everything?'

'I was halfway to the airport when he unrolled that one.'

'Halfway to the airport?'

'Tolly phoned me to tell me. I had to turn back. What did Luke want?'

She rubbed grimy hands down over the thighs of her jodhpurs. 'You'll never believe it…he wanted me back.'

'I believe it,' Rafael breathed very quietly.

'Poor Alice,' she sighed.

Rafael took a sudden step closer and then froze to the spot, as if someone had turned a shotgun on him. 'Are you taking him back?'

Harriet studied him in disbelief. 'Do I look that stupid and desperate?'

Rafael spread lean brown hands in a soothing gesture that was less expansive than usual. His behaviour was very low key for him, she thought, her brow furrowing. She watched him breathe in, very slow and very deep.

'I need to make that flight or my next deal is toast,' he shared, not quite steadily.

'You were halfway to the airport and you came back just to ask me about Luke?'

Rafael jerked his handsome dark head in mute acknowledgement.

'But…but why?'

Rafael shrugged and shifted fluid hands, as if he had no idea either. 'I have to go,' he said, and thirty seconds later he had gone and she was wondering if she had actually dreamt up the entire episode.

Thirty-six hours later Harriet was checking the fencing on a field boundary when she saw Tolly waving frantically at her from the gate. His car was parked at an angle behind him with the engine still running. Thinking that something bad must have happened, she hurried over to him, only to be handed a phone.

'Rafael…he says it's urgent!' the old man told her anxiously.

'What are you doing out without your mobile?' Rafael demanded.

'I forgot to bring it with me this morning. What's wrong?'

'I got the results. You're not my half-sister.'

'I'm not your half-sister…' Harriet repeated, dry-mouthed, feeling the blood drain from her face as shock, wild hope and an equally wild fear of being hurt again all coalesced into overload and destroyed her ability to reason.

'We're not related—except in so far as we are both human.'

'Not related... But are you sure?' she prompted shakily. 'Could the lab have made a mistake?'

'Take a deep breath and listen to me,' Rafael advised her with measured care. 'The tests were conclusive. You are not my sister. We do not have the same father. I even had my own DNA matched to Valente's to check that I am his son...OK? There is no margin for error in these results.'

Her mind was swirling. Her legs were hollow. She felt weak as a kitten. 'OK.'

'We'll have to talk to your mother about this result.'

Her eyes flew wide, for she had not yet managed to think that far ahead. 'Will we? But Eva's in Paris!'

'I'll get a flight organised for you. We'll meet in Paris tomorrow morning. Call your mother to let her know that you're coming, and that you're bringing someone you would like her to meet.'

'I can't believe what you've told me yet,' she whispered, suddenly finding her eyes filled with tears.

'You will. It's over. We'll never have to think about this nightmare again.'

When he rang off, that assurance kept on ringing in her ears: *It's over. We'll never have to think of this nightmare again.* She squeezed her eyes tight shut, impervious to the reality that Tolly was still lodged on the other side of the gate, much as if he had taken root there. Was Rafael letting her know that their relationship was still dead in the water? And, if he was, how could she blame him? What casual affair could survive such a misapprehension?

'Harriet…' The old man's face was deeply creased with dismay and concern. 'I didn't intend to listen, but I heard what you said to Rafael. Is that what's been wrong between the two of you? Is it possible that you picked up the daft idea that you might somehow be brother and sister?'

Harriet reddened as she realised how indiscreet she had been. She was grateful that Tolly could be trusted to keep that devastating misconception to himself. 'Yes, we did have cause to think that. But we had DNA tests done and thankfully… Well, it was nothing but the daft idea you just called it.'

'But where did you get that idea from?'

Harriet winced. 'Mum.'

'Will you come back to my house with me? I think it's time we had a chat about something that's been playing on my mind.'

She stole a worried glance at his troubled expression. When she had first met Joseph Tolly she had admitted that she was keen to find out who her father was. Now she was remembering her suspicion that the older man might know more about her background than he was comfortable admitting.

Tolly sat her down at the scrubbed table. 'I may

know who your father is. I feel I have to speak up, but I don't feel right doing it.'

'I'd be grateful for anything that you can tell me.'

'Your mother used to work weekends in the village shop. The family who owned it were the most prosperous for miles around. Their daughter was called Sheila. She was a bit older than your mother, but the two girls were very friendly. Sheila was engaged to my son Robert at seventeen, and married him a year later, when he was twenty-one. Eva was one of their bridesmaids.'

Sheila and Robert Tolly. All Harriet could think about was Sheila's hostility towards her and Eva. Tolly reached into a drawer and pulled out an old-fashioned photograph album.

'There's the three of them together.'

Her slim body tense, Harriet examined the colour picture of his son's wedding. Eva looked like a delicate blonde angel in an ugly pink satin frock. Her smile struck her daughter as false. Sheila looked nervous and happy, and back then Robert Tolly had been a surprisingly handsome groom.

'The bridal couple were very young—*too* young,' Tolly breathed heavily. 'My son has always denied that he was unfaithful to Sheila with your mother. He won't admit that anything happened. He won't even discuss it. I only have facts to offer you. No proof of anything, though.'

Harriet was hanging on his every word. 'Go on…'

'Sheila lost a baby a few months after the wedding. Eva stopped working at the shop very suddenly, and Sheila started spreading unpleasant rumours about your mother's morals to anyone who would listen. Much later I heard talk that Robert had been seen out with Eva in his car around that time. But it's only gossip,' he stressed carefully. 'A little while later your mother left Ballyflynn.'

'And you believe that your son may be my father?'

Tolly turned several pages in the album to show her another photograph. 'This is my late wife, Muriel. You're the very picture of her…and your hair is the same colour. But that's not a lot to go on, is it?'

The cheerful woman in the photo had died long before Harriet was even born but Harriet could see the resemblance and she smiled through her own tears to reach for Tolly's hand. 'I would be more than happy to settle for a grandfather in place of a father.'

'If only I had known you were getting tests done with Rafael, we might have found out for sure. Robert wouldn't have co-operated, but I certainly would,' Tolly asserted eagerly.

'Why didn't you speak up before now?'

'If your own mother didn't want to tell you, and my son was equally keen to remain silent, it didn't seem my place to interfere.' He shook his white head. 'Try not to think too badly of Robert. He and Sheila have had their problems and disappointments. Sheila never had another child, and that was a great cause of sorrow to her. If you are Robert's daughter, it would explain why my daughter-in-law felt the need to be so rude about your mother that day in the gift shop…Yes, Father Kearney mentioned it to me.'

Harriet winced with sympathy. 'Oh, dear…what a tangled web.' She sighed. 'When did you find out that I existed?'

'Kathleen told me a couple of years after you were born. She believed, like me, that Robert had been responsible, but there was no way of knowing for sure. Eva made it clear to your cousin that she didn't want contact with anyone in Ballyflynn. When I discovered you were coming here to live I was delighted, because I was hoping to get the chance to know you.'

A happy smile illuminated Harriet's face. 'I bet you were responsible for the flowers and the fire that greeted me the day I arrived at the cottage.'

'I wanted you to feel welcome. I was really hoping you would stay for good.'

Harriet stood up and gave him a hug. 'Thank you for being there for me ever since I arrived.'

She thought of phoning Rafael, to share what Tolly had revealed, but lacked the confidence to contact him. She would tell him when she reached Paris. She had a shower and fussed over her hair.

She was packing an overnight bag and agonising over what to wear when Una stumbled in and wailed in despair, 'Fergal's gone!'

Harriet sat her down and pointed out that Fergal would visit the stables occasionally and that she would see him then.

'Hardly ever, though,' the teenager gasped, stricken. 'I hate my brother!'

'Why? He's given Fergal a great chance—'

'How?'

'Fergal's a really nice guy, and hugely popular. I imagine he'll be equally popular on the stud farm and I bet he does really well there. Rafael will notice that. Here, Fergal was working as a barman, and I don't think that would have struck much of a note with your brother—'

'You're right.' Her attention fully engaged by Harriet's more optimistic outlook on the situation, Una swallowed back a sob and scrabbled for a tissue. 'Rafael wouldn't have been impressed by that at all.'

'This way Fergal gets to prove himself *and* do what he loves—'

'And meet some other girl!'

'That could happen here too,' Harriet pointed out.

Una looked tragic. 'I suppose it could.'

'But he's only twenty-two…I doubt if he'll go rushing into anything too heavy for a while yet.' Harriet watched the forlorn brunette pick up strength from that forecast.

'I love Fergal so much…' Una wiped her streaming eyes dry. 'I'd lock him up in a tower if I could.'

Harriet knew the feeling, but thought it wisest not to empathise too much.

'If I want to see more of Fergal I'll have to get Rafael to take me to the stud farm, and to the races…' Una remarked thoughtfully.

Harriet thought the teenager would find that a tall order.

Una heaved a sigh. 'That means I'll have to learn how to be a swot.'

Harriet blinked, all at sea. 'Sorry?'

'You have to know how to handle Rafael. He's always telling me about the rewards of hard work, so if I swot like mad he'll have to take me to the races if I ask. He can't say no if that's all I want.' Watching Harriet's face reflect sudden comprehension, Una sighed. 'When you want some hints on how to nail Rafael to the church door, and you're ripe for Father Frank's famous talk on the trials of marriage, just ask.'

Harriet knew how truly low she could sink when she found herself tempted.

'I mean, Rafael's a sitting duck right now.'

* * *

Rafael was waiting in a limo at Charles de Gaulle airport for Harriet.

Her dress was the colour of blueberries, and a neat fit over her bosom and her hips for she had rounded up a little in Italy, but the rich shade flattered her copper hair and fair skin. When she met Rafael's stunning dark eyes her heart literally jumped inside her chest, but he made no move towards her. As they drove through the busy, atmospheric streets of Paris he seemed preoccupied. He listened carefully to the story which Tolly had shared, and even smiled.

'I should have guessed there might be a link between you and Tolly,' he murmured.

She waited, but he added nothing more, and she thought that perhaps he was not that interested. She felt rather cut-off for imagining that he might be. Having been assured that she was not his half-sister, she reckoned that he probably couldn't care less who her father was.

'I should warn you that my mother can be hot-tempered.' Harriet felt she had to speak up before they entered Eva and Gustav's apartment. 'And Gustav is very protective of her.'

'Let me handle this.'

Eva's bored expression evaporated when she

caught a glimpse of the tall handsome male behind her daughter.

'My name is Rafael Flynn,' Rafael murmured softly. 'Rafael…Cavaliere…Flynn.'

Eva's jaw dropped inelegantly wide. 'I beg your pardon?'

Gustav did a doubletake at their visitor. 'Cavaliere? Valente Cavaliere's son?'

'You can't be *his* son!' Eva protested.

Without further ado Rafael settled a document on the gilt and marble coffee table. 'The results of DNA tests. Harriet is *not* my father's child!'

'That's impossible,' Gustav announced. 'I've known he was Harriet's father for several years—'

'But it's simply not true,' Harriet stated. 'Valente Cavaliere wasn't my father!'

'Why don't you tell your daughter the truth?' Rafael asked her mother.

'I'm feeling faint…' Eva gasped.

'Faking a faint won't get me off your case,' Rafael drawled icily.

'How dare you speak to my wife like that?' Gustav snapped furiously.

'I dare because after making Harriet live in ignorance for years your wife then chose to tell a disgusting and very irresponsible lie. At the time that lie was told, Harriet and I were lovers…'

Gustav was so aghast at that announcement that he stared speechless, first at Rafael and then with questioning force at his wife. 'Eva…is it possible that you were mistaken?'

'It's more than possible,' Rafael continued. 'My father didn't set foot in Ireland within five years of Harriet's conception. I very much doubt that he ever even met your wife.'

Eva burst into tears.

'Was it a lie?' Gustav pressed heavily.

Eva spun away from him and sobbed even harder. Gustav turned a mottled pink shade and walked out of the room.

'Mum…' The scene distressed Harriet. She hated to see her mother's frailty exposed in front of Rafael. 'Please tell me if Robert Tolly is my father.'

Eva's head flew up in dismay. 'How did you—?'

'So he is,' Harriet gathered tightly.

'You've got no future as an interrogator, Harriet,' Rafael said, very drily.

'Why did you lie to me?' Harriet demanded of the older woman.

'Because I told that lie to Gustav before we married and I could hardly change my story! You're right—I never met Valente Cavaliere. But I heard all about him in Ballyflynn. He was the most exciting thing that ever hit that dreary village,' Eva declared defiantly. 'I said he was Harriet's father because he was rich and important, and Gustav was impressed by that.'

'Why couldn't you just tell Gustav the truth?'

'Do you really think I was about to tell my future husband that I'd once fallen pregnant by the man married to my best friend?'

'I can see that that might have made him think twice,' Rafael murmured, without any expression at all.

An unexpected laugh fell from Eva's lips. 'My respect for Harriet is rising steadily. Are you as rich as legend reports?'

'Mother, please…' Harriet begged, squirming at the avid look in the older woman's gaze. 'Can I ask what happened between you and Robert Tolly?'

'Nothing much worth talking about. I did think I loved him.' The older woman gave her a bitter look. 'But he strung me along. He never had any intention of leaving Sheila. Her family had money. I had nothing to offer. When I got pregnant he panicked. Who do you think helped me get on that ferry and paid my fare? Your precious father. He also gave me the cash to go for a termination. But I met Will Carmichael and decided I'd rather get married.'

Harriet had turned very pale. Rafael curved an arm round her, mentioned a pressing appointment and whisked her out of there faster than the speed of light.

'Do you think Gustav will forgive Eva for lying to him?' Harriet asked worriedly as they boarded the jet for their flight back to Ireland.

'I would say that your mother is more than equal to the task of convincing him that he should. Are you planning to approach Robert Tolly?'

'I don't think so. But I bet his father will let him know that I know. Tolly would like a DNA test done for his own satisfaction, and no doubt he'll pass on that as well. I can live with my father's uninterest, though, and his wife's feelings ought to be considered. Maybe in time she'll come round to accepting my existence.' Harriet screened a yawn behind her hand. 'I'm sorry. I don't think I've ever felt so tired in my life.'

She had to be shaken awake when they landed in Kerry. A soft fine rain was falling, and lying like mist over the hills as Rafael drove them back to Ballyflynn.

'I'm taking you to the Court. We have one or two things to sort out,' he drawled softly.

Nervous tension infiltrated her. For some reason she felt she had to fill the silence, and she was chattering inanely about her plans for the vegetable patch as the Range Rover drew up outside the Georgian mansion.

'You must be bored out of your mind,' she muttered hot-cheeked as he led her indoors.

'You never bore me. But it is definitely my turn to talk.'

Before he could speak, Peanut and Samson rushed out to greet them.

'My goodness—what are they doing here? They *are* making themselves at home,' Harriet muttered in some mortification. 'I hope you don't mind.'

'Of course I don't. I see Albert every day after all.' Intent dark eyes rested on her anxious face and softened. 'I want to sign over my half of the livery yard to you. You deserve it—'

'No, I don't...don't be ridiculous. If we're not partners any more I'll not even have an excuse to see you!' Belatedly registering what she had let drop, Harriet went bright pink and clamped a hand to her mouth. 'Whoops...'

'Since when did you think you needed an excuse?'

'I don't know where I stand with you any more.'

'Are you still in love with Luke?'

'My goodness—how can you ask me that? I sent him packing!' Harriet reminded him with pride.

'That doesn't mean you don't still love him. Luke has haunted me ever since I met you.'

'How?'

'When I met you, again were still in love with him, and all you wanted with me was a fling…you shameless hussy, you!'

Her face flamed. 'I just thought about it. I didn't actually intend to do it…'

'And you didn't want to be photographed with me at Leopardstown,' Rafael enumerated.

'I explained why not—'

'But I wasn't convinced. And when you lay in my arms and called me Luke, any sense of security I had in our relationship was destroyed.'

Harriet was wincing double-time now. 'That was the most awful mistake. I know it was dreadful, and I still don't know how it happened—'

'But it did, and I believed you were on the rebound. Then in Italy you told me that I wasn't marriage material, which again led me into making unhappy comparisons.'

'Oh, that serves you right.' Her blue eyes sparkled. 'You went to great trouble to make it clear that you weren't up for marriage, so what did you expect?'

Rafael groaned out loud. 'You *still* haven't told me how you feel about Luke.'

Harriet collided with spectacular dark golden eyes that were distinctly anxious. 'I haven't loved Luke since I fell much more in love with you.'

Rafael looked stunned. 'Do you mean that?'

'I think it started the night of the bonfire…though of course I fancied the socks off you before that…'

'You love me?' His charismatic smile flashed out and he pulled her close and held her so tight she could hardly breathe. 'I was planning to propose on the flight home. I had the champagne all ready, and the ring, and you fell asleep…how *could* you?'

'You were going to propose? My goodness, Rafael, you should've woken me up!' she told him in reproach.

He laughed with rich appreciation. 'I am crazily in love with you, *a mhilis*.'

'But you said you didn't *do* love…'

'Then you ran across the lawn in those funky pyjamas and I went into hot pursuit. I've never felt like that in my life before. Everything with you was special…and Italy was magical… I didn't want to leave.' He looked down at her with tender intensity. 'But I didn't understand that I was in love with you until I thought I couldn't have you any more.'

'Eva's lie…the brother-sister thing…'

'I thought I would go insane. I never felt emptiness like that. I couldn't even trust myself near you at first. That's when I realised I loved you.'

'So you hit the brandy. Don't you ever do that again.'

'Is there anything you don't know about my flaws?'

'I know you love me, and I know I love you, and...show me that ring!'

It was a glorious diamond. While she was admiring it on her finger from all angles, Rafael suggested a wedding at Flynn Court.

'Before the point-to-point season kicks off? Good timing,' she agreed approvingly. 'Una will be over the moon. By the way, if she does start attending a local school, her sister might find it hard having a teenager around that small house twenty-four-seven.'

'I was concerned about that aspect.'

'Do you think Una might like to come and live with us instead?' Harriet asked.

His lean, strong face taut, Rafael gazed down at her. 'Wouldn't you mind?'

'No, I'm very attached to her.'

'How can I land you with a teenager when we're just married?'

'My choice.'

'I picked you good.' Rafael studied her with intense appreciation and a wicked smile curved his mouth. 'I picked you *very* good. Does this mean that I'm going to be getting my shirts picked up on a regular basis?'

She stretched up to him, bright blue eyes full of mischief, and whispered, 'Don't hold your breath!'

Feeling like a princess in her wedding gown, Harriet twirled in front of the full length mirror. Her strapless dress had a flattering basque waist, and the silk was overlaid with tulle embroidered with delicate crystal beadwork that caught the light. The emerald and diamond horseshoe brooch was clasped to the gold circlet that held her flirty short veil back, where it looked wonderfully appropriate.

'I'm so proud of you I'm walking on air,' Tolly confided as he escorted his granddaughter into the flower-bedecked church.

Her bridesmaids, Alice and Una, and her little flower girl, Will and Nicola Carmichael's daughter Emily, swarmed round her. Harriet skimmed an anxious glance over the rather tight expression on Alice's lovely face and gave her sister's hand a bracing squeeze. She did appreciate the effort it had taken for Alice to rise above her broken heart and act as her bridesmaid.

'You've really put my nose out of joint by bagging a billionaire,' Alice had admitted with a tearful giggle when the wedding was being arranged. 'No wonder you said you didn't want Luke back.'

Warm affection in her satisfied gaze, Una carefully removed a piece of straw from the train of Harriet's dress and twitched it straight with a proprietary hand. Clearly aware of Alice's sulky mood, she had taken charge. Little Emily stood by, sucking her thumb and clutching Harriet's hand.

On Harriet's passage down the aisle on Tolly's arm, Will and Nicola smiled at the bride and Boyce gave her an outrageous wink. Eva, her slim hand resting on Gustav's sleeve, watched her daughter with brimming satisfaction. For no less an event than the wedding of her daughter to the billionaire owner of Flynn Court her mother had been prepared to make a return visit to Ballyflynn. Harriet, however, only had eyes for the male awaiting her at the altar. An exquisite shrine to St Jude, patron saint of impossible causes, now embellished the chapel.

'You look like every dream I ever had,' Rafael swore huskily, and her heart sang.

By the time the photographs were being taken outside the church, Alice could be seen to have made a startling recovery from her earlier low spirits. Rafael's best man, Stephanos, the handsome heir to a Greek shipping empire, was making a great effort to make himself agreeable to her sister. Never had a broken heart been ditched with more sparkle, Harriet reflected with amusement. And Boyce, who was in the process of renovating his house at Slieveross, was talking to Fergal.

Two white horses pulled the fancy carriage that was whisking Rafael and Harriet from the church to the estate. A host of cameras clicked and whirred to record the event. The reception, to be held at Flynn Court, promised to be the biggest party Ballyflynn had ever known. The following day the bridal couple would depart for a honeymoon in the Caribbean. Harriet returned her emerald and diamond engagement ring to its position next to her new wedding ring and remembered when she had absently thought of imprisoning Rafael in a locked room in chains. She had never dreamt that it would not be chains but rings that bound him to her, of his own free will, and tender amusement filled her.

'Where are we going?' Harriet had finally noticed that the carriage had deviated from the direct route back to the house.

'You'll see.'

The driver brought the horses to a halt where the rough track narrowed down into the bridle path that led through the oak woods. Rafael sprang out and scooped Harriet from the carriage. She stared in amazement at the rich red carpet that had been laid to cover the trail.

'Am I dreaming?'

Smiling, Rafael drew her into the heart of the wood, where the oak, the ash and the hawthorn trees all grew together. Her fingers were secure in the firm hold of his. It was a moment when happiness took over and overflowed inside her, for the very beauty of their surroundings made her eyes prickle with tears.

'This is the place where I always remember being with you,' Rafael confessed. 'It's special…'

'Yes,' she agreed a little gruffly. 'Very special.'

Dark eyes held hers with gravity, and her heart started beating very fast. 'I brought you here to tell you that I love you as I never believed I could love any woman, *a mhilis*. That I intend to be a great husband, and the best father I can be…'

'Father?' Harriet repeated in surprise.

The faintest colour demarcated his proud cheekbones. 'Eventually—I hope.'

Harriet looked up at him, her face alight with unalloyed happiness. 'I didn't think you were ready for the pitter-patter of tiny feet yet.'

'Neither did I.' Rafael sighed, pulling her close. 'The fairies have had the last laugh. You're killing my womanising image.'

The teasing light in his beautiful eyes made her believe in magic. 'I love you to bits,' she told him

softly, and then he kissed her. There was silence—
until they recalled the vast number of guests awaiting their arrival at their future home…

Look forward to all these
★ ★ wonderful books this ★
Christmas ★

BETTY NEELS
MARGARET WAY
JESSICA STEELE

All I want for
Christmas

When baby's delivered just in time for Christmas

Precious Gifts

Marion Lennox · Josie Metcalfe · Kate Hardy

Together for
Christmas

Lynnette Kent & Sherryl Lewis

Christmas

Jasmine Cresswell · Kate Hoffmann
Tara Taylor Quinn

The
CHRISTMAS
VISIT

Margaret Moore
Gail Ranstrom
Terri Brisbin

SILHOUETTE
SNOWY
NIGHTS

XMAS/LIST V2

1105/059/MB146 V2

Experience the magic of Christmas, past and present...

Christmas Brides

Don't miss this special holiday volume – two captivating love stories set in very different times.

THE GREEK'S CHRISTMAS BRIDE
by Lucy Monroe
Modern Romance

Aristide Kouros has no memory of life with his beautiful wife Eden. Though she's heartbroken he does not remember their passion for each other, Eden still loves her husband. But what secret is she hiding that might bind Aristide to her forever – whether he remembers her or not?

MOONLIGHT AND MISTLETOE
by Louise Allen
Historical Romance – Regency

From her first night in her new home in a charming English village, Hester is plagued by intrusive "hauntings." With the help of her handsome neighbour, the Earl of Buckland, she sets out to discover the mystery behind the frightful encounters – while fighting her own fear of falling in love with the earl.

On sale 4th November 2005

researching the cure

The facts you need to know:

- **One woman in nine** in the United Kingdom will develop breast cancer during her lifetime.

- Each year **40,700** women are newly diagnosed with breast cancer and around **12,800** women will die from the disease. However, survival rates are improving, with on average 77 per cent of women still alive five years later.

- **Men can also suffer from breast cancer**, although currently they make up less than one per cent of all new cases of the disease.

Britain has one of the highest breast cancer death rates in the world. Breast Cancer Campaign wants to understand why and do something about it. Statistics cannot begin to describe the impact that breast cancer has on the lives of those women who are affected by it and on their families and friends.

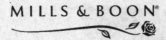

MILLS & BOON®

**During the month of October
Harlequin Mills & Boon will donate
10p from the sale of every
Modern Romance™ series book to
help Breast Cancer Campaign
in *researching the cure.***

Breast Cancer Campaign's scientific projects
look at improving diagnosis and treatment
of breast cancer, better understanding how
it develops and ultimately either curing the
disease or preventing it.

Do your part to help

Visit <u>www.breastcancercampaign.org</u>

And make a donation today.

researching the cure

Breast Cancer Campaign is a company limited by guarantee registered in England and
Wales. Company No. 05074725. Charity registration No. 299758.
Breast Cancer Campaign, Clifton Centre,110 Clifton Street, London EC2A 4HT.
Tel: 020 7749 3700 Fax: 020 7749 3701 www.breastcancercampaign.org

Celebrate the charm of Christmases past in three new heartwarming holiday tales!

COMFORT AND JOY by Margaret Moore
1860 Llanwyllan, Wales

After a terrible accident, Griffin Branwynne gives up on the joys of Christmas—until the indomitable Gwendolyn Davies arrives on his doorstep and turns his world upside-down. Can the earl resist a woman who won't take no for an answer?

LOVE AT FIRST STEP by Terri Brisbin
1199 England

While visiting friends in England for the holidays, Lord Gavin MacLeod casts his eye upon the mysterious Elizabeth. She is more noble beauty than serving wench, and Gavin vows to uncover her past—at any cost!

A CHRISTMAS SECRET by Gail Ranstrom
1819 Oxfordshire, England

Miss Charity Wardlow expects a marriage proposal from her intended while attending a Christmas wedding. But when Sir Andrew MacGregor arrives at the manor, Charity realises that she prefers this Scotsman with the sensual smile…

On sale 2nd December 2005